Humankind

Invasion Day series

Book 1

LC Morgans

ISBN-13: 9798389103733

For those who love us, and those who don't. Because in the end, neither will matter.

A Brief History of Earth, humankind, and its demise.

"The human race will ultimately be responsible for its own demise. It is with great certainty that I alert you of this now, and you heed my warnings. What we have called the 'benefits culture' for hundreds of years has caused profound chaos to our world and its economy, and it is damage I fear we will not return from." President of the USA, Harold Chant, the year 2465.

"We need to find alternative fuels and a cure for overpopulation. But short of a miracle or genocide, I fear it's too late…" Queen Anastasia of England, the year 2989.

In the year 3030 an alien species known as the Thrakorian's attacked Earth. On Invasion Day, the extraterrestrial race invaded the planet by force, however such influence was not needed. The Thrakorian's took control easily from the indigenous race that foolishly believed they possessed it, and any who opposed the new reign were killed instantly. Many were slain publicly to demonstrate that the invaders weren't interested in taking prisoners, and some lives were taken just show how uninterested the Thrakorian's were in negotiation with the leaders of the old world. Soldiers stormed the streets, homes, businesses, schools, and churches. They obliterated over half of all the human population on their first wave, and then enslaved the rest who would go on to either work or die under their new leader, King Kronus. They had travelled millions of light-years to Earth for the invasion, and the mission was carried out with precision and tact. It was by all accounts an easy harvest, and the humans were left ashamed by their lack of fight—and rightly so.

Thraks looked human, and spoke their various languages, but soon replaced the previously adopted concepts of both nationality and race with a simplified version. Those who survived were given one language to speak exclusively—English—and were henceforth simply called 'humans.'

Their lives as they once knew were shattered by the new powerful regime. In the days that followed, humans were split into classes and sectors, microchipped like cattle, and put to work. None could match the strength, skill, and intellect of the Thrakorian race, and their technology far surpassed that which the humans had once believed to be innovative and impressive.

From that day forward, every human knew their place, and they would learn to be grateful for all their powerful masters had given them, or else suffer. The foolish, lazy, burdens on society previously used to getting a free meal and a roof given to them died in the streets, while their hardworking neighbors were rewarded with food and shelter. Only those who worked for their amenities thrived, and the benefits culture was no more. Credits replaced currency, and the only way to get them, was to earn them.

Nothing was the same again, and their leaders enjoyed the order of things in their newly created world. Slaves were aplenty, and there was much work to be done, so every human had a role to play. They either did it willingly or died defying their powerful masters.

King Kronus had never once doubted the success of his mission, and quickly took his place on high for all to adore and worship, or else refuse and perish.

Rebels rose up to challenge his reign, and most were eliminated with no effort at all, but some remained. There would always be those who fought the regime, but the Thrakorian's loved a good hunt, so didn't mind one little bit.

And so, began a new era on Earth, where a savior came from the heavens, but at what cost?

<u>Glossary of terms, and general information regarding the
Thrakorian reign.</u>

<u>Earth's new class structure (in descending order):</u>

King Kronus
Kings Guard Service (a separate entity to the regular
Thrakorian army consisting of its highest honored
members.)
Thrakorian Royal Armed Forces
Thrakorian civilians
Mixed-breeds (those whose families were forged years
before Invasion Day to establish a presence on Earth prior
to the arrival of their species. Many ensured they were
appointed heads of state, or elected Kings and Queens of
countries due to be overruled by King Kronus on his
arrival.)
Gentry (Humans with extraordinary talent, intellect or skill
worthy of a higher standing above all others of their race.
They are handpicked by the King's chief advisors, and are
expected to work hard if they want to keep their place.
Many were branded as traitors to their race, while most
were envied for the strength of will and readiness to
serve—and their sinister tactics were well rewarded.)
Human Royal Armed Forces (dependent on rank)
Human upper-class
Human middle-class
Human lower-class
Convicts (those tried and judged by the Lawbringer for
crimes against their King. They are treated like vermin, and
ordered to work for nothing but basic food and shelter
rations in service to their overlords, and housed in
specialized areas away from the general human population.
In return for training and further provisions, many well-
behaved convicts are often given more responsibility if
they show willingness and repentance for their crimes.)

Rebels (the lowest of all humans, and considered to be of zero worth to the Thrakorian reign. They are hunted down and killed on sight, while their sympathizers are gunned down or exiled in the arid lands formerly known as South America, where the radioactive atmosphere and barren landscape offered nothing but a long and painful death.)

Human Royal Armed Forces rank structure
(in descending order):

Gentry Officers:
      General
Elite Officers:
      Colonel
      Captain
Secondary Soldiers:
      Lieutenant
      Sergeant
Primary Soldiers:
      Corporal
      Recruit
      Convict

<u>Thrakorian Royal Armed Forces rank structure (in descending order):</u>

King Kronus
Kings Guard Service:
(Only one of each title is awarded, and they are master's of all soldier's beneath them.)

> **Chief of Defense**
> **Lawbringer** (judge and juror of all who stray from the laws)
> **Besieger** (Capturer of rebels and rogues)
> **Master Protector** (the personal guard of the King)
> **Marshals of the Army, Navy and Air force**

Regular Thrakorian Royal Armed Forces:

> **Paladin** (the highest rank bestowed on a soldier, given to those renowned for braveness, intellect, heroism and loyalty to the King.)
> **Lorde** (a superior warrior, respected and heralded for their mastery in their field or fields.)
> **Duke** (the strongest fighters and most experienced conqueror's.)
> **Sentinel** (a soldier who guards their division and keeps watch over their comrades.)
> **Inquisitor** (a soldier who's highly trained to seek out information, by any means necessary. Nothing is forbidden, and a long and painful death would come for any human who refuses them.)
> **Master** (regular soldiers who work alongside humans to ensure they are following orders and not deviating from their given class and sector.)

CHAPTER ONE

"Kyra. Why don't you tell us your story of Invasion Day?" the kindergarten teacher, Mrs. Forrest, asked her with a wide, clearly glued-on smile. Kyra nodded and grinned back warmly at the woman, and took a breath, ready to begin her prepared speech. She was at the school for young human children to complete the final hour of the community service element of her high school diploma and had to admit she hadn't hated entertaining the kids at all. She worked hard in everything she did but had enjoyed the days spent with the energetic boys and girls, so it hadn't felt like work at all.

Ever since the world had been taken over by an alien race, society had drastically changed, and so too had the upbringing of human children. Schooling was now more about what you could contribute to civilization than getting high grades, and in their final year the students were expected to show support to their community as part of their progression into adulthood. Kyra had chosen to be a teaching assistant to try and help those who might've been like she was once upon a time ago—alone and afraid in this big, wide world.

"Absolutely," she answered cheerily, and ushered for the children to pay attention. Every tiny face peered up at her from their places on the floor, and she said the same words she'd uttered time and again over her life under the new rule. "I was born in the year three-thousand-and-twenty-five. That means that when the Thrakorian's came

1

to Earth, I was five years old. I was asleep in my bed, of course, and my parents were downstairs in the lounge when our house was hit with some sort of explosive wave. At the time, I had no idea what was going on, just that the house was beginning to crumble and fall around me. I was very scared, but I was also very brave. I went to find my parents, but sadly they'd both been killed." The children all nodded in understanding, and Kyra found it a shame that they were already so desensitized to death. Orphans were unfortunately very common in her generation and were almost treated like a separate level of society. They were raised in foster homes and given food and clothing, but were very low in the class system, and readily forgotten.

Everyone alive on Invasion Day knew their story well and were often called upon to retell it as a constant reminder of the day the Thrakorian's had come to save Earth. Every natural resource had previously been exhausted, and overpopulation had caused the planet's integrity to be forever compromised. It was a well-known fact that their world had been close to a cataclysmic event after all the damage humans had done to it over the many millennia they'd controlled it, and their race was now asked to evoke the guilt of generations forevermore via the retelling of their stories to the new ones.

Although she was used to telling her story by now, the memory of finding her father's burning body came back with a rush of nausea every time. Her mother's pained stare when Kyra had watched the final breath leave her lungs still haunted her, and she never wished that visualization on anyone, so didn't ever include that part in her retelling. She could still remember the awful smell of her dad's burning flesh but wouldn't convey that to any of the children either.

Kyra was convinced though that it was expected she should. She often wondered if the purpose of telling their Invasion Day stories was also to keep the fear of their invaders alive. The Thrakorian's were a superior race to humans in every way and had shown it by relentlessly murdering over half of the population the day they came to inform them they were taking over.

She certainly wouldn't forget that night, and for many other reasons than the strange combination of fear and gratitude. "I ran to my friend's house down the street, but they too had been hit. I had no idea what was going on, but knew I had to find somewhere safe to hide, so I climbed up onto the roof of a nearby building and simply kept going. I climbed and jumped, edging my way through the shadows away from the sound of gunfire and shouting. Eventually, I found a beautiful garden terrace. It seemed so peaceful and well kept, as if someone had loved it once. The flowers were blooming, and I stopped to catch my breath. That was when I heard what I thought was a helicopter approaching, but now I know it was a Thrakorian hovercraft."

"Whoa, did they land in the garden?" one of the children cried, holding his hand over his mouth in shock. Kyra nodded and grinned.

"Yes, and I was so scared that I leapt into the nearest bush to hide. Sadly for me it was a rose bush, and the thorns cut into my skin so badly that I sat there and cried. I tried to keep quiet, but the man who'd left the craft heard me, and he came to see what was going on. He had armor on so the thorns didn't cut him, and he pulled me free," she told the sea of awestruck faces.

She would never forget that moment, and instinctively put her hand on the scar in the shape of an X on her right cheekbone. There were more parts of that story she'd never told anyone, like how the man who'd helped her turned out not to be just any old soldier. He was one of the Thrakorian royals, and Earths new leader, King Kronus. His soft stare and caring hands had stayed with her even until now, and when he'd spoken it was with such a gentle, delicate tone she'd instantly forgotten about her cuts and bruises. Despite her fear, she'd edged closer when he reached out for her hand and trusted him even though she had been given no reason to. He'd stretched inside the bush and soothed her with encouraging words and that wonderful stare, and then yanked her free from the tangle of thorns into his arms. Kronus had then removed his glove and stroked her face, wiping away the blood before planting a soft kiss on her other cheek.

"The roses were trying to protect you," he'd whispered in her ear a second later. "They just held you too tightly and you got hurt, but they didn't mean it. This is just a kiss on the cheek from them, they don't understand how to be kinder to little girls and their delicate skin." Even now, she felt elation at the memory of his words and actions, but knew he'd probably forgotten all about her after he'd walked away.

"So then what happened?" the same child asked, pulling Kyra from her reverie. She pushed her glasses further up her nose and urged the smile to come back to her face and replace her wistful look.

"The Thrakorian soldiers took me to safety, and I was then given a place at a foster home for children orphaned in the invasion. They raised me, and I paid for their care by doing chores and helping take care of the babies and young children. When I started kindergarten, the foster home continued to take care of me. I'll live there until I finish school and leave to train for my chosen career."

"That's right, children," the teacher interjected excitedly. "When Kyra graduates she is required to give her bed to another child in need of care and safety. Our society now is very different to what it used to be, but does anyone know why?" The children raised their hands, and she picked a small girl to answer.

"The alie.. I mean, *Thrakorian's*, changed how our moms and dads work."

"Very good, however it is frowned upon to call them aliens. Why is that?" Mrs. Forrest asked her.

"Because the term alien means someone who is foreign

or doesn't belong here. The Thrakorian's saved the humans from a disastrous future, and we accepted the King for all his kindness and guidance. They belong here and we willingly share our world with them," she replied in the monotonous tone of a rehearsed answer. Adult humans would be charged with defamation if a Thrak caught them saying that word, and the teacher had put it nicely to the child. It was more than just frowned upon, it was downright forbidden. Humans had been carted away or beaten publicly for degrading the Thraks by calling them visitors who didn't belong on Earth. They saw themselves as Earth's saviors and expected to be treated as such.

"Why else?" the teacher asked. Another bouncing child with her hand in the air was chosen to answer.

"We don't use money anymore. We have credits for food and utilities earned by working. When you leave school, you start earning your own credits, before that our parents receive ours for us."

"Quite right. Every human in this new world must work or else they starve. There are a few who've managed to live on the streets on scraps of food or stolen produce, but they are soon reprimanded and made to work off their debt, as well as begin a job in the lower sectors," the teacher answered, wrinkling her nose. Kyra wondered if she'd always been such a snob, but then assumed Mrs. Forrest was well paid for her work so hadn't had to worry about going hungry or not having enough credits for a warm bath or a lamp to read by. "Have you chosen your profession yet, Kyra?"

"Not yet," she lied. "I'm majoring in computer and technological science but am planning on talking to the sector representatives at the school fair tomorrow. They'll help me choose, but I believe my grades and reports are good enough to pursue that route." The teacher seemed impressed at her skills and smiled across at her again with renewed interest. Kyra knew she was different to many of the other foster kids, and while she hated being stereotyped, it was always fun to have an opportunity to show people like Mrs. Forrest just how wrong they were to look down their noses at the unfortunates of their new world. They could be whatever they wanted, and she intended to follow her dreams with a clear head and an ambitious heart, regardless of where society had placed her after Invasion Day.

They soon wrapped up their discussion, and Kyra was signed off from her community service quota. She hugged and bid the children goodbye, knowing it would be a while, if ever, that she'd see any of them again. Coming to the end of her schooling was turning out to be rather bittersweet, but she was ready for the next challenge the world had to offer her.

Despite how she'd answered the teacher's question, Kyra already knew exactly which sector she was planning to join. She'd known ever since that night on the rooftop terrace thirteen years ago that she wanted to serve King Kronus in whatever way she could. She hadn't cared that because of the invasion she'd lost both of her parents. Her dad had been a drunk and her mom was a mess held together with borrowed makeup and a steady stream of black-market substances. Together they'd contributed nothing to society, only sponged off it, and their small squat of a home had said it all. They had no money for food or nice things, and Kyra remembered having to beg her cousins to swipe food from her working aunt's kitchen. She'd lost them in the invasion too, and still missed the only bit of kindness she'd known over those first few years of life. She wanted to forget them all, but the memories often haunted her dreams as a constant reminder of all that'd been lost. In some ways, Kyra wanted this new life to be the only one she knew, and she envied the youngsters of today for not having to remember how bad the world had become before the Thrakorian's came.

Humans had used up every natural resource and abused the world with landfill sites and overcrowding for hundreds of years. The Thrakorian's had killed millions of humans in their quest for world domination, and those who'd surrendered were treated with kindness, but it was only if they were ready to work for their food and shelter. Everybody contributed in one way or another, and Kyra had often watched in awe as each sector went about their business without money, power or greed influencing them or their decisions. There were still bars filled with drunks, but they were spending their hard-earned credits on their after-work drink, so Kyra had never judged them the way she'd judged her father. She often wondered if he would've even fit into the world as it was now, or would he have joined the rebels and fought the new regime? She doubted that either, as he wasn't the most active of men from what she could remember. Unless it was chasing Kyra's mother across the room to deliver her a beating, he usually stayed in his dingy old chair all day long.

Kyra had shaken off her melancholy by the time she reached the foster home in one of the most built-up areas of downtown Los Angeles and headed straight for her shared bedroom at the back of the cold building. After she'd tidied away her school things, she grabbed her computer and continued her research into the current rules and regulations of the Human Royal Armed Forces. Kyra had been preparing for years and was more than ready for the physical challenges involved in the training. Running miles upon miles was no bother now, even with weights on her back. She'd learned to fight well by the time she was ten years old, and mastered self-defense two years later in time for her body to start changing. Now at eighteen, she was stronger than most girls her age, and was grateful for having had a solid right hook whenever needed over the years.

Unlike Kyra, most of her peers weren't ambitious or talented enough to strive for more. Many of the foster kids were headed into the lower sectors, it was just how it worked, but she'd used her intellect to her advantage and pushed herself all the way through school. It'd paid off, and she was now top of her class in many of the computer sciences and other skills needed for a mid-sector role in the army. All Kyra had to do was get through primary training, shine in secondary phase, and she was sure she'd get selected for the Intelligence Division. There she'd earn enough credits to have a comfortable existence, while living out the rest of her life without having to look over her shoulder for the foster boys and their wandering hands or threatening stares. Many times over the years she'd had to sacrifice a meal to appease a bully, and she so looked forward to leaving that life behind.

The next morning's early alarm rang quietly beside her ear, and Kyra was up and off in a heartbeat. She ran a quick ten miles and was back in plenty of time for an early shower. As was her duty within the household, she then prepared breakfast for her dorm, and then ate a quick bite before catching the old train that would take her directly to school. Modern technology was a marvel, but traditional methods of transport were still used in the older parts of Los Angeles. Many original buildings still stood as landmarks across the city, while those that'd been destroyed were replaced by brand new designs, and with every new gadget known to man or Thrak. As she did every day, she watched out the window, and loved seeing the view of the dingy estate change to the business sector skyscrapers, and then reached their school.

Kyra had always loved going there. It was open, airy, and light, and it didn't have the musty, damp smell of the old world. The Thrakorian's had built the school as a gift to the humans ten years before, and she'd treasured everyday spent within its walls. She knew she'd miss it when she graduated, but still not enough to consider joining the educational sector.

She took a spot at the end of the queue heading into the main hall, where the careers fair was already going on inside. Kyra knew where she was going and headed straight for the corner dominated with posters for the Human Royal Armed Forces and browsed the brochures inside. Insignias for each division were all around her, and already she felt at home and ready to move on.

"You lost, little lady?" a deep voice asked from behind her, and Kyra turned to greet the owner with a forced smile. She got this all the time, thanks to her height of only five-feet-five, and knew exactly how to deal with it. She'd always followed the 'do no harm but take no crap,' mantra to life, and had developed a fun attitude alongside it over the years.

"No, but I was hoping you might find me a stool or something to stand on, these tables are awfully high." The soldier burst into laughter, smirked, and nodded in acceptance of her clever reply. "Kyra Millan, pleasure to meet you." She reached out her hand and he shook it, eyeing her with surprise.

"Sergeant McDermott," he replied. "Have you found something here you like?"

"Yep, Intelligence Division," Kyra said, pulling out her glasses to have a better look at the pamphlet in her hand.

"A geek, I should've known," the Sergeant rolled his eyes and shook his head a bit too dismissively for her liking. "You've got to get through a grueling few years of training first. This isn't the easy way into the science sector, you know?"

"I know full well what this is, and isn't. I want this," Kyra said as she looked around at the pictures of soldiers in their black uniforms with blue emblems signifying their division. She then reached out and stroked the lapel on the front of his jacket that indicated his rank. "I want to serve, and I'm not afraid of hard work. I'm ready to be a soldier first and a geek second."

Sgt. McDermott grabbed her hand and inspected the

scars on her arm. "Have you been in battle before? Because I guarantee this will be nothing like the street-brawls between kids, or Invasion Day. You will be pushed to your physical and mental limits and had better be ready to get up and ask for more, otherwise you will fail." Kyra pulled her hand back, breaking the contact.

"Well, I'd better make sure I don't fail then," she said with a sure smile. "When does recruiting begin?" she then asked, looking around at the other soldiers who were all talking with the jocks and other burly students that clearly suited their mold better than she. She didn't care if they thought she might not fit in, proving wrong anyone who doubted her had been a habit of hers all through high school, so why should she change it now?

"Where do you live?" he asked, flipping through the pages in his handbook.

"Old-town, Violet Street."

"The foster homes. Got it." He nodded, seeming to understand her drive at last. Most of the middle or upper-class sectors looked down on the kids from the more deprived areas. Their survival relied solely on the credit handouts from Kronus's new government, and it was seen by many of the wealthy as a charitable donation to offer up the scraps from their table to the poor little orphans. The very idea made her want to scream, but instead she accepted the handouts like all the rest—out of necessity. Kyra shrugged off his remark. She *was* a poor little orphan. Her family hadn't been well-off before the invasion, so she knew there was no reason why she would've been wealthier after without parents to work and make them so. All she had was herself, and that was fine.

He studied the chart and looked back up to meet her gaze. "August fourth. You've got a few weeks to change your mind, but if not, I guess I'll see you then." Sgt. McDermott gave her another cheeky smile, and then turned to talk with the next visitor to their stand.

Kyra watched him go and hoped she'd see him again.

There was no doubt about it; he was hot, probably in his mid-twenties and clearly fit and healthy. She found herself wondering how toned that chest was she just had her hand over when she'd touched his lapel and walked off before she was caught watching that cute ass of his walking away.

CHAPTER TWO

Kyra graduated a few days later with top marks in all her classes. She was offered a meeting with the guidance counselor regarding her choices, but knew she was in no position to carry on with her education without a scholarship, and they were almost impossible to come by. It was expected she at least entertain the conversation for a while, so she sat listening politely while the man droned on about the various sectors and opportunities each held, as though she hadn't already researched them to death. Joining the Human Royal Armed Forces was not just a dream she hoped might come true. She was going to make it happen, so humored him with her attention before heading off to her final class assembly. Their graduation ceremony was later that afternoon, and all the students were gathered around the vast hall, where they chatted excitedly and awaited the call to line up to receive their diplomas. Kyra found her small group of friends and joined them, greeting each of her fellow computer and technological science students before turning her attention to the tall girl beside her.

Samia, her best friend and part Thrakorian, was heading straight to college. The human schools were separate from the Thraks', not that there were many, but mixed-heritage children attended the human schools to show unity. Her family was more than taken care of by their new government, and her parents had funded Samia's lavish lifestyle without a care for credits or indulgences.

They had even ensured she had a wealthy future laid out before her, but Kyra couldn't begrudge her the easy road. She'd been the best friend Kyra could've ever wanted and knew she and Samia would miss each other once she disappeared off with the army truck in a couple weeks' time.

"You good?" she asked, peering up at her hugely tall friend. She knew Samia had just had her own meeting with a Thrakorian representative, and that the opportunities afforded to her were plentiful in comparison to the meager roads humans were offered.

"Yep, same old speech about how proud they are of me. He said the recommendation for inclusion in the advanced science group has been accepted, but my father already told me." Kyra's eyes widened with pride in her friend's accomplishment, but knew she was playing it down on purpose for her benefit. Being accepted into the advanced sciences program was a big deal, and almost certainly meant Samia would go far. She was getting everything she'd ever wanted, and Kyra could see through her relaxed demeanor.

"Don't be so modest, you deserve this. You earned it off your own back too," she whispered back, and Samia flushed. There were so many ways she seemed human, and it was easy to forget that an entirely different blood ran in her veins. Full-blooded Thrakorian's didn't associate much with humans, so Kyra hadn't had the chance to figure out their mannerisms or ways, but she knew her friend well, and had picked up a lot over the years.

Samia had told her a little about her family and the extraterrestrial community, but only what she could without getting into trouble. Her human great-grandmother had given birth to a half-Thrakorian child after falling in love with a reconnaissance soldier, and the bloodline had been kept pure with careful breeding ever since. Samia and her siblings were the youngest of an ancient lineage that could be traced back to the high-society men and women still atop the governing bodies back on their home planet, Thrakor, and had been well taken care of.

Like hers, many powerful and wealthy human families of the old world had revealed themselves to be part Thrakorian since Invasion Day. Most of them had run parliaments or even entire countries as Kings and Queens pending their willing abdication once King Kronus seized power. There had been others who oversaw the armies and other industries of old in preparation for the extraterrestrial incursion, and they too did their part to ensure an easy victory for the Thrakorian's. Their technology and experience of war was far more advanced than the humans, but from Samia's stories Kyra learned how they could've taken control easily regardless. Having the help of their men and women already planted around the globe in positions of power was evidently a mere tactical advantage should it have been necessary.

Samia's family and all the other half-breeds had then stepped up to their given place beneath King Kronus when he'd taken power, and the humans who'd surrendered fell in line beneath their control, or else became martyrs to their rebellious cause. Humans hadn't stood a chance, though. After years of abusing their planet, draining its resources, and overpopulating it, even Kyra knew the invasion must've been pretty easy. She could remember how it was only a matter of days before they were worshipping their new leader, and peace had come quickly once rules were in place.

Her half-breed friend had also told Kyra more of how the Thrakorian's had been establishing their place on Earth way before invading. Reconnaissance missions had gone on for centuries and had resulted in many of the half-breed families now prevalent in their new society. Many of the Thrakorian men and women had stayed on Earth to be with their offspring, and many had even settled down and married their lovers. It seemed like a strange sort of fairytale, but with aliens and spaceships rather than knights on horseback, and she often found herself wondering what it must be like in Samia's world. It was undoubtedly a very different one to hers.

Looking up at her friend's impressive frame, Kyra was reminded of how she'd once wondered if her mixed blood was how Samia had become so tall, and she'd confirmed it by telling her it was one of the Thrakorian traits that was often passed on. They looked no different to humans, but underneath they had differences on a cellular level. As well as being taller, their bodies also regenerated at a faster rate, and she'd never seen Samia with a cut of bruise that lasted more than a few minutes. The same cellular regeneration also caused them to age much slower—typically one year to every ten humans in a full-blooded Thrak. Those with mixed bloodlines added a few years to their lives, but not enough to have gotten themselves noticed for it before. When they'd revealed their true bloodlines and become the highest class in the new society, no one would dare ask questions, and that seemed to be how they liked it.

Thrakorian's were also visibly stronger, and broader than humans, especially the men. Kyra always remembered peering up at the incredibly tall King who'd taken her hand and led her to safety on Invasion Day but had wondered at first if he'd just seemed so big in comparison to her tiny and malnourished body. After watching him give a speech on television years afterward, she knew otherwise. Kronus had to be at least eight feet tall, and his shoulders seemed to span double that of a human man. Even now he looked exactly the same as he had back then, and Kyra knew he'd still be as intimidatingly tall if she met him again now. During his last televised speech regarding an overhaul of the credit system for teens, she'd marveled at how Kronus hadn't seemed to age a single day since she'd watched him step off that hovercraft, and she often wondered about him. Was he the same, kind man he'd once been? Or had years of sculpting the human race into a workforce worth more to him than just pets in his personal playground hardened him? Kyra guessed she'd never find out. He didn't make social visits or check in on the humans across the globe. In fact, she had no idea if he ever even set foot off the private island he resided in somewhere between England and France. Kronus was a face on the broadcasts and in his propaganda, but his orders were passed down via his Guard Service, their workforce, and the sectors beneath, never in person.

The only full-blooded Thrakorian she'd ever interacted regularly with took the stage—their school principal, Marta Mayne. She was a stunning woman, who looked to be in her fifties, however Kyra knew she must be more like five hundred years old if Samia's explanation of their slow aging was correct. Marta had been a good headmistress, but a firm one. She'd upheld every rule and regulation without ever blurring the lines or making allowances for any of her students, and the school had thrived under her tutelage. Kyra had never been in enough trouble that she'd had to be taken before her, but knew it was scary just finding yourself on the receiving end of her harsh stare. Those who did were often sentenced to extra work or community service to make up as punishment for their crimes, and Kyra didn't envy them for it.

Marta stood over them at the podium. She greeted the crowd in her usual warm manner and congratulated the students on their accomplishments.

"Over the coming weeks, your homes will be visited by representatives from each sector. You must join one, or else inherit the sector of a parent or guardian. And of course, you don't have to stick with one if it doesn't feel right. Raise your concerns with your leaders, and a transfer request can be made on your behalf," she added. Her clever gaze scanned the crowd, enveloping them all in her incredible, knowing stare. Although she was already aware of the law, Kyra had rarely heard of anyone changing their sector once they'd begun training. She wondered if

Principal Mayne always said that line to ensure her students didn't feel as though they were being forced to choose now and have to stand by that decision for the rest of their lives. It was scary, but for those sure of their chosen plan like Kyra, there was no opting out. "Those going to college must be taken to their new homes on campus before the end of the month. Good luck and always remember to serve your King with dignity and pride."

"Praise King Kronus," the crowd shouted in unison, which was the usual finale to their school assemblies, and they began filing out. At times it felt odd praising a flesh and bone being, but she spoke the same words as everyone else had, and like her peers, had never asked why they praised him aloud when he clearly wasn't there to hear them. Kyra knew nothing of the teaching methods used in the old world, but she did know they'd once praised an almighty entity called God for all he'd given them. She remembered the hymns and passages spoken aloud at her kindergarten a long time ago and found that concept even stranger somehow. God was apparently gone and had been replaced by their sovereign. There were times she wanted to question the reasons why, and to doubt a God could've been so easily replaced. If they'd been right to praise him for three thousand years before Kronus came to Earth, then why had he let their planet be invaded? Having an inquisitive mind wasn't a good thing nowadays, and though Kyra had her questions, she didn't dare ask them aloud. She always pushed those questions far from her mind, and never let herself revisit them later. They were the questions of a rebel, and rebels were the violators of their new world. She'd been taught to treat them as willful viruses to their perfect system, and to despise their need to question authority, not follow in their footsteps.

Rebels were murderers and deviants. They would rape and maim, steal from, and slaughter those human civilians loyal to King Kronus if his soldiers weren't there to protect them, and that was another reason she so wanted to serve in his army. Martial law had been in place ever since Invasion Day, and the soldiers not only kept the peace, but also protected it. The army was the policing, judicial system and department of corrections all rolled into one huge sector. Convicts were sent to a special division of the army that trained and rehabilitated them before putting them to work, and there was no appeals process or chance of early release. As a result, crime rates had reportedly gone down every year since its inception, and regular civilians were no longer afraid of gangs or thugs like those that had once ruled the more deprived areas like where Kyra lived.

Ever since the Thrakorian's had come to Earth, everything had changed. Humans now either worked or they died, much to the annoyance of some. There were many who wished for the return of the old days when they could sit around and do nothing, but Kyra welcomed hard work. It kept her busy and strong, and she'd been brought up to have a tremendous work ethic along with all the other foster kids in her home. Her entire life had led her to this, and she was going to do everything she could to make sure things went the way they were supposed to.

***

The forces trucks lined Violet Street a couple weeks' later, and crowds of humans came out to see which newly graduated teens might go and join them. Kyra watched from the sidelines as they knocked on every door and asked the same question as always.

"Do you have anyone in there that wishes to join his Majesty King Kronus's Human Royal Armed Forces?"

Kyra had heard them ask the same question year after year, and had watched each time as hordes of older foster kids took their seats in one of the huge trucks. She was finally old enough this time and had put all her worldly belongings in her backpack in readiness to leave, not that she had many. True to his word, Sgt. McDermott was with them. He climbed up out of the passenger seat but stayed high above the sea of people crowding around the trucks. He peered out and took stock of their surroundings, checking to see that everyone from the immediate vicinity was present.

"To be a soldier means more than just fighting human rebels or rogue Thrakorian's. It means policing the streets, maintaining high standards in our cities, and taking care of its citizens. It means always upholding the law, and most importantly—serving our great King Kronus. Who among you believes you can step up to the challenge and become one of our protectors? Who here trusts in the law and wants to serve it? Who is ready to fight hand-to-hand with those who wish to destroy the way of life we have been given and are thriving in? Come closer only if you truly deem yourself worthy of wearing this uniform," he said as he thumped his chest, and the pounding sound reverberated off the walls and into the ears of every awestruck face. Kyra took her chance to be the first in line. She stepped out of the crowd and peered up at him.

"I'm ready, Sergeant." He nodded and reached down to take her hand. She grabbed hold and let him hoist her up into the bed of the truck with an elated smile.

"Good to see you again, Millan. I'm glad you didn't change your mind," he told her with a cocky grin, before turning back to see who else was ready to join them. She took a seat and couldn't hide her smile at having evidently made a memorable impression.

The trucks were full by the time they sped away, mostly with the young men she'd known all her life, and Kyra looked across at them all, taking in the mixture of recruits.

"I've got five credits worth of supplies says she'll drop out in less than a month," one of the boys, Bran, called to the others close by, and he jutted his chin toward her. Kyra had never really liked Bran much, and he'd been all over her until she'd refused to sleep with him, so she guessed he'd never quite gotten over the embarrassment.

"You can give them straight to me in month-two, ass," she replied, earning herself a load of deep laughs, but nothing more from the man opposite. She looked around the truck bed some more. There were around ten other young women with them too, but each stayed quiet, and Kyra began wondering what'd made them want to enlist. She watched their fearful gazes and timid reactions to the banter going on around them and guessed they must've had no other choice. She was neither scared nor timid, and was clearly in a minority of the young women who wanted to be here. For some of those left behind, their only choice would've been to stay on at the foster home as an employee, but for many the sector recruitment week was their chance to escape and try something else—anything else. No career was out of reach if you were willing to work hard to get it. At least in the military, those with a lack of ambition could stay in a lower rank easily. If all they set out to achieve was a roof over their heads and food in their bellies it was a no-brainer, but of course they still had to get through primary training in one piece first.

When their truck came to a stop hours later, they were ushered off and separated into groups along with the numerous other buses that'd arrived from all over the west coast of America. Their training base, Fort Angel, was one of many all around the world that pumped out trained soldiers by the thousands, whether in the lower, middle, or upper ranks of the handful of divisions, and she suddenly felt rather small.

Kyra and the other women from her truck were split between the nearest groups to even out the numbers, and when she peered up towards the head of her line, she was pleased to see Sgt. McDermott standing there.

"Recruits!" a loud voice boomed from somewhere ahead and silenced them, and a tall human stepped out from behind the lead truck. "You will not get any warm welcomes here, nor will you have a shoulder to cry on or a pat on the back. I am Lieutenant Psy, the Commander of this establishment, and your judge, jury, and career executioner."

The chatter turned into fear-filled silence, and the stifling heat suddenly turned to ice as everyone paled at the thought of failing. "Welcome to Death Valley. This is Fort Angel, AKA—your home for the foreseeable future. First you will commence primary training, in which you will be taught the basics of the Human Royal Armed Forces. You will learn to fight, run, survive, and conquer. You will not rest or get sick. You will pay for your weaknesses until they are gone, and you will also pay for the weaknesses of your platoon." The Commander paced up and down the lines as he spoke, eyeing the recruits with a hard stare. "This year's intake has been split into twenty-six platoons, consisting of between twenty and twenty-five recruits per section. If you look down the long line of misfits and jocks to the front you will notice the smiling face of your Platoon Commander. He or she will be watching your every move. If you fail one too many times, it will be noticed. If you moan and fall behind, they are my eyes and ears. You will be kicked out, mark my words. If you cheat or knowingly hinder another recruit to advance further, you will be punished. This is not a threat. We are in this together, comrades until death!"

Kyra watched him intently, and his words began sinking in with every eloquently pronounced syllable. There was one thing she hadn't considered though, and that was putting the platoon before herself. She was in this for the long haul and had focused entirely on what she needed to do to succeed personally but hadn't even thought about the other recruits. She guessed only time would tell, but as she looked up and down the line of men and women who'd now become the closest thing she had to friends or family, she knew she'd have to try even harder if she was going to make it to the top of her game.

The group was then taken into a huge dorm that reminded Kyra of the foster home, but they didn't linger there. Instead, they were split across a few smaller male and female rooms towards the back of the building, and she was glad not to be sharing with so many. It was small, cramped, and dark, but she didn't hate it. In fact, Kyra felt at home already, and knew she'd made the right effort in preparing herself over the years. Basic lack of necessities could end up being some of the recruits' downfalls, whereas others it might be homesickness or lack of strength—but her past could prove helpful in ensuring she didn't suffer with any of them. She introduced herself to the other girls in her platoon, of which there were only four, and then they left their bags at the end of their chosen beds before following Sgt. McDermott out a door and back into the bright sunshine. He stopped, turned, and eyed each of his twenty-three recruits with a scowl.

They each stared back at him in silence, and Kyra took a moment to really take in the man who would be leading their training for the next year at least. The black combat boots and clothing he wore made him look taller, and the dark blue emblem on his chest showed his rank and position within the Infantry Division of the Human Royal Armed Forces. Sgt. McDermott was a powerful leader, Kyra could already sense it, and she respected the hell out of him before he even uttered a word.

"Welcome to Platoon Lima, my name is Sergeant McDermott. I'm your Platoon Commander, and in our platoon, we have some rules," he said, pacing left and right while he spoke. "Firstly, you do not fool around with each other, and you do not sleep with the other recruits. If you have time to fool around, then you're not training hard enough. Let's also get another thing straight; I hate each and every one of you. It doesn't matter if I was kind and helpful during the fair at your school, or if you think I'm some bad boy with a soft side you want to crack," he stared at the girls and Kyra was the only one not to shrink back in embarrassment. "I am not your friend. I'm your boss. You fail, I fail, and that is absolutely out of the question. I have successfully led three platoons through primary training and scored in the top five each time. I want the number one spot this year, is that understood?" The recruits all murmured their affirmations. "I said, is that understood?" his voice bellowed again, and this time it was met with a loud—"Yes, Sergeant!"

The next few weeks were a grueling set of physical and mental tests for the new recruits. They were put through their paces with each one, and every night as Kyra fell into bed, she ached from head to toe. It was an incredible time though, and she loved every crazy minute of it. Fort Angel had a state-of-the-art training facility that cut no corners with its endurance and harshness challenges, but there was an immense amount of satisfaction she felt when she managed to complete the trials, regardless of how hard they were on her previously undernourished body. Inside the simulated training grounds were areas dedicated to operational practice, and they were put through their paces in heat, mud, snow and even a virtual hurricane in just the first month alone.

During the physical trials, Kyra knew she'd surprised most if not all her comrades when she had performed excellently. At the end of the initial program, she outran all the men in her platoon, and even went head-to-head at the finishing sprint with Sgt. McDermott, or McD as he'd become known for short. He'd beaten her by just a fraction of a second, and punished her audacity by making her do press-ups, but it'd been worth it. He'd even given her one of his uncommon smiles when they'd run ahead of the others, and it was a beautiful gift that he didn't seem to give out very often, but one she'd cherished. After years of living in the system off meager portions of food and basic living provisions, affection wasn't something her caregivers had been paid to give her, so didn't. She had stopped pining for hugs and kisses a long time ago, and instead held the memories of moments like that smile closer to her heart than she'd ever admit to. Kyra knew he'd enjoyed the challenge and was eager to get more of those secret glimpses at the real him, or the McD she thought might just be underneath the scary and commanding persona.

***

Kyra loved her new job and held nothing back during each and every part of the physical and mentally challenging initiation phase of her training. She knew she was under great scrutiny from both Sgt. McDermott and the other superiors at Fort Angel, and she worked hard to make sure she didn't let herself, or them, down. One morning though, flu wracked her body with a force she'd never known before, and Kyra could barely lift her head off the pillow, let alone get ready for her morning parade. The other girls tried to help her, but she was barely lucid and could hardly stand. Her bunkmate Komali went off in search of McD, while the others tried to rouse her, and by the time he got to them she was babbling and so feverish she was hallucinating.

"Get up, Recruit. Time for training," she heard his deep and powerful voice from somewhere far away and groaned. "Don't make me write you up for being late. We don't do sick days, Millan."

She didn't respond the second time, so her friends evidently did the only thing they could think to snap her out of her poorly haze. Under their Commander's watchful stare, each girl took an arm and dragged Kyra to the showers, where she was left under an icy cascade to cool her fever, and the shock of it quickly brought her back to reality. Still in her pajamas, she reached out and grabbed McD's hand, desperate to make him see that she was trying her hardest to get back on her feet.

"We don't do sick days," she mimicked with a forced smile, and tipped her head back into the water. She took huge mouthfuls of it and gulped it down, savoring the icy goodness as it quenched her thirst and quelled the fire in her lungs. Kyra felt lightheaded but wouldn't let the heavy tiredness behind her eyes capture her again. Instead, she pulled herself to her feet and peered up at the man she'd somehow managed to soak while reclaiming her lucidity. "McD says we don't do sick days, so give me five minutes and I'll be ready, Sergeant."

"It looks like I'm gonna need to get changed into a new set of combats, Recruit. You're in luck, because I don't think I have any more to hand, so it'll take me at least an hour to get a new set." He turned to leave but stopped near the door and looked back at her over his shoulder. "That and I'll need a cold shower after seeing you in those wet pajamas," he added, and Kyra frowned. She didn't understand what he meant, but then looked down at herself and quickly realized that her soaked nightwear had not only clung to every inch of her so she looked almost naked, but they'd also turned see-through at the same time. Her cheeks burned with renewed heat, but not from her fever this time, and she grabbed a towel from the nearby rail to cover herself, but he'd already gone.

After popping her pills and swigging enough medicine to keep her going for the day, Kyra finally managed to get her ass to class, and was delighted to see that she was not the only one suffering with their latest wave of viral sickness. At least half of her platoon was ill, and thankfully McD chose to take it easy on them rather than insist on their usual regime of grueling physical training. They watched educational films outlining the new strategic methods for combatting low-morale, and she watched half-heartedly along with the others while hoping her body would kick its infection sooner rather than later.

When McD then came down with the same flu the next day, it was hard for his platoon not to act out their sadistic fantasies by making him pay for all the times he'd pushed them too hard or made their days too long, but they resisted. He'd protected his recruits the day before, rather than punish their weakness, and each of the recovering recruits was determined to repay the favor. Kyra was feeling better already, thanks to McD, so she gave him the idea of spending the day in the computer suite. There they could while away the hours working on simulations, while he rested in a dark corner out of sight from watchful eyes of his superiors.

"Sick days rock," she whispered in his ear when checking on him, and McD laughed. "Movies and computer games? Seems like the perfect couple days if you ask a geek like me." In a move so fast it shocked the hell out of her, Sgt. McDermott grabbed her wrist and pulled her closer. Kyra could feel the heat radiating off him but didn't pull back. His breath hitched in his throat, and he inhaled deeply.

"Every day can be perfect, if you let it." She wanted to ask him what he meant, but McD let her go and turned his face away. Part of her wondered if he was hallucinating, but he seemed perfectly conscious. Instead, she left him to rest, and got back to acquainting herself with the new computer system.

***

Weeks quickly merged into months, and they soon moved onto weapons training and other skills. Her shooting and knife yielding were good, as was her map reading, and although it wasn't easy, Kyra felt accomplished and ready to learn more. Their everyday routine was the same. The alarm went off the same time each morning, without a day off or a break in the schedule, and it was a constant program of training, lessons, food, training, training, training... she lived and breathed her new life, and woke up each day to begin it all over again under the watchful eye of her enigmatic Platoon Commander. Kyra felt drawn to McD in ways she hadn't with anyone in years but guessed he must have it from a lot of the women in his command, as he didn't seem to notice them all swooning over him in equal measure. Her conscious mind knew better than to think her attraction was anything more than a typical foolish crush on the person in charge, and it didn't help matters that he was truly a fine figure of a man. Those dark eyes and hair were mesmerizing, and when teamed with his hard and sexy stare, Kyra and the other girls melted every time.

Forcing all distractions aside, she continued working hard in her lessons and the specialized training program set out for them by the Thrakorian leaders. She excelled in some areas where others struggled, but it was during the first code-breaking session that she truly shone. Kyra not only broke through the encrypted firewall they were trying to get around in record time, but she also found a bug in the training code, which she fixed while she was at it. Shocked faces greeted her from the other recruits at the end of the task, and she simply shrugged before sliding her glasses back into her pocket, and then looking to McD for his next order.

Their team was ahead in almost all areas, and Kyra knew she was partly responsible for their incredible scores. There was no gloating though, nor did she want or need praise. All she wanted was a chance to show what she was capable of, and in that session, she'd got it.

Lt. Psy took her aside after the codex challenge and led her into his office.

"Why did you enlist, Millan?" he asked her with a scowl.

"To serve my King, of course. But also, because I believe I'm good enough to join the computer and technological science team within the Intelligence Division," she answered, being careful to mind her manners and talk clearly and respectfully to her

Commanding Officer. He offered her a seat opposite him, and then peered across at her with apparent intrigue. "I've wanted to be a soldier ever since I was a little girl. I know this is where I belong," she began to add, fearing the worst.

"You're absolutely right, this *is* where you belong. Make no doubt about that," he replied, cutting off her desperate ranting, and Kyra took a breath in relief. He watched her through wise eyes, the skin on his middle-aged face hardened and thickly lined with wrinkles. She had no doubt they were caused by too much scowling and time spent in the sun. "Complete your primary and secondary training in the overall top five, and I promise you your pick of career paths. We need soldiers like you, Millan. Keep up the good work," he said, and stood to indicate she was dismissed.

She quickly shuffled out of her seat. After a salute and a mumbled reply, Kyra stumbled out of Lt. Psy's office in shock. This was the ultimate dream come true. She'd been noticed by the top Commander of her intake and given her very own pep talk. There was no going back or stopping now, and she could've jumped for joy.

"Hey little lady," a deep voice rumbled from within the shadows to her right, and Kyra turned to find where the owner was hiding. The sound of McD's gruff laughter caught her ears, and she stepped across into the darkness between some storage crates with him. Strong hands grabbed her waist and lifted her off the ground, and a wall of muscle pressed into her small frame to hold her against the pallet behind. "Don't you know not to sneak into the shadows with men who have very questionable morals?" he asked, and as her eyes adjusted to the darkness, Kyra could just about make out his face above hers. He was mere inches away, and she guessed he was enjoying holding her near, because his soft, rapidly panting breath was so close it was tickling her cheek. She couldn't hide her surprise that he'd waited for her but was especially shocked by his apparent attraction. She'd watched him with a toe-curling craving for months but knew the rules and had never even considered that he might like her too.

"And who hates all his recruits. Don't forget that part," she teased, and he laughed. McD seemed to hesitate on how to act or what to say next, and she guessed he was feeling uneasy after having suddenly shown her how he felt. She was enjoying this small piece of affection more than she'd bargained for, though, and didn't want him to slope away in embarrassment. It'd been so very long since she'd been held close, and Kyra was beginning to feel like the only romance she'd find would be in her dreams when Kronus would come and deliver his light kisses to her scarred cheek.

She'd often watched Sgt. McDermott and his incredible body as he ran ahead of her during training. Many times it was the only reason she'd kept going through the mud and rain, but she'd never expected him to wrap her in his arms and share the same few inches of space between two storage containers like he was now. "What's your first name?" she whispered, filling the silence that'd descended. He seemed hesitant to answer and opted instead for a chance to sweep her off her feet, in the figurative sense as he'd already done so in the physical.

"I might be mean to you in the daytime, when I have to see you as nothing more than a piece of crap I'm to mold and polish until it's something worthy of a rank and a division," he conceded, leaning in even closer. "But at night when you haunt me, I'm the piece of crap, and you're molding me. You make me better, stronger, and with you around I'm more in tune with my desires. Your face is in my dreams every night, and when I see you the next day, it's all I can do not to kiss you good morning." Every part of her body exploded with heat without warning, and she couldn't quite believe her ears.

"Why are you saying this now?" Kyra had to ask. She was seriously swooning and knew that she was dangerously close to believing the things McD was saying to her. He had to tell her if this was all some sick prank, because she wasn't sure she could handle being messed around if it was. "Is this your idea of a joke?"

"Far from it. I've been fighting these feelings since the first day we met, but it's forbidden for the Training Commanders to have relationships with their recruits. I had hoped you might try to seduce me, but it seems I was the one who had to make the first move..." he let his explanation tail off.

His body was covering hers from head to toe, his breath invading her lungs, and Kyra could feel his heart beating in the chest he was pressing into hers. She craned her neck to stare into the darkness enveloping his face, and accidentally slid her lips across his lightly stubble-covered jaw. She was about to apologize, when he turned his face downwards and connected their mouths. Her lips parted, willing his tongue to invade, and it did. Kyra's legs were up and around his waist less than a second later, and their mouths didn't leave one another's in what felt like forever.

"Whoa," she breathed, and let him kiss her again.

"Silas," he finally murmured when he broke contact. "My name's Silas." He pressed against her and they both groaned.

"Well, Silas," she replied with a smile. "It seems we're about to start some trouble, doesn't it? Maybe we should call this off before it gets too out of hand?" Kyra hoped he wasn't about to agree with her and leave, but she was also terrified of jeopardizing her future, or his career as a Training Commander. He sighed and nodded against where he'd rested his cheek on her forehead.

"We've got at least another six-months to get through, so why don't we take it slow?" he offered, taking her aback. All the other boys she'd known seemed in such a rush to get their satisfaction and go on their way, but for some reason Silas was in no hurry to have her. She thought about how long they'd already known one another and guessed he really might just be a slow mover. It'd been almost half a year since that day at the careers fair, and they'd only just shared a first kiss. She liked going slow, and as long as she had some more stolen moments to keep her going, would happily forgo anything more. When she left the primary training program they could decide whether or not to pursue a relationship then. There was also the 'plausible deniability' factor if they abstained, and the sheer thought of waiting made that pang of fear that'd appeared in her gut subside.

"I like slow," she replied, kissing him softly again. "You are my boss after all. I guess I'll have to put up with you being an ass in front of everyone else, right?" she enquired, and he laughed.

"I'm afraid so, Kyra," he replied in a deep whisper, and the sound of her first name on his lips made her tremble. He'd never once called her by it, and she wanted to hear it again. "No one can know anything's going on. This will have to be our secret, are you okay with that?" she nodded.

"By day we're Sgt. McDermott and Recruit Millan. By night we're Silas and Kyra. I can handle that," she mumbled.

Silas let her drop slowly back onto her feet and Kyra ran her palms over his chest and down his arms. She took his hands in hers, and then kissed the back of one before slipping away and out of the shadows. There was no looking back, both literally and figuratively, or else she knew there'd be trouble. Their secret would have to be kept no matter what. Pretense in front of others was just another skill she knew she'd have to develop, but she didn't care. Silas was the first man to make her heart truly flutter since the King had pulled her from that rose bush fourteen years ago, and now she knew he wanted her back in a way she'd never dared to dream he might do. She didn't care if they never had more, but just knowing there was someone in the world that appreciated her enough to kiss and hold her close was truly a strange yet wonderful new feeling.

Kyra felt both liberated and grounded at the same time. Her entire life there'd been no hugs and kisses, except from the King and then years later the boys who'd taken a liking to her at the foster home. Kids being kids, they'd fooled around and had their fun, but it was never serious, nor did they make her feel the way Silas had just managed to.

He was an absolute ass when he wanted or needed to be. She'd seen it plenty of times, but he'd just shown her he was also capable of softness and affection, and she craved more.

CHAPTER THREE

"Are you *experienced?*" Silas asked Kyra a few days later when they were sat together under one of the huge trees that lined the perimeter fence. They had exactly forty minutes until the next patrol came around, so had used the privacy to take refuge from the hot sun together in secret. She snorted in shock but laughed when he took her hand and pulled her closer. "It doesn't matter either way," he assured her, wrapping an arm over her back where he kneaded the sore muscle in her shoulder. He'd worked them out hard that morning with a triathlon and seemed to know which muscles were complaining without her having to even say.

"I am," she eventually replied. "Growing up in foster homes, there wasn't much funding for locks on the doors or security for the girls. I held my own. When I was little it wasn't an issue, because I could run for miles if I ever needed to, but as soon as I developed a set of curves I learned self-defense. In the end it was a choice whether to give that part of myself up willingly and follow the rest of the girls, or hold onto it in the hope it was mine to keep." Her tone turned regretful as she recalled the stories of girls being pushed into sleeping with their boyfriends by the older teens. Despite the tough laws on adults regarding assault offences, minors often got away with a slap on the wrist if they played their cards right.

Kyra had been lucky. She'd found a small group of friends and ducked her head as a young teen. She hadn't been picked out by one of the older boys to be his arm-candy or doting little mistress, and she'd always been glad of it. Instead, a boy named Andreas had asked her to date him. He was kind and gentle, and hadn't pushed her to sleep with him. When they finally had, it was on her terms, and she didn't regret it.

"How old were you?" Silas's voice cut through her thoughtfulness. "I was sixteen when I lost mine. In the ten years since then I've only had a handful of women, I want you to know that." Kyra looked up at him from her spot nestled under his arm, and was glad he'd told her, and that she finally knew his age. They'd barely spoken in private since the night he'd made that first move, but already she felt safe and secure with him. She believed his story and trusted him to treat her with as much sincerity as Andreas had. At nineteen, Kyra wasn't all that younger than Silas, but in some ways felt more experienced, or 'street smart' as some called it.

"Almost sixteen," she answered and Silas seemed shocked, but quickly righted himself. "I've been with a few guys, but not many. I was never one of those foster girls who ended up pregnant or who was happy to get married and plod along in the lower sectors. I lived the way everyone lived in those homes, looking out for number one, while always feeling forced to fit in. I'm glad to be free of that place."

Silas pulled her closer and kissed her temple. The tiny affection in his gesture told her he didn't judge, and possibly that he didn't completely understand enough to answer. She wondered where he'd grown up and the sort of childhood he'd had in comparison to hers. Kyra reached up her hand and cupped his cheek with it, but was instantly mesmerized by his powerful stare. His incredibly deep brown eyes bore into hers, and she no longer wanted to talk.

She could see a huge resemblance in him to King Kronus and wondered if in some ways it was why she liked him so much. His dark brown hair was almost the same shade, as were his eyes. Silas clearly wasn't as tall as their Thrakorian leader, but when he peered down at her with kindness and sincerity etched across his face, the same feelings resonated within her that'd done the night of the invasion—acceptance and desire. As a child, she'd felt love for Kronus not based on the televised addresses that followed Invasion Day to inform them he was their new leader, but because of the way he'd made her feel on that rooftop. She'd taken him for nothing more than another alien soldier in that moment, and loved him anyway.

Kyra knew they only had a matter of minutes until they'd have to go their separate ways to the food hall, and she wanted more of what he'd teased her with the few nights earlier. "Kiss me?" she asked in a hoarse whisper, and Silas's eyes widened in happy surprise. He didn't hesitate in taking her mouth with his, and despite the heat of the day she felt an icy wave pass down her spine. It drove her insane with desire for more, but she'd promised herself they'd wait. Instead, she enjoyed the simplicity of their kiss. Her tongue flicked upwards while his caressed hers tenderly. His coarse, hardened lips pressed into her soft ones, but she loved the feel of his roughness. The five o'clock shadow on his chin was like welcome brashness to her smooth skin, and every second they connected made Kyra feel feminine and womanly. He was powerful and all male, and while she knew she was a more than worthy soldier, sometimes it was nice to remember she was also a woman. His kiss gave her that, and Kyra never wanted it to end.

After weeks of stolen moments and secret make-out sessions in one of the many shadows Fort Angel had to offer, the tension was so high between Kyra and Silas that she was sure she'd begun blushing every time he was anywhere near her, day or night. He maintained his cool, calm, and authoritative way perfectly, while she felt like she constantly had to keep herself in check.

One night after dinner, she and the other girls in her platoon headed back to their room but were intercepted by Silas along with four more of their male comrades.

"Follow me," was all he said, and after a quick look at each other in surprise, they immediately did as he'd asked. Not a word was spoken until they reached one of the smaller training rooms at the back of the building, where thick mats had been put on the floor and against the walls. Kyra wondered what sort of training could possibly require the use of a padded wall, and quickly got her answer. "Who here has done self-defense training?" Silas asked when they'd lined up before him, and he looked Kyra right in the eye. She raised her hand, along with one of the other girls, but he chose her, and beckoned her forward to join him on one of the mats. "What's the first rule of self-defense, Recruit Millan?"

"Hurt them first?" she asked, peering up at him questioningly. After all, she'd never had official training, just worked out at their local park with her friends practicing basic martial arts. They'd learned how to wrestle and use an attacker's weight or disadvantages against them, but never under proper tutelage, and she wasn't aware there were any rules.

Silas slid his foot beneath her legs in a movement so fluid she barely registered it until she was lying on the ground.

"Wrong." He gave her a hand up. "There are no rules. If you can run, you run. If you must fight, you weigh up everything you can in the time given, and attack as necessary. But what if they attack you first? What if they take away your basic senses? Like breaking your nose resulting in loss of vision, or punching you in the chest to wind you?" Before she could answer, Silas came at her. He grabbed her arm and swung her into the nearby wall. Kyra hit the padding with a thud that didn't hurt, but she knew it would've if the layers of foam weren't there to shield her from the concrete wall behind. Silas grabbed her wrists and held them at the small of her back and pressed into her. Physically she found it hard to breathe in his hold but was soon panting as heat bloomed between them. "You're an easy target, Recruit. Fight back, evade, and save yourself. If I were an attacker, you'd be dead or worse by now. Do not ever give up or give in," he took a step back and released her hands before turning to face the others.

Kyra was furious with herself for being beaten so easily. She lunged at him and ended up climbing onto Silas's back. She wrestled his arms with her strong thighs and twisted in an attempt to make him fall over, but he was too fast for her. He positioned her so she hit the ground first, and then pinned her arms above her head. Silas had ended up nestled between her open thighs, their faces close enough for Kyra to see the flash of need in his eyes. He reared back, pulling her arms down to her chest, where he crossed them over one another and effectively rendered her immobile.

"Asshole," she moaned.

"Do you give up?" he asked, pressing her hands into the mat while his hips rocked stealthily into hers.

"Never," she replied, and earned herself a smile.

"Good. Then get out of this hold," Silas demanded, and while she loved the heat in his stare, she was very aware of their audience, so assessed her position. After a wriggle and an attempt to twist away, she bucked wildly and heard the wind rush from his lungs as she successfully caught him in the chest with her crossed arms. In the split-second he relinquished his hold, Kyra pulled out of his grasp and clambered to her feet. She ran for the door and grabbed the handle, before turning back and accepting the round of applause from her fellow recruits. Silas stood and grinned at her, before letting his mask fall back into place. "Very well, Millan. The rest of you, pick a partner and start practicing. I don't want to see blood or tears; we're in this together. This is for your own benefit, for the good of the platoon—not personal enjoyment." He raised an eyebrow before rolling his shoulders in readiness for his second round with Kyra. She came back to the mat and watched as the others began their attacks, all the while eyeing the man she knew she was supposed to be fighting off warily. She didn't want to fight; she wanted him to take her. Damn, this promise she'd made herself to wait was getting harder and harder to keep.

"The final exercise for primary training starts at zero-eight-hundred hours. You'll split into your platoon's and your Commander will be given an envelope. Inside that envelope contains instructions they must follow in order for their platoon to succeed. You will not know what is inside that envelope, so must follow all orders as given to you by your Platoon Commander." Lt. Psy addressed the crowd of recruits in his usual, hard way. They were all stood to attention, ready for their last few days of primary training to be over with, so those who passed could move on to their secondary phases. Kyra would be one of the recruits asking to stay on at Fort Angel so she could try out for the Intelligence Division. In order to make their computer and technological sciences department she had to first prove herself in both the combat and tactical training areas. There she would learn about some of the confidential aspects of the Human Royal Armed Forces, as well as more in depth knowledge about their Thrakorian masters. Silas would go back to training the new recruits, but she hoped he'd still be around enough so they could spend their tiny snippets of free time together.

"Yes, sir!" the recruits all cried when Psy was finished, and they began checking their packs one last time to ensure they had everything they might need. Kyra was pleased with herself and her progress. She'd never doubted she'd make it this far, but there had always been the fear of failing that'd kept her going in the harder times. Silas had helped tremendously, and in ways she would always adore him for. He'd become a constant source of support she'd never once thought she'd needed, someone who made her feel wanted and beautiful. He told her every evening before sending her off to bed how gorgeous she was, even in her army combats, and she loved him for making her feel so good about herself. Kyra lived for the accomplishment she felt when he was impressed by her skills in training, and was also very aware of how the end of her primary phase brought with it two weeks of much needed down time. Summer leave was a beacon on the horizon, and she couldn't wait for promised long, lazy days spent without the pressures of training, or the scrutiny from her commanding officers.

Most recruits would go home to their families, but Kyra had none to go back to. There was no need for her to go to the foster home, and even the thought of going back to the L.A slums filled her with dread. It hadn't been an awful upbringing, but there was nothing and no one there for her to return to. Silas had told her very little about his home or family, but he didn't seem keen on going back either, and she hoped he might suggest them staying at the base together and hiding away if they could, or else find another hideaway they could spend their summer leave together in. Kyra pushed all thoughts of the break away though, and focused on the task at hand. First they had to get through the final exercise. They had no idea how their platoon was doing in the running for the number one spot, but felt confident they'd given McD a placing near the top. In order to ensure their success, they needed top marks for the final primary exercise, and she readied herself for anything the Commander would throw at them.

"Pack light, Recruits." In just three words, Silas had given them one of his codes for the exercise. Packing light meant they were headed for a landscape of heat or water, not snow or cold and wet conditions, so she quickly discarded her heavy jacket and waterproofs. Kyra then followed his lead and they regrouped at the entrance to the exercise area. They waited for the clock to toll the change of hour, and then followed behind Silas as he led them through a small entryway into a dark corridor. He only opened the connecting door once their path back out was closed, locked and secured from the outside. There was no choice but to move forward, and when the blaring sunshine hit her face, Kyra quickly pulled out her hat and sunglasses.

They formed a small semi-circle around McD, and listened intently while he issued his orders. "We need to scale this terrain and retrieve the flag with our platoon emblem at the finish. We then rendezvous back here, and the clock will stop once we are back out that door," he said, and pointed to the door behind them. "Follow my lead and do everything I say. Speed is of the essence, so we're not hanging around anywhere longer than absolutely necessary. Understood?"

"Yes, sir," the recruits replied in unison, and they fell in line behind him as Silas began running toward the huge sand dune before them. When they reached its peak all the recruits gasped in surprise. Their usual desert training area had been transformed into a route of sand, water and forest followed by a huge peak she guessed they must need to climb in order to retrieve their flag at the top. They'd been warned to expect soldiers on their secondary phase training posing as rebels, and she made sure her weapon was within easy reach should they be attacked. Any recruit that took a hit from one of their high-tech darts or was detained by the 'rebels' would lose points for their team, but a fast score would hopefully cancel out any demerits, so they all knew to just keep pushing on as much as was physically possible. Speed was key to passing their assessment with a good score, and if they had to, they'd put their personal needs like food and rest aside in order to achieve one.

CHAPTER FOUR

The platoon set off toward the mountainous structure in the distance. Kyra guessed it must be over ten miles away, and readied herself for hours of running. The heat from the sun was intense, but bearable, and she saved her water for future use—just in case. She tabbed alongside the others and scanned the areas to the left and right. No sign of trouble so far. The group then closed in and continued to check the perimeter as they reached the edge of a huge lake.

"Can we swim across?" one of her fellow recruits, Jonas, asked. They all looked to McD for advice, but he simply scowled. She could tell he wasn't able to help them more than absolutely necessary, and the others quickly figured out that his silence meant they had to decide for themselves as well.

"Too far," another of her comrades answered, and she agreed. Kyra then looked up and down the shoreline in search of an answer, and spotted something out of place just over a ridge. She grabbed the binoculars from her pack and peered through them, and beamed at what she saw.

"There are three boats to the west. Unmanned, but they must be guarded. I say we take a look, and relieve them from whoever is watching over them," she told the group, and many of the others followed her example by grabbing their binoculars to take a look.

"Friend or foe?" another recruit, Jett asked, and suddenly all eyes were on Kyra for an answer. Silas stayed silent, and she guessed he knew exactly when and where to offer help or guidance, but otherwise stayed out of the recruits' final exam. She wasn't sure she was ready to lead just yet, but it seemed there was no other choice, and so she took a moment to think it over, and gave the order.

"Let's take a closer look. Send in one recon recruit to check for rebel markings and if so, we take them out. Agreed?" she offered, and received firm affirmations. Regardless of it being an exercise, she knew they'd lose points if they attacked an allied camp, so knew it was worth spending a few extra minutes checking to be sure. She gave Jett a nod and watched as he opened his mouth to complain, but then seemingly thought better of it. He ran forward a few feet, and then ducked down before leopard-crawling the rest of the way. At the top of the next dune he stopped, watched for a few seconds and then retreated a few meters. Kyra watched through her goggles as he gave them the hand signal to signify he'd encountered rebels, and she immediately started toward him. The rest of their platoon followed, and took refuge at the base of the dune. Using only hand gestures, they agreed to spread out around the bank and attack in exactly thirty-seconds.

Soon they were charging over the ridge and into the base camp of eight secondary phase soldiers posing as rebels. Shots were fired, but they seemed genuinely caught off guard by the attack, and each took a simulated bullet from the recruits that registered as a fatal wound. The technology behind the new darts was a wonder to Kyra. She marveled at how they sensed the angle and placement of the bullet, before turning either green, yellow or red. Green meant it was considered a flesh wound and you could continue on. Yellow meant you'd had a serious injury so needed to play casualty, and red meant death for the supposed victim.

After checking the area and taking the boat keys from the men playing dead on the sand, they ran for the crafts.

As she climbed up and over into the closest hover boat though, a sharp slap between her shoulder blades caught her off guard. "Crap, have I been hit?" she shouted, showing her back to Silas, who nodded. His face told her everything, if this was a real life combat situation, she would be dead.

"Wait, it's not changing color," Jonas called from behind her and they watched her back while Kyra waited for what felt like forever for an answer. Silas was staring over at the beach thoughtfully, and then turned back to her.

He grabbed the dart and threw it overboard, and shook his head when she went to question him.

"It doesn't count, it was just one of the rebel players being an ass. That's why it didn't change color. His weapon has been deactivated because he's had a fatal hit."

"Thank you," she managed in reply, and he nodded. Relief swept through Kyra so fast she actually felt lightheaded. She wanted to jump back out of the boat, find the guy who'd shot her, and give him a swift punch to the nose, but knew there wasn't any time to waste. The main thing was that she hadn't been taken out of the exercise in the first few minutes, and she got her head right back in the game rather than dwell on her near miss.

Silas started the boat and steered them towards the opposite side of the lake. He didn't say a word, in fact none of them did. There was no celebrating or chatting to be done yet. That would only come after the flag had been retrieved, they were back at base, and their scores were tallied.

As soon as their boots hit the sand on the other side, the platoon re-grouped and looked to Silas for his orders. He stood with his back to the wilderness, and took stock of his men and women for a moment before addressing them.

"This area is a known rebel hold. We need to get to the

other side of this forest as soon as possible, so we do not engage unless absolutely necessary. A fight will only slow us down. Move stealthily and carefully through the paths, and watch your backs. Constantly check the periphery all around, including above," he pointed up into the treetops. "It is safe to assume there are only rebels in our path from here onward. Consider every person ahead as hostile. If they see us they will engage, so you shoot first. A dead soldier loses us valuable points, but if they capture you alive, they'll strip us of even more. Go down fighting. Never give up, and never give in."

"Yes sir!" they cried in agreement, and then filed in behind him.

Progress was slow through the dense forest, but after a couple of hours they eventually managed to reach a small meadow where they took a moment for a breather and to have a sip of water. Kyra pulled out her specialist binoculars again and fiddled with the settings, rather than rest. This felt too easy, and knew she'd only take a break once she was sure the coast was clear. After switching them to night-vision mode regardless of the sunshine, she stood on the edge of the small patch of grass peering into the dark woods. There was no movement out there, but something caught her eye and she zoomed in as far as the glasses would allow.

There was an intricate carving on one of the trees to the west. It resembled a star, but had one point slightly longer than the others, as if it was an arrow. She slowly followed the trajectory east and eventually spotted another, and another. The final star shape had its elongated edge pointing upward, and it was only when she lowered the goggles that Kyra realized they were heading straight for an ambush. The arrow pointing up was directly in their path to the mountain, and every synapse in her brain fired in warning. The rebels might be located above the ground in that area, and would attack if their platoon wandered underneath their camp on their way to the summit. If they were ambushed by ten or more rebels, they'd easily lose half of their men, no doubt about it, and she quickly scanned the east side of the woods to check for more symbols. There were none.

Going east might take longer, but she was sure it would result in less casualties and a higher chance of success when it came to the climb for the flag.

"Something to say, Recruit?" Silas was in full Commander mode, and Kyra knew he'd picked up on her findings.

"Yes, Sergeant. We're headed north, correct?" he nodded. "I believe an eastern approach would be better." A smile curled at his lips, but he quickly hid it away. He was impressed, and she reveled in that tiny glimpse of pride he'd shown in her tactical instinct.

"Why? A northern route will be quicker and more direct. The eastern woods are darker, indicating that they're denser. It will take us longer," Silas replied, and made sure he said it loud enough for the others to hear. The rest of their platoon began shuffling and murmuring, clearly interested in their conversation, and Kyra took a deep breath. She knew she had to be sure of her intel, and of her ability to lead their group safely if she were to voice this opinion, and took a moment to gather her thoughts. This was an exercise, so no one would really get hurt, but she knew that in a real-life scenario she'd do the right thing and follow her instincts. If this were her platoon, she would lead them east, no doubt about it.

"I believe that straight ahead is a rebel stronghold, and by continuing to head north we'll walk directly into a trap. They know we're going for the flag, and this is the most direct route to it. Also, there are clues, directions of sorts for the rebels to follow to their base, and it leads there." She pointed directly ahead and the others followed her gaze into the forest. "I say we change course. Head east and then follow the curve back before taking the mountain from that side rather than head-on."

There was silence as the others deliberated over her given opinion. They seemed torn, and rightly so. After all, McD had given them an order to head north, and now Kyra was offering an alternative based on clues they hadn't seen. Silas had stayed quiet, and she guessed it was all part of his brief to let the recruits decide things like this for themselves, but she hoped he might at least give her a warning look if she was going way off course or making a huge mistake.

"Let's do it," Jett answered with a kind smile, and he stood to join her on the eastern edge of the small meadow. Many of the others joined them, but a final few hovered by the northern edge.

"But, what if it takes longer? Surely speed is more important than evasion? If we fight our way through the rebel camp we'll be at the rock face before nightfall, if we go east it could be morning. I say we keep heading north," Jonas was the one who spoke for them, and she couldn't deny him wanting to voice his own opinion. Kyra appreciated his honesty, and was glad to see he was airing his concerns. They could all agree there were two very viable options, and so they all looked to Silas for his final decision. As Platoon Commander, he was their leader, and had the last say. Kyra told herself that if he said they should continue north, she would go without any argument. This final exercise was their chance to showcase all the fundamental things they'd learned throughout their training, and she'd done that just by offering up an alternative route, whether they took it or not.

In order to complete their primary training phase, following orders and maintaining discipline were two of the key principles. Showing skill in combat and surviving in the field were next, and then their tactical and intellectual skills came after. She knew she'd potentially skipped ahead by trying to be clever with her code-breaking skills now, and if that wasn't the point of this exercise, then she was willing to show her understanding in the matter. Kyra wondered if the ambush was exactly what their chain of command wanted to happen. They were perhaps required to show how they tackled a rebel combat scenario, and it was no-doubt Silas's job to get them there. She knew she was winding herself round in circles, and hoped he would speak up soon and save her from the inner turmoil she was having.

"Two teams. Millan," his voice pulled her from her thoughts and she snapped to attention. "You take four recruits east and meet us at the waterfall." He showed her the point on their small map that indicated the falls, and she nodded. "If we aren't already there, you wait until sunrise and then climb. Do not attempt to scale that mountain in the dark, is that understood?"

"Yes, Sergeant," she replied, and she could hear the shakiness to her voice. He trusted her to lead a small team away from the main group, and she couldn't begin to explain how amazing it felt to have her idea rewarded with a show of faith in her deciphering skills. Kyra chose the four recruits closest to her, the ones who had joined her first, and together they turned and walked into the forest. She didn't dare look back, but heard the murmured voices of the rest of their platoon as they too gathered their things and headed north.

After two hours of slow progress through the dense forest, their team came upon another small clearing. They secured the perimeter and took a drink of water, while remaining quiet and on guard for any sound of life around them in the trees. Kyra took a look at her map and located the small gap in the forest that she was sure must be where they'd stopped, and she knew it was time to head north again. She used her goggles to check for any sign of rebel activity, but found none, and after devouring an energy bar from her pack, she led the others on through the trees.

By dusk they were exhausted, and by midnight they were ready to sleep where they fell, but Kyra pushed her team onwards. It was too risky to sleep, at least until they reached the waterfall, and she knew there couldn't be much forest left for them to clamber through. The trees were already thinning out, and she could hear running water in the distance. Every muscle and bone in her body screamed for rest, but she engaged her brain and told her aching limbs to shut the hell up. There was only one goal, and that flag was it. Sleep and rest were for the following day when they'd retrieved their prize and passed the exercise.

As if she'd willed it, moonlight hit Kyra's face and her boots squelched into softened mud. The others then broke free of the woodland, and they too peered up into the simulated moon overhead. Sometimes she had to remind herself that the hot sun or howling winds weren't real, and that they were nothing more than elaborate training grounds provided by the Thrakorian's. They'd been created to ensure their human soldiers were trained in all aspects of earthly warfare, regardless of where they were stationed, and it worked. Troops could then be sent to every corner of the world dependent on their division, and thanks to the intense training could survive and work on any terrain.

Kyra checked her watch, and it was three-am. She wondered if the others were languishing by the cool waterfall already, laughing and joking with each other about their sub-team and her foolish plan. The sheer thought of being ridiculed for her idea made her stomach ache, but it also urged her onwards. She had to know for sure if she'd been right or wrong, but would hold her head high regardless, and knew Silas would be proud of her initiative.

It wasn't long before they found the waterfall, and the cool mist coming up from the pool was heaven on her sweat-covered brow. The team then scoured the area from top to bottom and found no sign of their platoon.

"Do you think they were hit?" one of the other women

recruits named Brona asked when they dropped their packs and took refuge by one of the alcoves.

"Maybe they got here hours ago and went for the flag rather than wait for us?" Jett asked, fiddling with his pack to squeeze it into a pillow-shape.

"Surely they would've left us a sign if so? And McD said to wait for sunrise before scaling the mountain," Kyra answered quietly, feeling pensive, and the others murmured in agreement. "Let's rest now, and at dawn we head for the flag. Follow orders, complete the exercise," she added, telling herself as much as the others. Sleepy affirmations met her ears, and she settled down beside the others to take first watch. She held on as long as she needed to before rousing the next in line, and then stared down at the water for a while before letting her lids fall closed.

CHAPTER FIVE

Just before dawn, Kyra woke from her light sleep, slid on her glasses, and quickly scanned the area around their small alcove. It was clear. There was still no sign of the rest of their platoon, and she began to wonder if their micro team would have to go for the flag alone. She moved her aching body slowly, and climbed out of their huddle to stretch her legs and arms in the cool morning air. The water was rushing to the small pool beneath, and she loved the calming sound it made. It was kind of like white noise to her frenzied thoughts, and soothed her. Brona roused too, and she asked if it was clear. Kyra nodded.

"I'm going to do a quick sweep. Come and find me if there's any sign of them," she told her, and Brona nodded before turning back into the shadows for a few more minutes of rest.

Kyra grabbed her weapon and checked the waterfall and its surrounding area. It was still clear. There wasn't any sign of McD or the others, and she knew that dawn was less than thirty minutes away. If she were going to climb that mountain with just four recruits for company, she would need to be fresh and alert, so she decided a wash in the cool water of the falls would do just the trick. She stood staring at the cascade, but it was coming down fast and hard. Kyra was sure it'd feel more painful than relaxing to stand beneath the heavy downpour, so she decided a splash of water to the face from the pool below would have to do. She grabbed a small pouch from her pack and threw one of the beans it contained into the water. After waiting the few required seconds, readings from the pool began to appear on the screen of the device she'd kept in her hand. The bean was a clever piece of equipment designed to check the water for dangers such as temperature, acidity or poison, and animals that might pose a risk to anyone considering a swim. It came back as clear, and Kyra reached down to stroke the surface of the cool water with her hand.

"You can take a dip if you'd like? I'll keep watch," Brona's soft voice called from the direction of the alcove, and she climbed out of the shadows. She'd clearly thought better of having any more sleep, and Kyra was glad. The thought of getting a cool soak was so inviting she couldn't bear refusing the offer. She beckoned her over and Brona quickly followed her lead. When she was standing beside her, she followed Kyra's gaze out and away from the pool towards the forest.

"Stay here and watch, if they come from the woods you'll see them as they breach the tree line. Shout me as soon as you see anything," she instructed her, and her comrade nodded in understanding. Brona crouched and rested against one of the boulders so she could watch the area to the south, weapon poised and ready, and Kyra quickly stripped down to her underwear. She left her combats folded in a neat pile above her boots, but put her weapon right beside the water's edge in case it was needed.

After one last peek around, she stepped forward into the water. It felt freezing on her sweaty skin, but was also a welcome relief from the heat and grime from the day and night before. The trek through the forest had given her scrapes that stung with the freshness of the water, and her sore feet throbbed, but slowly eased as she took the weight off them and lay back in the pool. She peered up at the mountain of rock they still had to scale, and saw that the morning sun had now hit its peak. It was almost time to get ready to move.

Kyra rubbed the skin on her arms, legs, torso, and back with her hands to clean as much of her dirt away as possible without the use of soap or towels. She rinsed off a few times and then swam back to the edge, where she stepped up and began twisting her waist-length, dark brown hair around itself to squeeze the water out. The warm air was drying her skin nicely, and she begrudged climbing back into her dirty uniform so stayed away from the small pile as long as possible.

"They're here!" Brona's voice called from her spot as lookout, and Kyra quickly poked her head above the rocks to take a look for herself. Her friend was correct. Of the ten recruits McD had taken north, only six followed behind him. One of them, Jonas, was on a crudely made stretcher being carried by the others, and Kyra wondered if he'd been injured for real or as part of the role-play. Those who were fatally wounded were expected to play dead and would've stayed behind with the other soldiers who'd played the rebels, while those with serious injuries had to also carry on in the role of casualty. She hoped it was the latter in Jonas's case, but was happy to see them regardless. "Hadn't you better get dressed?" Brona then asked with a surprised expression. Kyra looked down at herself and realized she was right. She wasn't shy about her body, but knew this was not the time or place to be sauntering around half naked. She hurried back to her pile of clothes and was hopping on one foot, trying to push the other damp one into the leg of her combat trousers, when Silas rounded the boulder and stopped dead.

"Nice to see you had time for a swim," he told her with clearly forced seriousness. His eyes roved over her skin and she felt herself prickle with heat under his gaze. It was then that she realized he'd never seen her with so few clothes on before, and she felt her cheeks burn. The incident with the wet pajamas was a blur now that her fever had passed, and this time she was more than conscious of what she was showing off. She also noticed when he stopped to peer questioningly at the scars on her arms and torso. He'd only ever seen the ones on her hands and face, and he was clearly wondering about them.

Kyra hadn't told him the story of the rosebush and its thorns that'd 'kissed her' the day King Kronus had come to Earth with his troops, and knew he would have his questions about her scars. Now was not the time for that talk, though.

"Just a much needed rinse after our long trek. How did your team get on?" she asked as she buckled her belt and grabbed her shirt.

"You were right, Recruit. We hit a rebel camp and lost three soldiers. One was taken hostage, and the rest of us got away. Jonas was injured, broken ankle I believe." He seemed annoyed that one of his men had been hurt, and Kyra guessed he blamed himself in some way.

"So, it's a real injury then? Not a yellow dart?" Silas nodded and frowned, but his scowl did nothing to hide the fact he was still staring at her. He watched her every move as though he'd missed her and was reacquainting himself with her again, and she enjoyed having his eyes on her. Kyra felt like the sexiest woman alive, despite the fact she was giving him the opposite of a striptease. The air buzzed between them as she buttoned her shirt, and his eyes lingered on her cleavage before she hid it away with the uniform he was so used to seeing her in. When her hands dipped beneath the waistband of her trousers she was sure his breath hitched, and Silas seemed mesmerized by the so innocent act of watching her tucking in her shirt. "My eyes are up here," she joked, sliding her glasses into place, and he gave her one last grin before shaking off his momentary lapse of Commander persona.

"We're going to leave the others here and take only the strongest up the mountain. All we need is for one of us to retrieve the flag, and then we can come back down for the others and head back to the door. I'll instruct the others to make Jonas a splint and crutch for the trek back, and we'll go your way."

"Yes, sir," was all Kyra said in response to his order, but she couldn't hide the small smile she had at knowing she'd been right. Silas had known he was taking the others into an ambush, of course he did, but he'd still made the choice to let some of them take the alternative route, and it'd paid off. Kyra's team were rested, fed, and hadn't endured both a fight and a long trek with a wounded comrade. They were ready to scale that mountain, and she hoped she might even be the one with her hands around that flagpole atop it.

It wasn't long before Kyra and her team was scaling the rock face with Silas. Jonas had apologized profusely for doubting her, but there was nothing to be done other than for him to be ready to head back once they returned with their prize. The others seemed grateful for the respite, and cheered the small team when they started hiking up the trail towards the summit.

Kyra climbed, trekked and even had to jump over the rocky terrain, and free-climb up sheer faces of the mountain in order to scale it, but she didn't complain once. Her hands were bleeding from climbing, and her muscles screamed in outrage when she'd forced them to move her body upwards using numerous static movements to ensure she didn't fall, but she refused to stop even once. There were no ropes securing them, just their strength and will to succeed, and by mid-afternoon she was stood staring down at the flag emblazoned with a huge L against the army's incredible emblem. Every part of her wanted to reach out and be the one to grab it, but she forced herself to wait. The team, their platoon—that came first this time, and Kyra finally felt like she understood the solidarity they shared. Silas, Brona, Jett, and their other sub-team members, Liza and Andy weren't far behind her, and then together they reached out and lifted the flag from its hold. Each of them beamed, pleased with themselves and each other in a way no one could ever take away from them, and even Silas grinned from ear to ear as he roared with happiness at having achieved their goal. The small group followed his example, and each of them let out battle cries that they knew would be heard from their platoon below.

The climb down took half as long as the ascent, but this time it was with a light and happy sense of pride. They'd done it, and in good time too, so were keen to get back and find out how well they'd placed overall. When the small group reached the waterfall, shouts of praise and happy faces greeted them, and Silas passed the flag to Kyra so she could be the one to show the others. She beamed, and accepted hugs from her comrades when she joined them, before letting the flag go to be passed around. There was still the hike back to get through, but for now the biggest hurdle had been conquered, and even Silas stood back and let them enjoy the moment.

"Last one in stinks of McD's sweaty undies!" Jett bellowed as he ran past Kyra and the others, stripping as he went, and dove straight into the pool beneath the falls. Laughter ensued, and each of the recruits stripped down in record speed so as not to endure the torture of being called names by the others on the route back to base. Her discarded mess of clothes resembled nothing of the neat pile she'd left that morning during her swim, but Kyra didn't care. The only thing she was careful to discard were her glasses, and then she jumped into the blissfully cool water below with the others. Brona was too busy trying to find somewhere to put the flag, and was unfortunately last to jump in, so was teased from the instant her head broke the surface.

"No! Technically Jonas is the loser," she tried in vain to save herself the torment, but it was no good, and she eventually accepted her taunts with a smile. The group swam, splashed, laughed and play-fought, and all the while Silas stood and watched from the edge with a smirk.

Kyra was up on Jett's shoulders having a wrestling match with Brona when his voice finally rang out from above them.

"You have five minutes and then we're off," he called, and was met with groans from the group. "But you can't go anywhere without your clothes…" They all looked up to find their Commander stood with a wicked grin on his face and a pile of clothes in his arms. "And you say *my* undies stink," he added with a grimace, before walking away and out of sight. The platoon cried out in unison for him to bring back their clothes, and after a few excruciating seconds, Silas returned but was empty handed. He took a seat next to Jonas overlooking the pool.

Kyra and the others watched as he chatted with his fellow spectator for a few minutes, and they seemed to agree on the terms of their game. "You can have your clothes back, but only if you answer a question correctly," he called, and the group collectively moved closer to the bank. As eager as they were to stay in the water, they were also very aware that they were still being timed, and therefore needed to get back to the start of their exercise sooner rather than later. Silas shot questions at each of the recruits in turn in a quick-fire test of their skills, and those that answered correctly were told to get out of the water and retrieve their clothes. She didn't know if he'd done it on purpose, but Kyra ended up being the last one out of the water. The others were all getting dressed over the ridge, talking so loudly it was hard to hear anything over the din, and Jonas had been helped up and was starting off towards the forest. She liked knowing they had a stolen moment amidst the chaos, and let herself enjoy his gaze now that they were effectively alone.

Silas stepped down onto one of the rocks by the water's edge. His gaze warmed her skin with its intensity again, and Kyra yearned to kiss or touch him, but didn't dare. She simply stepped within reaching distance and peered up at him through her soaked lashes.

"What's my question?" she asked, her voice quiet and haughty.

"Where are you going for summer break?" Silas asked, and every molecule of her body screamed in excitement. Was this his way of asking her to spend it with him? She sure hoped so.

"I don't know," she answered. "Our credits are allocated so we can go home, but I don't have a home to go to. I was thinking of staying here."

"You can't stay, they use the time to prep for secondary phase and the new intake. Why don't you use the credits to go somewhere else?" His lip curled into a half-smile. "Somewhere like... Hawaii?"

"Hawaii sounds nice, but I'll be bored there alone."

"Oh, you won't be alone," he whispered, and took a step back. "Well done, Millan. Grab your things, you're holding up the rest of us."

Silas was gone before Kyra even took a breath, but she didn't care. All she could think about was that he'd finally asked her the question she'd been desperate to hear come from his lips. He wanted to spend their summer break together, and she knew damn sure they wouldn't spend it seeing anything of the island other than the inside of their room.

CHAPTER SIX

Platoon group Lima reached their door late that night, and quickly headed into the same corridor where they'd entered the exercise the morning before. Silas led the way, and pulled a key from his pocket to unlock the door that would take them back out to the base. There they would find out how many others had completed their assessments as well, and hopefully judge where they might come in the rankings. The lock clicked, and the door swung open while every one of them held their breath in anticipation.

On the other side stood Lt. Psy, and his grin told them everything—they were the first ones to complete the exercise. He greeted each member of their unit and congratulated them before slapping Silas on the back and shaking his hand.

"First platoon back, McDermott," Kyra heard him say. She was buzzing with pride for both Silas and their unit, and knew they'd rank highly regardless of any demerits. She was then swept up in the celebrations with her fellow recruits, and it took a few minutes before they calmed down and regained their composure, but Lt. Psy seemed happy to let them celebrate.

It was a full thirty minutes before another platoon emerged, and soon after more and more completed their exercises. Word got around quickly that Lima Platoon had won, and their fellow recruits congratulated them, despite the competitiveness. Their fallen comrades were also released from the exercise area and came out to join them, each one full of apology for having been caught or killed in the simulation, but none of them cared. Morale was at an all-time high, and regardless of their exhaustion, the recruits spent hours telling the other platoon's their stories from inside the training grounds.

"Hey, little lady," Silas whispered from beside Kyra, but it didn't matter anyway. Everyone was so pumped that they'd completed their primary training that they were shouting, laughing and joking loudly to one another and wouldn't overhear them. "Come with me," he added, before ducking behind some of their well-known crates in search of a hidden spot. She followed, and soon found herself being pinned to the wall by Silas's immense frame. His mouth found hers and he kissed her with such fervor that it took her breath away.

"Hawaii?" she asked when he finally pulled back, and he nodded.

"Hawaii. I'm not going home, so I've arranged for somewhere to stay on the island instead. I want you to come with me. Our credits are good for return travel anywhere. As long as we come back when we're told, there's no need for them to look into where we went, or with whom. Tell me you'll come?" he sounded like a lovesick teenager, not a powerful and successful soldier in his mid-twenties, but she could hear the need in his voice. It echoed her own. The angst she felt deep within wanted so many things from him, and it seemed he wanted her the same way too.

"There's literally nowhere else on this entire planet I'd rather go than with you," she reached up and stroked his stubbly cheek before kissing him again.

"After tomorrow I'm no longer your Commander, so we can officially date after summer leave. No more hiding in the shadows stealing kisses," he told her, nuzzling her neck.

"But I like stolen kisses," she teased, arching into him.

The deep growl he gave her fueled her even further, and Kyra planted a kiss against his earlobe. "I can't wait." She then slid sideways to escape his hold, and ducked back out into the crowd before he could keep her there any longer. They were so close, and she had to keep her cool if she was going to make it through the next day in one piece.

She'd left her entire world behind to come here, and now looking around at Fort Angel and its inhabitants, Kyra knew she'd done the right thing. She wasn't a leader or a specialist yet—she was simply a recruit. But, she'd worked hard, and had helped her platoon reach that flag and get back in record time. They'd succeeded regardless of the setbacks, or the times others might've thought they'd fail, and she felt immense pride in herself and her comrades.

Lots of changes were ahead; it was inevitable. Some of the other recruits would stay at a primary level to carry on with their careers as infantry soldiers, while others like her would move on for a further two years of secondary training, and a pass would ensure they were chosen for one of the middle or upper-class military divisions. Kyra had her sights set on the Intelligence Division, and knew she'd already shown proficiency in both her computer skills and tactical ability. Lt. Psy had already said so himself, and all she had to do now was keep going, keep winning, and keep pushing.

***

The next morning, Kyra and the others lined up in the yard and sat in wait of the final results. The top fifteen platoon's would go through to secondary phase training, but the top five units were also awarded extra credits as an award, and the honor of knowing they'd succeeded above all others. Competition was a surprising part of the camaraderie, but they all felt it, and were eager to hear who had placed at the number one spot. The scores for the entire year were tallied and added to the results for the final exercise, so there was no real way of guessing who'd come out on top.

"From this moment forward you are no longer Recruits. You are Corporals in his majesty King Kronus's Human Royal Armed Forces. You serve, fight and lead. You preserve and protect our way of life as was given to us by his highness, and above all—you wear that pledge with pride," Lt. Psy told them from the podium set above the crowd. He then began informing them of the scores, starting at the bottom. Moans and unhappy murmurs could be heard from the unsuccessful platoon's, clearly disgruntled at having to remain in the lower-class division of the army. None cried or refused their position though, and Kyra knew that no matter where they'd placed, it would be better than going back to the lower-class civilian sectors to try and live on measly credits and hard work. The army was a better alternative no matter what, and they were no doubt grateful just to have made it through with a role at all.

The middle groups were then called, and the members of Lima Platoon were growing restless. They each wanted to hurry up and find out their position, and Lt. Psy seemed to be enjoying his casual speed, or at least it felt that way. It was wonderful knowing that no matter where they placed now they were returning for secondary phase training, so Kyra's goal had already been achieved for her first year. It still didn't stop her hoping they might come in the top five, but to reach the number one would be wonderful. "In fifth position… Delta Platoon." The group next to them erupted in exultation, and Kyra watched them with a smile. She turned and risked a glance at Silas, who didn't look back at her, but smiled. She and the others had given him his top five placing, and the sense of pride she had at giving him his dream was immense.

They weren't fourth or third place, and Kyra started to sweat. She'd never dreamed of doing so well, and grabbed

61

Brona's hand beside her. They watched as Lt. Psy read the autocue and smiled. "It gives me great pleasure to announce that second place goes to… Juliet Platoon." The group across the way began cheering, and she suddenly felt sad. It was only when she registered that her own platoon were celebrating too that it dawned on her. "And last but certainly not least, after a superior year's training and a tremendous final exercise, first place goes to Lima Platoon!"

There were people hugging and grabbing her from all around, and Kyra was in utter shock. By the time it all sunk in, they were ushered to sit back down, and she kept hold of Brona's hand. Their smiles didn't fade for even an instant, and it was all Kyra could do to concentrate on what she was hearing from the podium above. Their Commander was saying something about the designated transports and return dates for secondary training. She picked up on some of it, but knew Silas would go over the details again when they returned to their rooms in Lima Platoon one last time, so didn't worry too much. It was the end of an era, and although it saddened her, Kyra was pleased to be coming back after the break. She would get to see Silas on a night after her training was over and he'd finished with his new recruits for the day, and knew he'd make time to be with her. They would be a real couple, able to walk together during breaks and sit with one another for meals. They could laugh and joke without having to worry who might see, and she couldn't wait.

"Where are you all going for summer leave?" Brona asked when they were packing their bags and clearing the dorm room a short while later. "I'm heading home to Atlanta, my parents have missed me something rotten, but it'll be nice to see them and tell them all about our adventures," she added excitedly. They hadn't learned much about one another's families, but she knew the other girls were all close with theirs. Once upon a time ago she'd envied them, but not now. She had somewhere to go, and someone to go with. There was no sitting in downtown Los Angeles whiling away the next two weeks like she'd thought.

"I'm going home too," Liza answered. "My sister is getting married and she had a baby this year so I'll get to meet my nephew." She had a smile that screamed she'd once been a small-town girl before running away with the soldiers on sector selection day, and Kyra was pleased to see the real Liza she had kept hidden away the past year. She was clearly itching to get home, and spoke of her family with such love and adoration Kyra envied her.

"I'm visiting a friend on the west coast. I've no family in Los Angeles, but further south I have some distant cousins I can stay with," she lied. "Sun, sea and sand— here I come!" the other girls beamed, and seemed to believe her. She knew they'd never ask Silas where he was going for summer leave, and even if they did he'd more than likely tell them to mind their own business. No matter their achievements and the changes they'd all made during the past year, he was still a hard-ass, and their superior. Kyra did wonder where he was from though. His accent was full of southern lilts and influences from the east, with a hint of wealth, but she hadn't learned where he'd come from yet, and hoped that over their break he might open up about himself some more. Even just thinking about spending the next two weeks with him made her cheeks burn, and she had to turn away from the other girls until it subsided.

The platoon was no more, and it was a bittersweet moment disbanding their small unit so each soldier could carry on without one another in the secondary phase. They said their goodbyes and grabbed their things, but not before giving one another one last hug and wishing everyone well. They weren't sure if they'd be together again in the next phase, so said their goodbyes now, just in case they didn't have the chance later.

Kyra boarded the bus heading to Los Angeles, and when she spotted Silas in the queue a few feet behind, her heart began to race. She was excited, and a little bit scared about the couple of weeks they had ahead of them. She hoped they hadn't put too much pressure on themselves to have a wonderful time, or for everything to be perfect, and was determined not to let her expectations ruin the reality of their time together. Kyra had done that her entire life with her fantasy of King Kronus she'd held dear to her heart, no matter how fictitious she knew him to be. Every man she'd been attracted to since had been compared with him, and so far none had measured up. But now, she had the real thing, and had been trying her hardest to forget about the Thrakorian who had kept her company in her dreams and helped her escape reality through the years. What she and Silas had was real, and their connection had been forged over days of clandestine kisses and glances, the gentlest of touches, and the unadulterated need to connect on a spiritual level.

Kyra watched as he climbed on board and took the seat across the aisle from her, offering nothing but a brief hello to her and the others, while she swooned and fiddled nervously with her hands. The next five hours were going to be torture, she just knew it, but it was the sweetest of torments, and because she knew what was on the other side, she was ready to endure them.

Kyra ended up falling asleep halfway through the bus ride. The motion and her exhaustion sent her body into sleep-mode quickly after finally leaving Fort Angel behind, and many of the others did the same. She woke up just in time to see the signposts signifying they were a few miles out of Los Angeles, and quickly smoothed down her hair and popped a mint in her mouth to freshen up her sleep-breath. Kyra felt very aware of the ache in her neck, and knew that she'd probably been nodding her head or rolling it left to right on the cushion of her seat whilst asleep. She didn't dare look over to see whether Silas was giving her one of his masked smiles, because she was getting used to seeing right through those stern looks by now, so watched out the window instead of admitting her embarrassment with a shy smile.

After they arrived, it was a case of swiping their wrists over a customs gate so their embedded microchips could be read and their credits checked. Then the designated travel sector staff began directing the hoards with ease and in a clearly practiced organizational manner. They were processed and sent on their way, and at one point Kyra lost sight of Silas in the crowd. She panicked, looking from left to right amidst the huge wave of people, but she didn't see a single face she knew. She went to call out, but no sound left her lungs, and she had to tell herself over and over again that it was all in her head. She wasn't lost, and they had plenty of time yet. All she had to do was stay put, and he'd find her. Once the terminal building started slowly emptying, Kyra took refuge in a corner. Never before had she been afraid of crowds or felt claustrophobic, but she'd never been in such a bustling throb of people at one time either, and knew she wanted to avoid it at all costs on the return journey.

"There you are, I thought I'd lost you," Silas called as he rounded the corner and caught sight of her. He frowned and pulled her into a hug when he saw how disheveled she was. "We missed the early hovercraft, so how about we go and wait for the next one where we can relax just you and me? I'll even buy you a coffee," he then offered, and immediately pulled Kyra from her somber state.

"That sounds wonderful," she replied, and let him lead her to the dock where they'd catch the next hovercraft to Hawaii a couple hours later.

When it was time, they boarded the hovercraft headed to Kailua-Kona on the Island with hardly any other passengers. Not a single soldier joined them on the craft, and both Kyra and Silas took it as a sign of good fortune.

They sat close together and talked while the small craft took them across the ocean. Silas held her hands in his and leaned in close, while each of them still felt forbidden from doing so, but it also felt so right. Kyra had never been so alive, and the short drive from the airport was like a breath of fresh air. She discarded her hair tie and combat cap once they were on the road, and let the warm wind send her dark hair flying around her shoulders as the cab drove them to the destination Silas had given the driver.

"Here we are," the man called from the front seat when he came to a stop. Silas swiped his hand over the payment screen, depositing one of his credits to cover the fee, while Kyra took a look at their home for the next two weeks. What he'd said was nothing more than a place to crash for summer break turned out to be a secure mansion set back from the street behind a gated fence. It was huge, like some monument to days of old, but with modern edges all around, and it screamed of wealth and power.

Kyra was in shock. She gawped up at the house while Silas grabbed their bags and punched in a code to open the gate to the walkway, and then immediately followed him into the house in silence. Once clear of the garden and inside, the emptiness of the vast mansion was daunting, and she felt uneasy. She'd never lived alone in all her life, and never spent the night in such luxury as this. After having been brought up in dorms and then a block room with her female platoon-mates, the silence was deafening. Privacy was a comfort she'd never had before, and she wasn't sure she'd be able to sleep with so little sound.

"I know it's a lot to take in, but just relax. We're here to block out the rest of the world and have fun, so let's enjoy ourselves, okay?" he asked, reaching out a hand for her to take, and Kyra took it. Silas led the way, and showed her to a bedroom filled with nothing but pale blues that were the exact same shade as the sky outside. "This is your room for the duration of our stay, I'm next door," he told her with a shy smile.

"We're not sharing?" she blurted out, and loved how his eyes flew to the bed in response.

"We can if you'd like, I just didn't want to rush you," he answered, pulling her in for a kiss. The act of chivalry did nothing but make her want him more, and she grinned up at him, but first a shower was in order, followed by a stiff drink and a chance to take all of this in.

"Let's see how we feel, yeah?" Kyra eventually answered, and Silas nodded in agreement before ducking out through the connecting door to his room. Strangely, she didn't feel uncomfortable in the bedroom like she had the rest of the empty house, but still needed to know why he'd brought her to this beautiful and very large mansion, rather than a hotel or small apartment by the beach like she'd envisioned. Kyra took a minute to get her bearings, and pulled out the only clothes she had, her old and scruffy jeans and shirt she'd been wearing the day she'd climbed aboard Silas's truck and left for the army. Everything else had gone to the other dorm girls, and she knew it was time to check her credits so she could buy some more. It hadn't mattered when all she needed was her combats and boots, but now that they were on summer leave her uniform wasn't necessary, and it was a welcome thought not to have to wear her combats for a couple of weeks.

She showered and pulled on her old clothes, which were surprisingly snug now that she'd piled on some muscle mass, so was forced to leave the top button undone on the jeans. There was a knock on her door, and Silas entered a moment later. He looked amazing out of his combats, having clearly done the same as she just had, and he looked relaxed and comfortable in shorts and a t-shirt.

"You'll be far too hot in those. Don't you have anything else to wear?" Kyra guessed her embarrassed look must've said it all, and he quickly reached for a nearby drawer. "This is my sister's room, so I'm sure there must be something you can borrow," he added as he rooted through the belongings inside. Silas pulled out a stunning white summer dress and threw it to her with a smile. "You'll look beautiful in this, and we can go shopping tomorrow for some new civvies for you." She nodded in agreement, and while it felt strange borrowing his sisters bedroom and clothes, she knew they were just on loan for the time being, so sucked it up and got on with it.

While he turned away, she slid off her jeans and shirt and put them straight in the trash. They were the old Kyra, and she never wanted to wear them ever again. She slid on the dress, turned and looked in the mirror, and could see he was right—it looked stunning. The strappy shoulders and fitted collar fit tightly over her average sized bosom, but made them look bigger somehow, and the material fell around her waist in layer after layer of delicate white cotton that was flattering yet comfortable.

"Will I do?" she asked, and Silas turned back to check her out. He opened his mouth to speak, closed it again and coughed. "I'll take that as a yes." He nodded and stepped closer, wrapping her in his arms as he went, and Kyra immediately climbed up onto her tiptoes to reach his mouth with hers. He kept his hands to himself, but she could feel them both heating up in their embrace. *Not yet*, she told herself. She needed to know some more about the real Silas McDermott first, and especially how it was he had this house at his disposal, while the rest of their friends had gone back to their tiny family homes or on vacation with nothing more than a backpack and a tent to sleep in. There was also part of her that needed him to see and respect the young woman she was beneath the combats, not just the soldier he saw every day. When they were on the base, it was too easy for him to assume the role as her superior, but not here. Away from Fort Angel they were just like any other young couple, and they needed to get to know each other properly for a little while before exploring their relationship any more.

Kyra stepped back and peered up at Silas. "Why don't

you give me the tour, and tell me what on earth we're doing in such a luxurious place?" she asked, and grinned.

"Yeah, I guess I wasn't very forthcoming about all this, was I?" he asked as he took her hand and steered her back out into the hallway. Silas then stayed quiet about the how's and why's as he showed her around the large house, along with all its six bedrooms, state of the art kitchen and living room, and numerous dens.

They finished off at the private pool at the back of the house. "My family is all in the military. I always knew I'd join, my father informed me so as a child, and I never questioned it. He's now a General in the Legal Division, along with my mother who's a Colonel. My big brothers are both Captain's in the police force, and my sister is a nurse specializing in genetic research with the Medical Division." Kyra was in shock. She'd heard that many of the middle-class sector families joined the army, but hadn't realized how they could also be made up of service men and women throughout. She guessed she'd been more out of touch with the real world than she'd realized during all her years of living in the downtown slums of L.A. They'd been fed and raised safely, but that was where any care or consideration ceased. Now, she was just getting a taste of how the upper-classes lived, and in all honesty she wanted more. This world felt good, the quality clothes and the quiet cleanliness of it all felt nice, and it seemed welcoming if you were hardworking enough to achieve it. She knew she could do it, and that there was a part of her that felt like she deserved it.

"How come you're in a lower sector of the army? Didn't you want to climb higher?" she asked, hoping he wouldn't take offence to her query. She hadn't meant to question his ambition or anything, but it seemed surprising that with such a high standing family he hadn't also ended up in one of the upper ranks alongside them. Silas nodded and handed her some fruit he'd just plucked and peeled from a nearby tree.

"I was a typical youngest child. I didn't concentrate, and I didn't care," he replied, and Kyra was surprised. All she'd seen the past year from him told her quite the opposite. She flopped down into one of the chairs on the patio with a thud. "I thought I'd get through on my name alone, but I was wrong. I learnt a huge lesson on the final day of my primary exercise. Our platoon was one of the bottom, and I wasn't even offered secondary training. It was only when I came back after summer leave and begged the Commander to give me one last try, that I picked my ideas up out of the gutter and actually started working on proving myself. I'm still on that last chance, and I'll never be able to thank Lt. Psy enough for giving me it." Silas bit into his own piece of fruit, and watched Kyra with a thoughtful expression. "I'd like to continue up the ranks eventually, and he's the man who'll decide when. I'm also hoping that perhaps the results of this year's intake will help me, and I've you to thank for that." He slid to his knees before her and cradled her face in his hands.

"Not me!" she shrieked, and was taken utterly aback. "Our platoon did well and won together. You were a great leader, Silas. You pushed us all every step of the way, and we were lucky to have you." She meant every word, and was pleased to see the pride in his stare.

"I doubt you'll ever realize just how incredible you are," he told her, leaning closer. Silas pulled her face down to meet his and ran his thumb over her lips while staring at them thoughtfully. "It's a beautiful trait, modesty. Your innocence and passion are contagious, and I know you've infected me. I want more. I want to do better—to *be* better. I didn't want any of those things before you came wandering into my life and downright told me you weren't settling for anything less than what you deserved. All your life you've been held back because of your bed in that foster home and the status it gave you, but now the world's your oyster, and I can't wait to see what you do with it."

Kyra was his. Gift-wrapped, claimed, and ready for collection. Silas had been a constant source of affection and kindness all wrapped up in a grumpy hard-ass package, and one that'd pushed her to her limits, but then kissed away her bumps and bruises at the end of it. She'd needed all of that throughout the entirety of her transformation from foster kid to soldier, and Silas had known it. With those words, he'd truly set her free. He'd done in a few sentences what flying all the way to Hawaii or refusing to return to downtown L.A. hadn't been able to, he'd given her proof that she belonged and was accepted in this world.

In his eyes, Kyra had found the person she wanted to become, and evidently so had he in hers. They'd built each other up in a time where humans no longer had their own say or took charge of their lives. Under the reign of an entirely different species that could crush them if they so desired, they'd found purpose and a reason to serve and succeed. She didn't know whether to laugh or cry.

"I think I just fell in love with you, Silas McDermott," she said with a lump in her throat, and tears prickling in her eyes.

"I've loved you from the very first moment I saw you in that school with your glasses on your nose, and a chip on your shoulder." Silas grabbed Kyra and pulled her up off her feet. He wrapped her legs around his waist and sat down on the huge outdoor sofa so she straddled him, and Kyra followed his lead.

Leaning with her long hair covering them both, she kissed him with every ounce of the emotion she was feeling from within. Their bodies were screaming for each other's, and when his hands slid from her ankles up to her curled knees and higher, she moaned into his mouth. He pulled her into him by her hips, and her lips crushed even harder against his. Their breathing was ragged, and when she pulled away to finally take a deep gasp of air, Silas kissed his way down her neck rather than do the same. He held her tightly to him by the arms still wrapped around her waist, and he buried his face in the love heart shape of her chest created by the figure-flattering dress.

"You never showed me your bedroom," Kyra managed to moan in her sweet agony, and she could hear rather than see the smile on his lips when he groaned in response. There was no more waiting. They had to be together, and Silas took the hint without her having to say another word. He carried her up to his room still wrapped around him. Her hair was draped over his shoulder while she kissed her way up his freshly shaven neck and cheek to his mouth, and he knew the way without having to watch where he was going, which was lucky because she wasn't about to stop for anything.

Inside the room he was gentle as he placed Kyra on the bed, undressing her slowly while watching her body like he was appreciating a prized piece of art. She did the same, watching as he pulled his t-shirt over his head and revealed the stunning body she'd always guessed was beneath those misleading combats. Every muscle was defined and toned. He was stronger than anyone she'd ever known before, and hadn't suffered during training one little bit. She could now see why. The veins in his arms bulged as they flexed with each movement, and Kyra was mesmerized by the perfect masculinity of him.

Silas climbed onto the bed with her. He slid between her thighs and she giggled as she remembered the evening when she'd been meant to fight him off from the exact same pose, but only served to remind them both of how they'd wanted this exact scenario.

"Tell me to stop and I will," he murmured, and leaned up onto his elbow to peer down at her. "I'll never force you."

"Don't you dare stop," she demanded in response, and reveled in the grin he gave her. Kyra wasn't shy, but his touch made her tremble and heat bloomed from within in a way she'd never known before. It made her blush. She craved him, and hoped he felt the same way about her too.

Once upon a time ago he might've been an arrogant rich kid, but now he was a leader that was respected and feared by the recruits he took under his wing. Silas had given her endless days of harsh training without ever giving her a break, and she'd worked hard to keep up with him, but now he was soft and slow in his pursuit of something more. The strictness of Fort Angel was gone, and only the real him remained.

Silas was gentle and sweet, and when he finally made love to her he was neither hurried nor selfish. Nothing else mattered, and the world could just go on turning without them.

CHAPTER SEVEN

It was noon before Kyra and Silas finally left the bedroom the next day. When she padded down to the kitchen in search of food, it was with a definite spring in her step that even the independent woman within didn't bother to try and hide. Silas had made her feel on top of the world, and together she knew they were capable of great things.

"Something smells good," he told her, sniffing the coffee-scented air as he too wafted in on an invisible cloud with a smile. Kyra could see the difference in him, and was pleased to see she'd left him feeling the same as she did after their night together. The pair had barely slept, and had instead made up for all the stolen kisses and tension left unsatisfied. They'd explored each other in a way she'd never known before, and Kyra knew she wanted more of it.

"Vanilla latte," she answered, sliding the mug of frothy coffee under his nose. "I wish I could say I made it myself, but all I did was press a button." Silas pulled her into his embrace and nuzzled her ear, clearly not caring whether she'd made it by hand or not.

"Whatever you touch turns to gold, Kyra. Everything I taste with you is like it's for the first time. You've awakened something in me I cannot ever forget. Thank you," he reached out and snagged her hand, and placed gentle kisses all over her palm and fingertips, before carrying on further up over the back of her hand to her elbow. She giggled and tried to pull away, but Silas held on even tighter. "You remember where else I kissed you?" he teased, and she groaned in affirmation. "Would you let me kiss you there again?"

"Yes," she breathed. "You can kiss me anywhere you'd like." She meant it. What little she had to give was for him, he didn't need to ask. Silas scooped her up and took her back to the bedroom, and the coffees went cold in wait for mouths that were busy elsewhere.

***

"Tell me about your scars," Silas asked later that day, and he trailed his hand over a particularly deep mark on her collarbone. They were laid in bed, resting together in blissful silence, and he'd finally asked the question she'd known was coming ever since he'd seen her half-naked at the waterfall.

"Invasion Day," she answered, lifting her arms to show him the silver marks in the dimming sunshine. "I was five, and terrified. When I heard a ship coming, I hid in a rose bush, and it cut me to pieces. A Thrakorian soldier saved me, but the cuts were deep and they scarred." There was never a logical reason as to why she'd still not told anyone that her savior had been King Kronus. She'd told herself time and again to come clean, but the truth always stayed firmly on the tip of her tongue. Even with Silas, she didn't want him to know how she'd harbored a deep and foolish attraction for their leader since that day—and perhaps even more so now that they were well and truly a couple.

"Did it hurt?" he asked, and she nodded.

"Yeah. My crying was what alerted them to my presence, but it was for the best really, because they took me away to safety. I'm not sure where I might've ended up if they hadn't taken me to the foster home. I'll always be grateful." She meant it. Despite her elation at having escaped her childhood this past year, she would be forever indebted to the Thrakorian's for the chances she'd been given by staying there and being a loyal servant to King Kronus's regime. It'd been a hard upbringing, but she'd been sent to school and had been given three square meals a day, which was more than could be said for some children that still fell through the cracks, even with their new society. "How about you? What's your Invasion Day story?" she asked, looking up at him. Silas looked older somehow, tired and burdened, and she wondered if he felt sorry for her. She wanted to ask him the question again, but decided to leave him be. Everyone had their demons, and she certainly kept her secrets close to her chest, so didn't want to push him if he wasn't ready.

Silas had a story; everyone older than a toddler when the Thraks attacked knew where they were that day. It was forever engrained on their memories and minds. For Kyra it was the first day of the rest of her life, but for the rebels it marked the end of civilization. They would overthrow King Kronus and take back the Earth if they could, but she couldn't see why they'd want things back the way they were before. Yes, they were being ruled by an otherworldly race, but from what she could tell, Kronus had taken a planet used and abused to near extinction by its inhabitants, and had made it thrive again. The Thrakorian's had given them renewable energy and food sources that weren't a drain on the Earth like they'd had to use before. They'd given the humans purpose and a system that worked, and every time she even considered things going back to the way they were, Kyra was filled with even more desire to succeed in the army. Part of her wanted to be the one who cracked their codes and destroyed the rebels once and for all. She wanted to be regarded as the best in her field, and knew it was nothing but a dream, but one she held dearer than many others. She'd never wanted to be a wife or mother. Computers were her calling, and science was what she loved. They were her future, well at least until Silas McDermott had gotten in the way, but he was fast becoming a welcome addition to the dream.

"My dad knew it was happening. We were already safely inside a bunker when the invasion began, and didn't come out until King Kronus had taken control. I was only twelve, but even I could tell that it was an unfair advantage," Silas seemed embarrassed to say so, but Kyra envied him for having had an advantage over the others of their kind. "My father was left as the highest ranking surviving officer on the west coast, which was no accident. He was called into the King's service the next day, followed shortly by my mother and older brother, Tarquin. My sister Lasiandra, and my brother Pedro and I were taken into the central refuge area for service children, where we were cared for until they returned, and then we were free to go. Our family was given more credits than they could ever use in return for my parents' pledge of allegiance. Their work in ensuring the human soldiers followed them into Kronus's army only added to his worth, and it turned out my father had already been given this and many other houses across the world in return for his assistance prior to the invasion. Since then, my parents have been kept wealthy and powerful in payment for their continued service beneath the Lawbringer's headship, which suits them perfectly. I've no doubt my mother will be invited to join the Gentry before too long as well." He took a deep breath and sighed, and Kyra didn't like the way he spoke of his family. It really did seem like he was an outcast, the black sheep, and had never fit in with them. She wondered if he ever would.

"Don't you agree with what they did?" she asked.

"I do, of course it was simpler to take the offered path if it meant we were safe and taken care of for life. But sometimes I wish we didn't have it so easy while people like you were left orphaned, scarred for life, and left to be raised in foster home dorms where you were never truly safe."

"There were always differences in society, Silas. Don't

pity me because my parents were worthless nobodies who lived and died in the slums, while yours worked hard to secure their place in the new world for themselves and their family," she replied. "I remember a world in which I had to beg for food or line up for hours to get my families rations, and all the while my parents did nothing to better themselves or try to make my life better. They didn't care about leaving a safe world for me or any further generations to come, only what they could get from the world before they left it. I envy you."

"Your parents weren't worthless nobodies. They brought you into a world it was impossible to survive in unless you had money, or were willing to do anything it took to get it. They weren't given the chance to better themselves, whereas you were. I too remember what it was like before. We lived in a world where my family was given permits to drive, while everyone else had to take buses and trains thanks to overcrowding on the roads. We were privileged and greedy, but because of who we were, we got away with it." He shook his head. "How can you envy me? People like me deserve nothing but hatred. We cowered in a corner while you fought to survive, and all because my father was willing to betray our race so readily."

"Well, maybe I hate you a little bit," she conceded, but laughed to relieve the tension that'd swept into the room along with their intense conversation. "But then again, I always did think you were an ass. This story hasn't changed anything."

Silas rose to her bait perfectly. He pinned her to the bed by her arms and planted kisses all over her face and neck, while she giggled and writhed before surrendering. She looked up into his smiling face, and basked in the warmth from him. Yes, there were vast differences in the way their lives had gone, but Kyra only wanted to focus on the here and now. Her choices and intelligence had brought her here, not Silas or his families wealth. There was no debt she owed, and it felt good not to carry around heavy burdens like he seemed to.

Kyra had gotten through primary training on her own merit, and vowed she'd never stop until she'd found her natural place amidst her comrades. She was determined she'd never accept a bribe or take the easy road. Instead she'd stay strong and trust her instincts. No matter what, here was a lot better than where she'd been a year ago, and she wasn't letting it go for love nor extra credits.

"Two weeks isn't long enough," Silas told her, peering down into her eyes in the deep orange glow of the sunset. "I want you to myself. Now…" He kissed her lips. "And always." They hadn't left the bedroom since her attempt to make coffee that morning, and Kyra guessed food was off the cards for another few hours at least, but didn't care. In their training they'd gone without during simulations of rations or natural food sources, and now her body craved nothing but the man keeping her wonderful company.

***

A loud crash downstairs had both Silas and Kyra jumping out of bed and pulling on some clothes early the next morning. In silence, they each tiptoed to the hallway and peered out. There were lights on at the end of the hall, and raised voices.

"Oh, great," Silas whispered and he huffed. He then gently grabbed Kyra's arm to pull her back into the bedroom with him, and closed the door. He didn't need to explain, it was obvious he knew the voices owners, and was not impressed at their arrival. "It's my brother, Tarquin. Clearly he didn't get the memo that I had the house this leave. Either that or him and his girlfriend have had yet another row." Kyra could tell he was annoyed at the idea of having their seclusion shattered, especially by his older brother, but couldn't blame him. She found herself wondering if they could be close at all, or if he'd been too much of an outcast due to being the baby of the family, and the one who'd rebelled and been less ambitious in his career.

"The house is big enough for us to share. We can simply stay holed up in this room for the next week or so, I don't mind," she replied, and stepped close to slide her arms around Silas's back. He seemed to relax a little, and laid a soft kiss to her temple.

"It's not just him though, you can guarantee that wherever he goes my other brother follows. If Pedro's here then his wife will come too, followed quickly by…"

"Darling. Are you awake?" a soft voice asked, and a hand tapped on the bedroom door. Silas flinched. The voice was older, and surely couldn't belong to his sister, which only left for it to be his mother. "Silas?" The door started to open.

"I'm not alone, mom. Give me a minute and I'll be down, please." There was no response, but the door, which was only opened an inch or two, quickly closed shut again. "We'd better get ready for the inquisition," he said to Kyra with a frown. Silas went to the door that connected his room with his sister's, gave a knock, and then entered when he'd checked it was empty. He grabbed Kyra a pair of shorts and a shirt to wear, and the way he deliberated over which ones to give her spoke volumes. She quickly realized she needed to be careful around his family. He was on edge, and if just their presence had him acting this way, then she knew she'd better be ready for some serious scrutiny.

Kyra had a shower and braided her hair. She took time to ensure it was neat and tidy, and gave her teeth an intense scrub to make sure her breath was fresh. She suddenly felt uneasy, and looked to Silas for a way to dispel that strange pang in her gut, but he too seemed wound tightly.

When they were ready, he took her hand and led her down the hall, and through to the rest of the house. They found his brothers and mother sitting at the huge table in the kitchen, drinking coffee and talking quietly to one another. They all looked up as they entered, and Kyra's initial instinct was to shrink back, but Silas wouldn't let her. He kept her beside him, and immediately introduced her to the others.

"Kyra, I'd like you to meet my mother, Freya McDermott," he said. She smiled and greeted her timidly, and felt the iciness in his mother's stare despite her plastered on grin. "And my brothers, Tarquin and Pedro," he indicated with his hand.

"It's a pleasure to meet you all," she said, shaking hands with each of them, and the two men looked back at her with mischievous grins. Freya on the other hand remained poised and closed-off, a stark contrast to her three children.

"We had some issues with the Manhattan apartment. Rot in the building, so we had to come here. I knew you wouldn't mind, darling, but I admit I wasn't expecting you to have company," Freya told her son in a soft tone, but eyed Kyra warily. "Tell me a little about yourself, and how you know my son," she added, indicating for her to take the empty seat to her left.

She did as she'd been asked, and accepted a much-needed cup of freshly brewed coffee from Tarquin with a smile. Silas opened his mouth, presumably to tell them about her himself, but Freya raised her hand to silence him. Kyra had never seen him cower before anyone, not even Lt. Psy, but under his mother's scrutiny he seemed to retreat so much into himself that she could no longer see the powerful soldier she knew so well.

"There isn't much to tell really," Kyra replied, stirring her drink intently. "Silas and I met at the sector fair at my school, and then again at Fort Angel. I've just completed my primary training, and will return for secondary at the end of next week. He and I grew close this year, and when it was time to go on summer leave he invited me here with him."

"You didn't wish to return home?" Freya asked, sipping on her drink.

"I have no home to return to," she answered, and hoped that honesty was the best policy. Silas and his brothers watched their exchange in complete silence, and she wished they'd join in, or at least strike up a conversation of their own to help break the tension, but they seemed to think better of it.

"Oh you poor thing," Freya's voice warmed slightly after hearing her answer, and Kyra hoped it was sincere. "Do you mind me asking why?"

"I was a foster kid, so since I left I have no need to go back. That's not where I belong."

"Oh? And where do you belong?" There seemed to be an edge to Freya's tone again, and Kyra wondered if she was suspicious of her motives for being with her son. Perhaps lots of young women over the years had tried to ensnare a McDermott boy in the hopes of getting their hands on their wealth, and she couldn't blame Silas's mother for being distrustful.

"At Fort Angel with the other trainees. All I ever wanted was to enlist and serve the King. Meeting Silas has been a wonderful addition to my new life I hadn't counted on, but not my sole reason for pursuing my dreams."

"Aw, she's really hung up on you, little brother," Tarquin said, cutting some of the tension between her and Freya. Kyra looked across the table into his deep brown eyes that matched his brother's, and admired their likeness. In fact, all three McDermott brothers looked very alike, and she was pleased to see the same mischievous smile on each of the older siblings' lips she'd come to know well.

"The feeling's mutual, don't worry," Silas replied, immediately silencing any further banter from either of his brothers. Kyra appreciated that he'd managed to shut them up, but soon found herself wondering why they were so surprised that he was seeing someone. Even his mom looked stunned by the declaration of affection, and she watched him for a moment before turning back to Kyra.

"Lovely," Freya said, and she took another swig of her coffee. "Were you in his platoon?" The tension rose quicker than the temperature, and fear sprang to life from deep inside Kyra's gut.

"Yes, but we didn't start seeing each other until I'd passed primary training. There's no way either of us would jeopardize our careers that way, and that's the honest truth." Despite her dread, she stared right into Freya's bottle green eyes and urged her to believe that what she said was true.

"*Tsk, tsk*, bro. Always gotta push the boundaries, don't you?" Tarquin teased Silas, but he didn't seem ready to rise to any of his bait.

"She's telling the truth. We've done nothing unlawful," he replied flatly.

It was his mother who answered.

"Be that as it may, she's still a junior rank to you. Also, judging by the fact she's wearing your sister's clothing and smells as though she's been washing with your toiletries, she clearly doesn't have more than a few credits to her name."

Kyra tried to stay calm, but her blood was boiling. She wanted to scream and shout at Freya for daring to put her in the same box she more than likely put every young woman who went near any of her sons in, but forced herself to stay calm.

"Kyra had no idea where I was bringing her, and would've come with me to a shack on the beach if I'd asked. We arrived in our uniforms and I offered her the use of Lasiandra's clothes until we could go shopping for some of her own, as her old jeans no longer fit." Silas was clearly having the same reaction to his mother's words that she was, and Kyra was pleased he'd decided to stick up for her. He knew there were absolutely no motives in place as to why she was here, and she hated that the assumption had been made so readily simply because of where she'd come from. "I'm finally serious about a girl, and instead of being happy for me, all you want to do is interrogate us?" he then growled, and stood from the table. Silas stormed away, and Kyra followed him without even a backward glance at his family.

He finally came to a stop under the gazebo where they'd sat together a couple of days before, and marched up and down while she took a seat. She watched and waited, hoping he might say something, but he simply continued to pace and seethe.

"We knew we'd be questioned as soon as we revealed our relationship, Silas. I know we thought we'd have more time together first, but at least we can use the rest of the summer break to show them we meant what we just said in there. They don't know me like you do. They weren't there when you told me about your past, and I told you about mine. They didn't feel what we felt the other day when we accepted each other for who we are, and they certainly don't seem to know the man you've become despite their constant criticism and expectations." Kyra was desperate to find their way back to the happy, carefree and loving couple in the first throes of passion they'd been the day before. Soon they'd be back to training and exhaustion, and she knew they'd struggle to find time together when they were at the base again. Silas stopped his pacing and peered down at her.

"How do you do that?" he asked as he took the seat beside her and pulled her into his arms. "How did you just manage to tell them off and stick up for them at the same time?" he let out a gruff laugh that told her he'd understood why she'd played the fence a little with her words.

"Momma bears are always hard to win over. Don't worry about her questioning me—you're worth it. Why don't we go to town so I can check my credits and buy some clothes so she can stop complaining, and then we'll get drunk and eat a stupid amount of junk food on the beach? We can still use this time to have fun, just me and you, however it seems we can't keep the house to ourselves any longer."

"That's the best idea I've ever heard," he replied with a huge smile.

Rather than calling a cab, Silas presented Kyra with a crash helmet and led her into a garage to one side of the house. She found an astonishing sight inside, and gasped at the sheer amount of gifts and bribes the McDermott's had clearly taken over the years in the form of classic automobiles and modern vehicles. Back in the old world, humans with money to burn spent it on expensive toys like those lined up before her, and she felt like she was standing in a museum filled with relics from those days. Manufacturing of cars or motorbikes for sale was now a thing of the past, and the sectors that once created such things for pleasure were now solely in the business of making cars, trucks, trains or other old-school equipment to keep the human civilians mobile and troops well stocked.

Despite the new technologies that were readily available on Earth since Invasion Day, only the use of certain Thrakorian equipment by humans was allowed. The use of computers at school and on base were all in the service of King Kronus, so were deemed necessary to help further their society, but there were plenty of services that weren't, and the use of them always came at a price. The hovercraft that'd delivered them across the sea to Hawaii was one of those luxury expenses, and unnecessary travel would quickly eat away at any stock of credits a person had accrued. They were lucky, because as a yearly bonus each member of the Human Royal Armed Forces was allowed to travel to one destination and back for free. Kyra still didn't know how many she'd earned during the past year, and was eager to find out now that she and Silas had been forced to leave the solace of their short-term home.

Like her, most credit-conscious humans worked close to their homes, and didn't stray farther than the free trains allowed during their time away from work. It was considered more than just dangerous to run out of credits while far from home, but most low-paid humans couldn't accrue enough to travel anyway. There was no longer such a thing as holidaying for pleasure. Humans went only where they were allowed, and the system seemed to work perfectly to keep everyone in their place, without ever building walls or physical barriers to keep control of the classes. By keeping the poor on the breadline, their new society ensured the middle-class humans didn't have to see or think about them. Their food was made and their streets and homes cleaned, but they were busy working their own toil for the credits afforded to them, so didn't see the dirt below.

Kyra felt she'd finally crossed over into that void between those two classes, and didn't like the realizations she was coming to about just how bad the human race still was. They were following orders and doing as they were told, but life was simply passing them by. She hadn't noticed it before, but for the lower-classes, life seemed more about survival than actually living—and it was undoubtedly on purpose. Here she was, standing in what had to be one of the wealthiest human families' homes, and she despised the luxury and the power they'd been given. They had to have servants who'd cleaned the house in preparation for their visit, and who right now were dealing with the rot in what Freya had called their 'Manhattan' house. They probably didn't appreciate or even care for them, and Kyra hated how far she was feeling from her old roots. She felt torn, dithering between the world she'd known her entire post-Invasion Day life and the world she had within reach if she continued to progress in her career.

"I wonder if this is how Samia felt all those times I was eating rationed lunches, while she had her choice of the best meals," she whispered to herself, and knew Silas would want her to explain. She looked over at him, and had to smile at thinking back to the old friend she hadn't seen in over a year. "I had a half-breed friend at school. She taught me a lot about the Thraks, and I was always interested by her stories. Samia taught me to understand the divides between us, rather than hate them, and now I feel like I can appreciate even more. She was a genuine friend, but at times I felt like she took pity on me, and my lowly status. She was so kind, and had everything while I had nothing, but never let me see how vastly different we really were."

"What do you mean?" he asked, laying a hand on her shoulder. Kyra knew she must look pretty vacant, and peered into his dark eyes. She felt at home in that stare, and he brought her back to Earth again from her haywire thoughts.

"Every day when she came to school, Samia crossed over from the highest class system humanly possible into a middle-class sector, while I came up from the lower-class. She chose to be my friend, even though I was so poor I could never be allowed to visit her home or meet her family. She encouraged and helped me decide on my chosen career, yet she knew that one day I might come to look at the world the way I'm seeing it right now."

"Seeing it how?" he seemed really lost, and Kyra laughed.

"Divided in ways I could've never guessed," she answered as she wandered over to a nearby sports car and ran her hand over the delicate leather hood. "I keep asking myself where I fit in, wondering if I should strive for anywhere other than a lower rank of the army. What if I don't belong higher up? What if everyone treats me the way your mother did? Will I always just be the poor foster kid from downtown L.A." Questions were rolling off her tongue in waves, and she didn't really need them answering, only to say them aloud.

"Everyone has a chance in this new world to reinvent themselves, Kyra. I'm the other side of the coin, and ashamed to say it. I wanted to get rid of the shackles of wealth, but slowly I'm learning to accept it. You've helped me to come to terms with who I am, and I'm going to help you too," Silas promised, and she felt some of the weight lift from her shoulders. "You can be both the girl from the foster home and the soldier on her way to greatness. They aren't exclusive. Your past will stay with you in your kindness and the compassion you'll certainly never lose, but your strength will help you fit into those circles that might've once looked down on you, and that's because you belong there on merit."

His words hit her hard, and Kyra knew he was right. The world didn't owe her a thing, and neither did the Thraks, but she would earn her place regardless of what anyone thought or the box they tried to put her in. In a world where wealth and power should no longer be a factor, she would make sure it wasn't, and get her credits through hard work and determination.

"I love you," she whispered, lifting up onto her tiptoes to kiss him when he reached for her again. "Now, take me shopping. I want to check out just how much I get paid for being in this army thing," she added with a giggle, and then followed him over to where a huge black motorcycle sat waiting patiently for someone to ride it. He laughed at her feigned ignorance, and she appreciated that he didn't believe she could be such a scatterbrain. Silas walked the bike outside, fiddled with it for a minute, and then jumped on a lever to the side.

It roared to life, and Kyra watched with a smile while he checked that the components were working correctly, and then frowned when the front door of the house opened. Tarquin wandered out with a grin, and nodded at them both before leaning in to talk in her ear over the sound of the engine.

"You survived round-one, well done," he said, and she

turned to look up at him in surprise. "It took over a year before she accepted my girlfriend, and she's the Police Commissioner of the entire US. Hang in there, midget. She'll thaw eventually," he added, and gave her a light knock on the shoulder with his fist.

"Hey, who're you calling a midget?" she answered with a wink, and he shrugged before patting her on the head as if to prove his point. He might be taller than her, but she was used to that by now. "But thanks, and I guess I've still got a lot to prove before I'm allowed in, yeah?" He nodded, and Kyra knew she'd been right earlier when she suspected Freya would be hostile to anyone seeing her sons, no matter where they belonged in the classes or sectors.

"She'll soften. My girl even offered to take her out for dinner one night, but that went all kinds of wrong. The end result was her threatening to get Deena fired 'cause apparently she was being aggressive.'"

"She *is* aggressive!" Silas shouted over the loud engine, and Tarquin laughed. He shrugged and nodded, not denying his girlfriend's apparent ways.

"So, are you into butch chicks then?" Kyra asked, and earned herself a deep belly laugh from the huge policeman beside her. He was too busy howling with laughter to reply at first, but soon righted himself and peered over at his brother.

"This one's definitely a keeper, Si," he told him, and Silas grinned and gave him a nod. "I won't tell her you called her butch, but yeah, muscles turn me on, midget. She fights like a man and takes it like a Thrak—all night long." Kyra was shocked, but he laughed it off and she wondered if he was talking from experience or simply going on hearsay. It was a well-known fact they were bigger and stronger than humans, so it stood to reason that they'd have a longer endurance when it came to all things physical. Either way, she had the sneaking suspicion he wasn't about to tell her his history with human lovers, or otherwise.

"Nice, Tarq," Silas muttered when he put the bike in neutral. He climbed down off the humming beast and headed over to them with a smile, and Kyra could see he and Tarquin had a much better connection than either seemed to have with their mother.

"Come on, don't tell me you're all sweetness and light these days, bro? I know you've probably put this girl through hell in training, and judging by the fire in her eyes, she did nothing but come back for more, right?" The look Kyra and Silas gave each other must've said it all, and he snickered. "He gets results, but isn't afraid to beast his soldiers to get them. There was a time when I warned every girl who took a second look at him to stay away. Bad boy, black sheep of the family—whatever title he was aiming for, he got it and took no prisoners while doing so."

"Don't push it," Silas snapped. "We're the ones leaving our little piece of solitude for a few hours because you three turned up unannounced. We were quite happy whiling away our summer leave with nothing but a roof over our heads, and could easily find an alternative. Don't make me stay away for good next time."

"Hey," Tarquin replied, and lifted his hands in apology. "I was just teasing, baby brother. And, anyone can see it's not her who needs to be warned to stay away from you, but perhaps the other way around." He leered at Kyra, and she scowled at him. What did he mean by that?

Silas grabbed her arm and turned her toward the bike, breaking the eye contact and the tension that'd just descended, thanks to Tarquin's loaded comment. She wanted to ask him just what he was on about, but was well aware of the bristling man standing beside her, and how close he was to the edge. She somehow knew there wasn't much more Silas could take, so opted to salvage their day rather than let it be ruined by his oppressive family.

Kyra climbed onto the back of his bike and secured her

helmet, then wrapped her arms around his waist and held tight. He checked she was ready and then sped out through the barely open gate while she screamed excitedly, and was happy to leave the tension behind. The speed and danger were a thrill she felt all through her body, plus the wind felt good against her skin as it rushed through her clothes. She loved the ride, and knew she'd take him up on the offer of a proper tour of the island if he fancied it on another day of their trip.

Once in the small nearby town, Kyra went immediately to the credit station to check her balance. She knew there wouldn't be much in the way of clothes to shop for or treats she could buy, but she wanted to find at least something of her own she could take back to that mansion. Borrowing clothes hadn't been on her mind when she'd come to the island, and she was looking forward to having more things of her own to put in her half-empty backpack. Just like with cars and bikes, clothes were a luxury most people couldn't afford. Each human was provided with work uniforms, and in the lower-class sectors the adults she'd known usually wore those day and night because they didn't have anything else. Now though, she was trying to embrace her newly found freedom from that rut. She would be able to buy at least two outfits, she was sure, and then Freya couldn't moan about her borrowing her daughter's clothes.

The chip-reader loomed over her, and Kyra hesitated. After living on scraped credits as a kid earned solely by doing small jobs above those expected of her, she still felt nervous checking her balance. She rubbed the scar on her arm, and could feel the small lump beneath the surface where her chip was. As a child, she remembered having it placed inside her wrist by a huge Thrakorian nurse with no care for the scary equipment, or how much it'd hurt. She and the other kids had cried for hours, and had eventually been bribed with cake made especially to cheer them up by their caregivers.

After shaking away the memory, she pushed her arm into the rounded slot in the wall and waited for the reading. Seconds ticked by, and she nearly shuffled in case it wasn't being read properly, but then the figure appeared on the screen that made her want to scream. She'd never had more than twenty credits to her name in all her life, and yet now she seemed to be worth over five thousand of them. Kyra tried to work out how many she should've tallied up over the year. The actual figure was far more, and she wondered for a moment if it was a mistake.

"Silas?" she asked as she wandered back over to him. "How many credits should we get for primary training?"

"Didn't you get enough?" he asked, and was clearly ready to take her to the nearest police station to speak with the clerks there regarding the issue.

"I think I got too many," she mumbled, feeling embarrassed.

"You should get four thousand, give or take. Minus your food and board, but then add the bonuses for your scores. You did really well this year, that'll be the extra." He grinned and squeezed her shoulder. "Our platoon came first, so we all got a gratuity for that."

"That must be it, then. I've never had so much before," she could feel her cheeks burning with embarrassment, but was glad when Silas wouldn't let her fret over it.

He grabbed her hand and led her to a nearby clothing store. The manager there seemed used to serving those with credits to spare, and quickly got to work measuring her up and advising her on the best choices for her frame. The clothing would need to be custom-made, as the rules regarding wasted fabrics prohibited the tailors from mass-producing them, but she would do it within a few hours, and Kyra couldn't quite believe it. She'd never had service like this before, and after choosing just a simple dress, shorts and shirt for herself, she was ready for a strong drink. There hadn't been a chance to buy anything new in all her life, and it felt odd being able to afford just a few essentials now that she was working hard, and seemingly getting rewarded for it. They left the seamstress to her work, and she focused on procuring their first drink of the day.

"You're a wreck, what's the matter?" Silas asked when she steered him towards one of the bars that lined the beach in search of something to take the edge off. He came to a halt and peered down at her, fixing Kyra with that stern stare that sent her right back to training. "Do you feel bad for spending your hard-earned credits on yourself?" He grabbed her by the shoulders and shook her. "You're not off spending stupid amounts on foolish things. Get over your guilt."

She took a deep breath and knew he was right. There had to be a break away from the old her, and now was the time to fully take that last step. She did need those clothes, in fact she should've gotten more, and decided not to beat herself up about using some of her credits. She would spend them wisely, she had no doubt about it, and that was all that mattered.

Instead of ducking into a bar, the pair decided on a coffee shop instead. Patrons were invited to work for a free brew or pay with their credits, and Kyra smiled at the concept. Hawaii seemed rich and full of middle-class humans, but there were still those in the lower-class, and with limited credits. It was wonderful to see how they could be rewarded with hot coffee or tea after just a small amount of work to help the storeowners out, and she admired their initiative. Silas ordered the drinks, and Kyra couldn't resist grabbing them a chocolate muffin each. She hadn't had cake in years, and her mouth started watering immediately.

"What can we help you with?" Silas asked the clerk, much to Kyra's surprise, and she was filled with renewed love for him. Instead of buying the drinks for her, he was offering to work off the credits for the order, and she appreciated the gesture. She was too hungry to work though, and instead paid the bill with her own credits.

"This muffin cannot wait until we've worked it off," she told him with a wide smile, which he instantly returned. The clerk shrugged and went to the next customer in line, and Kyra demolished the cake in just a few bites while Silas carried their tray over to an empty table. "Oh, wow. That was amazing," she sighed. It felt good to have been able to buy them, and that she'd gladly paid the bill without worrying about her balance. Thanks to Silas she was changing with every minute that passed, and she watched him with a contented smile. He leaned over the table to wipe her mouth with his thumb, and then handed her his muffin.

"Have mine if you'd like. I'm not hungry," he said, and she knew it was a lie, but accepted the second mound of chocolaty goodness without argument. Kyra liked this new life she was making for herself, and even more so because of the people sharing it with her. She was happy, and that was more than she'd been able to say for a very long time.

CHAPTER EIGHT

By that afternoon, they'd whiled away the hours by the beach, drinking coffee and chatting about everything and nothing. Kyra was starting to feel more and more relaxed in Silas's company, and soon stopped seeing him as the grumpy Platoon Commander she'd slowly gotten to know during the past year. He was hers, just as she was his. The love blossoming between them already felt so pure and real, and she didn't care if she had a fight on her hands with his mother if she wanted to keep it.

They collected her new clothes, and when she tried them on so the seamstress could check the fit, Kyra felt amazing. She swished her dress around her knees and even asked to keep it on, much to the shopkeeper's delight.

"Would you like to add anything else to your order? We have underwear available in your size," the woman offered, and Kyra knew she needed them. She'd been wearing the same few sets of trusty underpants and bras for years, and they were in desperate need of replacing. She nodded and accepted a handful to try, while Silas browsed through a magazine in wait for her. He didn't seem to mind at all, and especially so when she flashed him glimpses of her chosen items from the changing room.

With her purchases complete, Kyra felt amazing. They stowed the bags in a locker at the back of Silas's motorbike, and soon they were on their way back to the house. She felt light as a feather as they breezed down the quiet streets, and was sad to see the mansion appear over the horizon a short while later. Silas seemed the same, and when he sped right past the house without any intention of slowing, Kyra squealed in excitement. She gripped him tighter, but leaned back slightly to let the hot, salty wind seep into her skin.

Here they were free. On the road and in the breeze there were no extraterrestrial overlords ruling them, nor was his family rich and powerful enough to intimidate her. They could be anyone they wanted to be, and knowing they accepted each other either way was all that mattered.

Silas slowed the bike near the peak of a ridge, and eventually stopped. They were near the edge of a huge cliff, and Kyra discarded her helmet so she could peer out at the stunning view. She climbed off the bike and edged her way forward just a couple of steps.

"Why didn't you go to New York with the rest of your family for summer leave?" she asked, her eyes on the horizon. "Why did you come here with me instead?"

"Because no matter what I do, I'll always be the family screw-up. You heard Tarq earlier, always teasing and pushing at me for what I was like years ago. We get on better than we used to, but they've still put me in a box I'll never escape from, just like you. Did you notice how not a single one of them congratulated either of us for coming in first place. They didn't mention it, even though I know they would've been informed the outcome by Lt. Psy." Silas was right, and Kyra knew there was no sticking up for them this time.

She nodded and took his hand in hers. Despite his failures, Silas truly had seemed to learn the error of his ways. If they couldn't see what an amazing man he'd become, then they were the ones missing out, and she told him so.

***

The smitten couple avoided the others as much as

possible over the next few days, and opted to stay in the bedroom wherever possible. The need to explore their love hadn't diminished one little bit, and they kept each other busy day and night with their unashamed affection as they gave into the love that'd accompanied their adoration.

The last couple of days in Hawaii were bittersweet. Freya had softened a little and even Tarq's taunts weren't as harsh, so the atmosphere was better, but the progression also brought with it the end of their break from Fort Angel.

They climbed back into their combats and headed for the hovercraft in plenty of time to get back to base. Kyra was sad to leave their island behind, but this time they wouldn't be heading back to secret kisses stolen behind crates in the shadows. She knew they'd need to come clean to Lt. Psy first, but then they'd be free to act like a proper couple when they were ready, and part of her couldn't wait to get back so that conversation could be over with.

Kyra was also apprehensive about starting her secondary training. She knew the harder and more physical work was done in the primary phase, so now was her chance to really shine in the lessons to come, but she was still terrified of failing.

"It's good you're so scared, it means you want it bad enough," Silas told her mid-flight when she was clearly still fretting. He seemed to have picked up on her unease without needing to ask her what it was about, and she loved how intuitive he was towards her emotions.

"I guess so, and even if I stayed where I am now it's not the end of the world. I'm earning credits and will have my own room in the block now, plus food and utilities. Everything is falling into place at last, so I just need to keep going."

"Exactly, but knowing you you'll never need to settle for anything less than what you deserve," he replied, and pulled her close.

The long ride back to Death Valley was hot and hard. Kyra and Silas sat together, but she had to keep from holding his hand or leaning in for a kiss. They were quiet the entire journey, and she welcomed the sight of the base when they approached.

"Meet me outside Psy's office in an hour," he told her before grabbing his pack and heading off into the huge building. She watched him go, but tore her eyes away. She had to focus on her training again. Kyra knew she'd never forgive herself, or him, if she failed thanks to her absentmindedness during the next phase.

"Corporal Millan," a voice called from the head of the group ahead, and she raised her hand. Before them stood the voices owner, a soldier she'd seen around base during her first year. "You've been assigned to C-block, room twelve." She thanked him and took the key he offered, and then stood back in the ranks with the others. When they were all given their assigned rooms, he addressed them again. "Welcome back to Fort Angel, and to the secondary phase of your training. I'm your Commander, Sergeant Parker. We'll get you all back into the swing of things with a kit inspection and a ten-mile run tomorrow from oh-seven-hundred. Until then, get out of my sight."

She did as he'd ordered, and ran off to check out her room. C-block wasn't far from the main buildings of the base, and she was pleased to find it clean and comfortable inside. They each had new combats and a full kit hanging in their closets, plus linen for the beds and toilet rolls in the bathroom. Basics covered, Kyra had almost everything else she needed, and pulled her toothbrush and personal items from her pack. She stashed the clothes she'd bought in Hawaii in a small cubby space designated for their personal items, along with some shells they'd collected from the beach and a photograph of her and Silas a man had taken in exchange for some food and water. They were both smiling so brightly, and Kyra loved how they'd captured such a beautiful moment forever.

Fort Angel's Commander's office was a few minutes' walk away, so she checked her things over one more time, locked the door behind her, and then went across to meet Silas there. He was already inside, chatting to Lt. Psy casually and in such a relaxed way she hoped he might've been given some good news, but neither of them said anything when she appeared in the doorway. Kyra stood as tall as she could and saluted.

"Good afternoon, Commander. I was hoping to have a word if possible?" she asked, and he nodded.

"Come on in, Corporal. Sergeant McDermott was just leaving. What can I do for you?"

"Well, sir. We were hoping to talk to you together," she answered, and his courteous half-smile quickly turned into a full-blown grin.

"Took you long enough," he said as he indicated for them both to take a seat. She closed the door behind her and followed his instructions, and her heart was beating so hard in her chest she was sure it might explode. Lt. Psy leaned forward and rested his elbows on the desk. "The two of you have begun a relationship and would like permission to see one another while on my base..."

"Yes, sir," Silas answered. "And I can assure you we weren't together before summer leave."

"Well you were, but not in *every* way," Psy corrected him, and she guessed he'd known all along what they were up to. "I allowed it because you weren't disrespecting this base, the army's rules, or my orders. Now? You are no longer her Platoon Commander, Silas. You're free to date one another just as long as you continue to respect this base and the soldiers in it. Do not flaunt your relationship or act like lovesick teenagers, and I certainly don't want reports of late-night shenanigans keeping your block-mates awake. Is that understood?" Kyra let out the breath she'd had no idea she was holding.

"Thank you so much, Commander. We won't let you down, I promise," she replied, and they both stood.

"Thank you, sir. And I meant every word I said before," Silas added.

"All you two need to do, is continue to impress me, the rest will come in time." Lt. Psy replied, and took one last look at Kyra. "And you. I asked for a top-five placement and you gave me a number-one spot. I hope you're planning on keeping up the hard work this year?"

"No doubt about it. You have my word." She meant it, and appreciated his acknowledgement of her hard work the year before. Lt. Psy really was the mentor Silas had told her about, and she could see why he looked up to him so much.

Outside in the corridor, the pair of them beamed and Kyra had to stifle the tiny, girly shriek threatening to burst out of her. Their conversation had gone better than she could've imagined, and it was clear to her now that their Commander really did see everything that went on in his base.

"We'll tell the others in time, but for now let's just get into our new routines and wait for the perfect moment to come clean to our friends. Some of the guys training you for secondary phase are buddies of mine, so you'll most likely have to put up with a little teasing I'm afraid," Silas said as he walked her towards the door. "But I'll tell them to go easy on you."

"I can take whatever they've got. I guess you're worth the hassle, or else I'll just finish things," she teased in response, and he shook his head. They both knew their relationship was worth fighting for, and her words were empty taunts. "What were you talking about before I got there?" Kyra had to ask, and Silas grew instantly serious.

"I told him I thought I was ready to earn my next stripe. I want to be Lieutenant." She was more proud of him than ever before, and couldn't stop from touching his cheek with her palm for just a second before letting it drop. "It's not about proving everyone else wrong anymore, Kyra. It's about proving you right. I want to be the man you believe I can be, and I'm starting by leading a group of secondary soldiers this year instead of primary recruits again."

Kyra's eyes widened, she was so pleased for him but at the same time wondered if it would impact on the approval Lt. Psy had just given them. "I'm moving into combat and weapons specialism, so wouldn't take your geek group anyway. That's what I assured him of, that I'd never be your instructor again. That way, we'll never break that rule, and he was happy with that."

"Phew, I was worried for a second there." She pushed her glasses up her nose and peered into his deep brown eyes. "And there's nothing wrong with being a geek. I didn't see you complaining when I fixed your computer..." Kyra sauntered away before he could respond.

She stepped out into the bright sunshine and felt elated. Everything was falling into place at last, and it was incredible.

CHAPTER NINE

Weeks of grueling physical endurance assessments combined with intense specialty testing meant Kyra was soon lacking in her energetic glow, and even stolen kisses with Silas were getting fewer and farther between. Many of the recruits had hoped secondary training would come a little easier, but it was as hard if not worse than primary in many ways. The units were now fully-fledged members of the army, and were now expected to not only train for their physical duty, but also mentally prepare for a coveted place in their chosen division.

"If you wanted it to be easy, you should've stayed in the Infantry. You chose to be here, you accepted your spot on this next phase. Do not cry and moan, 'cause this is exactly where you wanted to be. You should be thanking me for making you a better soldier," Sgt. Parker roared while pacing up and down as his training group was doing push-ups in a freezing cold area of one of the simulated training zones. Kyra was covered from head to toe in an icy, clay-like mud, and she hated every moment of it, but pushed her way through the pain and the discomfort. He was right, and as her body grumbled in response to their harsh workout, she forced her mind to switch off from what her body was doing. She began preparing for her computer science test scheduled for the following morning, planning out algorithms and rehearsing codes she'd learned during her study of their made-up mainframe and its bugs.

After hours spent behind the screens of their state-of-the-art computer suite, she was sure she could tackle anything the assessors threw at her, but wouldn't take any chances. She'd been alone in the suite many of those times, and could tell there weren't many looking to join the Intelligence Division this year, but competition was still fierce.

"Check the system, take out the firewall and scope for codes," she was talking aloud without realizing it, and Sgt. Parker stopped beside her.

"What did you say, Corporal Millan?" he bellowed. "You have time for a conversation during my workouts, do you?"

"No, Commander. I just wanted..." she shouted as loud as she could through her icy lungs while still pushing up and down into the mud. "To thank you."

"Very well then," he said, and she could hear the smile in his voice. "Everybody stop, but don't get up. I'd like you to stay exactly where you are. Lie down, get comfortable, and enjoy the cold. I'll be back in thirty minutes. Anyone who has moved in that time will be on laundry duty, so can enjoy cleaning the muddy combats all afternoon."

"Yes, Commander," they all shouted, and each groaned as they settled down on the thick, goopy mud that was so cold it made their teeth chatter.

"Always check for fake connections in the encryption. Double-check the code against the source." Kyra carried on reciting her practiced method to herself. In her mind she envisioned the computer sitting in front of her and as many different scenarios as she could, in which a virus had gotten into their system, or the opposite where she was planting a virus in a rebel network.

Boots crunched by her ears in no time at all, and Sgt. Parker congratulated them on their willpower. They were then released, and each of the Corporals welcomed the heat that hit them when they emerged from the arctic simulator. They each basked in it for a few minutes, and she felt like a lizard warming under a lamp.

"Please tell me I won't have it this hard once I make it into the Medical Division?" Brona asked, pulling Kyra from her thawing haze. She laughed.

"Worse. I've got three words... combat medic training," she replied with a smirk.

"Ugh!" Brona shoved her and wandered off back to her block. Kyra turned away from the heat of the sunshine and started in the direction of her room, when a small cough alerted her to the fact she'd been being watched.

"I'm not sure why, but this whole mud-bath thing you've got going on," Silas said as he approached her with a cheeky grin. "Turns me on."

"Safe to say I don't believe a word of it," she replied dismissively, but grinned. "Please tell me you're staying?" she asked, and hoped the answer was yes. It felt like so long since they'd had some time together, and she hoped he might at least have enough of a break for a bite to eat or a coffee. No one had asked them outright whether they were seeing each other yet, but they'd been seen spending time together here and there, and knew the questions were coming, however they no longer cared. They weren't flaunting their relationship, or making anyone feel uncomfortable with public displays of affection. They were simply being friendly in the open, and far more so whenever they could get away with it in what little private time they each had. Lt. Psy seemed happy with their behavior, but Silas's hectic schedule of combat and weapons training in preparation for his move into the Tactical Division was making it hard. He seemed to love every minute of it, as did she with her computer science training, but it made it hard to maintain a new relationship while they were both so busy.

"I'm here for an entire week, little lady," he replied, and his grin broadened. "So go take a shower and meet me by our tree. Bring your books, we're studying."

Kyra pouted, but was actually glad. He knew she had her exam the following morning, and had clearly planned on not selfishly taking her away from her much-needed study time. She gave him a quick salute and ran the rest of the way to her block, where she threw her muddied combats in the wash and took a blisteringly hot shower. With her wet hair tied back in a braid, and a fresh set of combats on, Kyra then grabbed her laptop and books. She stuffed them in her pack and was out the door a moment later. She had a date with a certain Sergeant, and was not going to keep him waiting.

"Tell me, what exactly do you have to study again?" Kyra teased as she watched Silas sprawling out under the warm autumn sunshine like he was about ready for a nap. She, on the other hand, was sat reading through her course materials while running simulations on the laptop her tutors had loaned her for the process of the evaluations. There were no games or fun browsing to be done, it was a simple processor loaded with computer-generated hacks and viruses ready for tackling.

"It might look like I'm not doing much, but I'm actually stripping, cleaning and rebuilding various weapons in my mind. I'm very deep in thought, and hard at work," he said, folding his hand underneath his head to act like a pillow as he snuggled down lower.

"Any deeper in thought and you'll be dreaming," she groaned, and then laughed when he sprung up and grabbed her around the waist, pulling her into his arms. She wriggled half-heartedly and then gave in. She figured allowing themselves a few minutes of snuggling wouldn't hurt.

"I knew it!" Brona's voice chimed from a few yards away, and they both groaned. Kyra didn't spring up in shock, but instead she rolled over and lay with her head on Silas's chest, peering up at her smiling friend. "Caught you, I told Jett you were seeing each other, and he wouldn't believe me," she added, slumping down on the blanket Silas had procured for them to lie on.

"So it's true, you two are seeing each other as well?" Kyra asked, and Brona blushed.

"Yeah, just the past few weeks. We were friends first, but lately I think we've all grown up a lot. Seems the same with you guys," she said, and Kyra knew she was fishing for details, so decided now was as good a time as any to finally spill their half-true version of the story.

"We've been seeing each other since summer leave. I ended up on the same bus, train and boat as McD heading to Hawaii. We've okayed it with Lt. Psy, and he's fine as long as we don't make a big deal out of it. So you need to stop yourself going all girly if you see us together," she told her, and Brona nodded energetically.

"I will, and it's the same for me and Jett. We're keeping things under wraps for as long as we can, but things feel good so far," she replied with a shy smile.

Kyra was happy for her friend, and didn't mind that she and Silas had finally been caught together. It was in everyone's best interest to keep things from escalating into becoming the base gossip, and she trusted Brona not to go squealing to anyone who'd listen about their confession. The three of them then chatted for a while, but thankfully she took the hint, and left them to it after a few minutes. They'd taken the first step forward by telling her friend the truth, and as Silas pulled Kyra in close and kissed her temple, she sighed happily.

"It feels good to have things out in the open," he told her, and then grabbed one of her books and slid it into her hands. "Now, back to work, geek." She both giggled and groaned, but did as he'd instructed.

***

Kyra walked into the examination room the next morning, and sat down in front of her chosen computer screen. There were only a handful of other recruits in there with her, but she paid them no attention as she prepped her area and made herself comfortable. After a short while, the screen came to life, and a simulated network appeared on the vibrant display.

Envelopes were then given out, seemingly at random, to each of the trainees. Each was labeled with numbers one-through-five, and left in a neat stack beside her keyboard.

"Welcome to your assessment. You must now attempt to complete all five challenges given to achieve consideration for the Intelligence Division. You will be marked on speed, accuracy, knowledge and skill. Please open your first card and follow the instructions as given," a computerized voice echoed through the small room, and Kyra grabbed her first card.

Inside were instructions to infiltrate the system on the screen before her, and plant a tracking code. She had to get in and out undetected, and knew exactly how to do it. With her hands flying over the keys and mouse as fast as she could move them, she created a fake digital signature, and breezed through the firewall protecting the simulated server effortlessly. She covered her tracks every step of the way, and completed the first task in no time at all.

Each envelope then contained a harder or more intricate challenge, but she kept her cool and ploughed through every one of them as fast as she could while maintaining her accuracy. She hacked systems and took them down, and planted simulated viruses to slowly infiltrate, copy, and then destroy them. Every one was a success, but she didn't take any of it for granted.

The final task was, of course, the hardest. Kyra had already been sat for hours with no food, drink, rest or a toilet break, but she didn't care. She'd planned for this, and knew she had to keep her mind sharp and focused, and away from anything her body might be saying she needed right now.

She heard some of the others moaning or cursing at their screens, but blocked them out again. This was it. She had her chance to shine, and wouldn't waste a single moment of it. Within seconds of reading her card, a system warning flashed on her screen. A simulated rebel was trying to hack into her mainframe and steal official documents. It was her job to stop them as fast as possible, and she quickly began defending each of her networks with a method she'd devised to send potential hackers to the wrong place. She carefully wove a tangled web of decryptions and codes that she alone could follow back, and only when every area was covered did she go after the rebel.

She found the hacker, traced it to the source, and then shut down their entire operating system. The intruder was toast, but she still had her interwoven path to follow back, so Kyra then spent a few minutes bringing her system back to its original state.

With her hands shaking, she then peered at the screen, eagerly awaiting the verdict. The warning ceased, and the operating system returned to normal. Nothing else happened, and she found herself staring at the screen in readiness for another challenge, but it didn't come. It was only when she felt a light tap on her shoulder that she tore her tired eyes away, and peered up at the man who'd done it. A mountainous Thrakorian soldier stood peering down at her with a smile, and with a wave of his hand beckoned for her to leave the computer suite. Kyra's aching bones protested when she stretched and stood, but then relief washed over her, and the need to pee suddenly became very apparent.

Kyra looked around, and paled as she realized she was the last one left in the suite. In the build up to her assessment she'd been so sure of herself, but now a wave of nausea caused her mouth to flood, and she gazed up at the huge man waiting patiently by the door.

"Am I the last to finish?" she asked, and he nodded.

"So, have I failed?" He didn't answer. The Thrak simply opened the door and held it for her, and Kyra stepped slowly out into the hall. She forced her fear of failure away, and stood to salute him properly. "May I use the bathroom, sir?" she asked timidly.

"Of course. When you're finished, you may go back to your room. Report back here at zero-eight-hundred hours tomorrow for the results." He smiled again, but she didn't feel put at ease by it. Kyra ran for the bathroom the second his back was turned, and proceeded to puke up the barely-there contents of her stomach. Bile stung her throat, and tears streamed down her cheeks. Was it over already? Had her dreams been stomped on at the first hurdle? Not knowing was agony, and she didn't know if she could survive the wait until morning to find out.

When she finally made it out of the building, Kyra was shocked to find herself engulfed in darkness. She checked her watch, twenty-two-hundred. She'd been there all day, and her mind slowly caught up with the exhaustion in her body. Every step was with feet that dragged, and her mind was still fraught with her fears of failure. She took the quickest shower she could and fell into a heap in bed. Sleep washed over her in seconds, and it felt like only a minute had passed when her alarm chimed the next morning.

"Wow, you look like hell," Brona said, watching as Kyra nursed her coffee with a scowl. She was in a bad mood, and understandably. It was all she could do not to curse at her, but none of this was Brona's fault, so Kyra bit her tongue. "Did it really go that bad?"

"Worse than bad," she replied. "I was last to finish, how did that happen? I'm screwed, I just know it. All this hard work and I'll be stuck doing admin for the rest of my life."

"Did you complete the tasks?" Brona asked as she tucked into her bowl of cereal.

"Yeah, and thought I'd done well. I used my own algorithms and codes, which I guess takes time, but not once did I think I'd be the last one there." Kyra let her head fall onto the table before her with a small thud. "Ouch," she groaned, and Brona laughed.

"That bad, huh?" Silas's voice broke through her despair, and she lifted her head up to look at him as he took the seat beside her. Tears pricked at her eyes, and she wanted to slap herself for being such a girl. A nod was all the answer he needed, but he didn't seem ready to give her a pity party just yet. "They told you so, or you felt like it went badly?" he asked, and Kyra guessed her empty expression must've said it all. "Stop feeling sorry for yourself. Walk in there, demand to know your score, and fight your corner if they dare tell you you're not good enough." Tears welled in her eyes again, and she was almost about to throw her arms around him, but then thought better of it.

"Oh, Sgt. McDermott, you know all the right things to say," she teased in her best attempt at a sarcastic reply. He was right, though. She hadn't been told yes or no yet, and until she got her explanation or was offered the chance to appeal, wallowing in self-pity wasn't getting her anywhere. Kyra finished off her drink and slammed the mug down on the table. "I did everything I could, and if it's not good enough—so be it." Her friends all nodded in agreement, and she silently thanked Silas for his little pep talk.

With more than twenty minutes to spare, Kyra headed straight for the Intelligence Division training building and took a seat in the waiting area. She forced herself not to fiddle or pace, and instead watched as the other trainees inside wandered around with happy smiles on their faces, and a clear sense of purpose. Each of them had gone through this ordeal, and they'd made it. She wanted it so much, and knew that was why she'd gotten so wound up about her lengthy time in the suite the day before. She hadn't once doubted her skill before that, but knowing she'd taken longest was a real kick in the teeth, and Kyra vowed to herself that she would never let it happen again.

"Corporal Millan, you're early," a deep voice that seemed to bounce off the walls and shake the seat beneath her called. She looked up and found the same soldier from the night before peering down at her with a smile. Kyra felt like that little girl again, and it took her a second to force all thoughts of King Kronus and Invasion Day back out of her mind. Her neck ached with the effort it took to look into the huge Thrakorian man's face, and she jumped to her feet and saluted him.

"I like to be punctual, sir," she replied, still staring up at him despite standing. "And of course, I'm eager to get the results of my assessment."

"I'm sure you are," he told her with a smile that lifted her spirits. "Follow me." Kyra did as she was told, and before long was ushered inside a huge doorway she assumed must've been installed by her gigantic superiors. She was ordered to sit on one side of a large table in what she now realized must be a meeting room, while three elite human officers and a Thrakorian Lorde stared across at her from the other side. She'd heard of the Thrak opposite, and knew he was the Intelligence Division's formidable leader—Lorde Sharq.

The man in the center, whom she knew was called Capt. Carlton, perused her file for a moment before he spoke. He gave nothing away, and Kyra could feel herself starting to sweat.

"Eleven hours, that's quite a lengthy timeframe. Care to tell us why you think it took you so long to complete your assessment, Corporal?" he asked, and his ice-blue eyes bore into hers.

"I prioritized getting it right over getting through in the fastest time, sir. Some of my methods take longer to implement than traditional counter-measures, but I believe that they work better at securing the systems and stopping the hackers from stealing any information." Her voice was surprisingly calm, and she forced herself to sit upright in front of the assessors. If this was her last chance, she was going to go out with her head held high.

"We noticed that," Capt. Carlton continued. "In the final trial you successfully stopped not only the hack, but also ensured no data was leaked. Well done."

Kyra went to thank him, but was instantly bombarded with questions from the others. They wanted to know how she'd come up with her algorithms, and why she'd used certain codes when typically a set standard would be used. Every second of her challenge was picked apart and criticized, and she felt utterly drained by the time the human officers had finished their questioning.

"Why do you want to join the Intelligence Division?" Lorde Sharq asked at last, and they all looked at Kyra for her answer.

"Because I know I'm good enough, and I've wanted it my entire life. I believe I can use my skills most effectively in serving the Intelligence Division, and what I demonstrated yesterday is just the beginning of what I know I'm capable of. My brain naturally works like a computer. I have the ability to see things differently to others, I always have, and when something is out of place I often notice it right away," she said, talking from her heart rather than with any prepared speech she guessed he would find insincere.

"A natural code-breaker," Sharq replied, and she nodded.

"It says in your file, you successfully led a team away from an ambush in your final primary exercise based on a system of symbols you found, and where no others had done before you?" Capt. Carlton said, and she nodded again. They each looked at each other and then at Lorde Sharq, and Kyra knew his decision must be final.

He fiddled with his papers for a few minutes, and it was agonizing. All Kyra could hear was the thud-thump of her heart in her ears, and her stomach ached with the tension she knew she was holding tightly. Sharq looked back up at her, to the others, and down at the page in front of him, and she wanted to scream.

"Welcome to the Intelligence Division, Corporal Millan," he finally informed her, after what felt like an hour had passed, and she wanted to scream. Kyra felt light-headed at the realization she'd made it after all. She wanted to ask him why, how, and all the things her brain was going crazy picking apart from her interrogation-style assessment, but he didn't give her the opportunity to ask. Sharq signed the top piece of paper in his pile, which he handed to Capt. Carlton. He then wrote on another form, which he held out for Kyra to take. "I expect nothing but great things from you, Corporal. I assume you're planning on trying out for the elite course at the end of your secondary training?" he asked, and Kyra nodded. "Well then, you'll require three personal recommendations. Here's your first," he added as he let go of the paper, and she could do nothing but stare at him open-mouthed.

CHAPTER TEN

Brona had gotten through her assessment with an acceptance into the Medical Division, as had all their other friends from Lima Platoon with their chosen fields. They celebrated their victory with a contraband bottle of booze in the block, and after just two shots, Kyra was already feeling fuzzy. She declined any more, and fell into bed with a satisfied sigh. She'd done it, and was already on the right path to completing not only her secondary phase training, but also the potential of an elite position in the division she'd dreamed of joining for years. Most soldiers peaked in the secondary phase, and slowly moved up the ranks as far as possible whilst in their chosen career. Elite training was offered only to those who showed expert potential, and if she passed the training she knew she'd be on the right path to becoming a Captain by the time she hit her thirties.

Kyra wished Silas could be with her to share in the celebrations, or at least spending the night wrapped in his arms would be the perfect prize. He'd managed a few hours, but was called away after dinner by his new platoon. She'd watched that cute ass of his all the way to the door, and hoped they'd get some proper alone time soon.

Sleep claimed her quickly, and it was the dawn light that roused her before the alarm the following morning. Kyra showered and changed, and went for an early breakfast in the canteen. Inside, she spotted Lt. Psy talking to some of the higher-ranking soldier's in his front office team, and greeted them all politely. He beckoned her closer, and she smiled respectfully while internally freaking out.

"Can't sleep?" he asked. His voice was stern, but somehow gentler than she'd ever heard, and it was a surprise.

"Something like that, Commander," she replied with a smile.

"You certainly made an impression, Corporal. Keep up the good work, and you'll find out what wondrous possibilities await you," he told her. "Finish secondary training in the top-five, and I'll recommend you for elite myself," he added, and she was taken aback. The Lieutenant had been an impenetrable wall of hard-ass and strict mentor, but she was starting to understand why Silas spoke so highly of him. He'd provided the pep talk in her primary training that'd given her hope, and a reason to work hard, and now he'd simply moved that goal post.

"Thank you so much, sir," she replied, and was unable to hide her smile. Lt. Psy simply nodded and walked away, and she guessed he wasn't much for the soppy side of the human psyche. She promised herself she wouldn't let him down, or herself. She would get that place, and her recommendation, even if she had to work around the clock to achieve it.

Once Computer and Technological Science training began, time lost all meaning, and was soon nothing but routine and studying. Physical training became just a regular part of their week, rather than for hours or even days on end like before, and Kyra enjoyed the break from working on the computers or in the codex labs. She was pushing herself so hard in lessons and their regular assessments, that it was a welcome escape to run a few miles or work out in the simulated environments of the training center, and found she needed the balance.

Time with Silas was few and far between, but somehow they were managing to make it work. Stolen moments were no longer necessary, as everyone seemed to know they were a couple without actually asking or making a fuss about it, and she was pleased. They sat together every mealtime if they could, and she would sneak into his block when it'd emptied out, or he'd bribed his fellow Sergeants for some privacy. It wasn't perfect, but when the training was over and they could apply for a house of their own to live in, it would all fall into place, she knew it.

"If you go elite, you'll spend another few years in training," he told Kyra one night, peering down at her in the dim light of his room. She snuggled deeper into his embrace, but couldn't let herself worry about how long it might take for her to reach her peak. If she got the recommendations, she'd go no matter how long it took. "I want you to know, I'll support whatever route you decide," he added, and it was exactly what she needed to hear. The prospect of having a row with him over it had actually been worrying her the past few months, and it was a relief knowing he supported her. Elite training would take her to a dedicated Intelligence Division base in Alaska, whereas Silas seemed to be staying in Death Valley for the foreseeable future. Like her, he wanted to proceed, but his chosen path was here, and it was inevitable that they'd be separated at some point.

"We're meant to be, Silas. We'll make it work," she replied.

"Yeah, we'll find a way. I won't lose you, little lady. I couldn't live without you," he told her, and kissed her tenderly before turning out the light.

***

"Today you will be starting an element of training that contains classified information, so be warned and remember to keep your mouths closed regarding what you've seen," the Course Commander, Captain Quinn said as she stood at the head of the class and watched them all with her usual hardened stare. She took no prisoners when it came to her teaching methods, and had so far covered the entire course content single-handedly and with apparent ease. It was almost the end of the year, and in that time they'd learned a tremendous amount under her guidance. They'd fit in more than Kyra had ever thought possible before dedicating every waking moment to her training, but she was always ready to learn more.

Quinn began firing questions at the students, asking what they knew, or thought they knew, about the superior race who governed theirs.

"They're all very tall," one soldier said, and was met with a nod.

"They don't mix with humans socially, nor do they train or study with us," said another.

"True, and why is that?" Capt. Quinn asked, but was met with blank stares. Kyra guessed everyone was thinking the same, but didn't want to say it, so she raised her hand.

"Why should they?" she asked in answer, and was met with a booming laugh from the back of the class.

"That's exactly right, Corporal," the Thrakorian soldier she'd met during her assessment replied, and she jumped, not having realized he was there. "Thraks did not come here to make friends, we came here to lead." He walked through them towards the front of the class. "Humans in the lower-class sectors serve all of us. Middle-class humans still serve, but by hard work and provision to the King. Upper-class humans also operate for the same purpose. Above your human class system is none of your concern, and why?" he asked, staring at them all with an intimidating look.

"Because we are grateful to King Kronus for liberating the humans from our lives of excess and greed?" one recruit asked, and it earned him a snicker.

"Rehearsed propaganda is for the lower-classes, you know better than that!" he replied. "Don't give me your practiced lines, give me your gut response. You're in the

Intelligence Division now, act intelligent…"

"We aren't important enough to know," one soldier asked, and the Thrak nodded.

"We only know what we have to in order to do our jobs," Kyra added, and he gave her a wink.

"Absolutely right. Now we're getting somewhere. Does that annoy you? Do you feel like a pawn in a game where none of your teammates could possibly win? Or do you accept your position and readily move on?" he asked, pacing the small room. Stunned silence met his words, and they all seemed unsure how to respond. "If you want to question your place in our society, then you need to walk out of here right now and join the rebels. You are the clever ones, the geeks and the nerds. You are a precious commodity, but only while you serve King Kronus. If you don't want that, go now…" He paused for effect, and Kyra was pleased to see that none of her classmates left the room.

After his explosive entrance, the Thrakorian soldier then took them through various details of their race. There was a lot she didn't know, despite having had some insider knowledge from Samia in their school days. She'd known that their people all stood far above the humans in Earth's new reign, but never dreamed there were so many levels in their triangular government that led all the way to its one leader, King Kronus. "So, at the bottom we have convicts. They are tried and sentenced by the Lawbringer. He is an appointed Thrak who oversees the judicial system, and whose say is final. Convicts are brought to train and work in the lowest level of the army, and ninety-nine percent of them stay there. Then we have the lower, middle and upper-class humans, or soldier, officer and elite members of the Human Royal Armed Forces. Between them and the mixed-heritage sector is the Gentry. They are handpicked humans who are specialists, or have performed extraordinarily in service to his majesty. They are given a higher status, wealth and position than other humans, but still no higher standing than any Thrakorian."

Kyra was writing notes furiously, and was surprised she'd never heard more about the how's and why's of becoming a Gentry officer before. Part of her remembered how Silas had described his family, and knew the McDermott's were prime examples of humans of such high standing. The title also explained their wealth and power in an otherwise dictatorially ruled existence. "Next you have the mixed-breeds, then Thrakorian civilians, and the Thrak army. Above that is the King's Guard Service, and then King Kronus himself." He paused just long enough to watch their hands moving furiously over their notepads with a satisfied smile. "Do any of you know where the planet Thrakor is?" Every soldier shook his or her head. "Or how about why we came here?"

"To colonize and rule?" one girl asked, and the soldier shrugged.

"Yes, but more than that?" No one answered. "We started out the same as the humans, and our planet is like Earth, but superior in every way. Our species evolved millennia ago, whereas yours crawled from the primordial ooze, evolved and then diminished over time. That's why our leaders decided to begin an invasion hundreds of years ago. Earth was a gift to King Thrakor's youngest son as his inheritance, and he came to take control when he reached adulthood. I'm talking, of course, of King Kronus."

Murmurs erupted in the class, and Kyra watched as he scanned them with a sly smile. She knew they were all lapping up his tales of how the Thraks saw the humans as nothing but cattle tending to their world while they reaped the benefits, but she didn't believe it. Her hand instinctively went to her cheek, and she rubbed the scar there. She'd been treated with the loving and gentle hand of a man she was sure hadn't come to crush and rule the humans with fear.

"So are we simply inhabitants of a world solely existing as a trial run for if he eventually inherits the Thrakorian throne?" she asked, and silence quickly descended on the class.

"You could say that, yes," the soldier answered. "But also, Earth is an extension of King Thrakor's reign, and his offspring have every right to rule it as they see fit. Some colonies of ours are ruled with an iron fist, and in others the previously populating species was obliterated before colonization. You should count yourself lucky King Kronus came looking for peace here."

"Oh, I do," she replied, feeling like a deer in the headlights. "And perhaps one day my service will be proof of my gratitude," she added, to ensure he knew she wasn't questioning their ruler, just his motives.

They went on to learn more about the Thraks as a race, and the differences between them and the humans from a genetic point of view. Kyra learned how the planet Thrakor had been created in the same big-bang explosion that'd formed the Earth billions of years ago. The two species' were similar from the start, but the Thraks had thrived and advanced to be far more superior to the human race over the millennia. They'd gone in search of planets like theirs centuries ago, and had placed reconnaissance units on each before deciding to lay the foundations of various colonies. Mixed-breeds were essential to ensure the Thraks had a stronghold already on Earth, and they had caused a wave of immigrants from Thrakor to come and stay.

"When a Thrakorian chooses their partner, nothing will come between them. Not surprisingly, many of the first waves of soldiers' fell in love with their human child-bearers in the same way, and requested permission to stay. Their lovers grew old and died, but they stayed to care for their children, and see to it that they kept within the mixed-breed families," he told them, and Kyra remembered how Samia had said the same about her own family tree.

There was a lot to take in, but by the end of the day she was well versed in the sectors, classes and Thrakorian way of life. The detailed truths were more than she'd ever expected to be taught so openly, and she understood Quinn's opening warning now. It was a shock to discover how closely related the humans and Thraks were, but also how complicated that distant relationship had become after centuries of interbreeding, and the colonization process.

Kyra walked back to her room deep in thought, trying to figure out how she was feeling. The soldier, who never had given his name, had worked hard making them feel inferior to his race in a way she'd always known to be possible, but never believed true. Part of her wondered if the Thrakorian civilians hated the humans, or saw them as pesky vermin on a planet they were trying to call home. The few she'd met in her life had been all about purpose, and had never shown care or consideration to her or the other humans in their stead, but she'd seen the importance of family values and racial prejudice in Samia's upbringing. None of it seemed to add up, and the confusion was making her head sore. Kyra was well aware by now how exhausting the training was, and found herself counting the days until summer leave came around again. This time she wouldn't have to complete a grueling exercise, and in fact many of her fellow trainees had been tasked with playing rebels for the primary assessments, so she welcomed the chance to get to the end of the month and take it easy.

"Can you believe almost an entire year has gone by?" Brona asked as she plopped down on the end of Kyra's bed. "Where are you going this time, Hawaii again?" she then asked, and Kyra shrugged. She and Silas hadn't had much of a chance to discuss it yet, but she hoped he was planning to take her away again. It would be nice to just hide out for the break, but she'd take whatever she could get, just so long as she spent it with him.

After a bit of small talk, Brona seemed to take the hint that she was tired, and left her to have a power-nap before dinner. Kyra set her alarm for twenty minutes later, closed her eyes and quickly began dreaming about the Thrak who still had her very confused—King Kronus.

He approached her cowering form, but this time she stood and was an adult. He reached out and stroked her bloody cheek, and then kissed the other side without so much as a word. Kyra swooned, and stumbled backwards to where the thick thorns threatened to hurt her again. Kronus immediately lunged, and caught her in his arms. He pulled her close, and she inhaled deeply. He smelled of roses combined with the sharpness of metal from his armor, and a faint tang of blood from her cuts.

"Do you love me?" he asked. She jumped back and peered up at him in shock. His face had turned into the hard stare she'd seen on television, and she shook her head. "Good, because you aren't worthy anyway. Why would a King love a common foster kid like you? You're just playing a game, and it's a game you'll lose. No one wants you to succeed, and you'll soon be back in the gutter where you belong." Her ears were ringing, and she tried to shake the sound away. It wouldn't stop, and as she focused on it, Kronus started to disappear, until eventually she jumped awake and dismissed her alarm.

"Talk about messed up..." Kyra mumbled, and climbed up off the bed. It was hard to admit, even to herself, but everything was starting to get on top of her, and she was in a bad mood as she wandered the short distance to the food hall. Silas was there to greet her, having saved her the usual spot beside him, but Kyra still found it hard to pull herself out of her melancholy. She sat down and devoured her meal in silence.

"Struggling with the workload?" he eventually asked, and she nodded. "It'll get easier, I promise." She knew he was lying, but appreciated the effort anyway.

"Everything I thought I had figured out doesn't seem so set in stone anymore. How do I stay strong when the pieces of the puzzle aren't fitting?" she asked, and then it clicked. Her doubts and beliefs were getting in the way of the knowledge she was being given. Her mind didn't work that way, so the conflicting messages weren't sitting right in her gut.

"Will a trip to New York help?" he whispered in her ear, and the sheer thought of making plans for summer leave again had a smile forcing itself back onto her lips. Kyra nodded, and offered her gorgeous man a wink.

"That would help very much, how soon can we make it happen?" she answered, and leaned back in her chair. She watched as Silas moved with careful, fluid movements, as in control of himself as ever, while she felt like an excited puppy, desperately trying to keep calm or else get a tap on the nose.

"T-minus twelve days, and counting," he replied, and he put a hand on her thigh. The small touch sent a shiver down her spine. No matter what strange infatuation she seemed to still hold in her heart for King Kronus, Silas was the one who'd become the real love of her life. He was the real deal, not the daydream, and she would show him how dear that love was to her as soon as they were alone.

CHAPTER ELEVEN

"As part of the Intelligence Division, you must learn to weed out anomalies and help in the capturing of rebels, but you must also be ready to fight, should the need arise. There are also times in combat where you might come upon a Thrakorian opponent, why?" the soldier, who had revealed his name to be Sentinel Gron, asked in class later that week. He eyed the students impatiently, and picked a hand at random to answer.

"Rogues," the girl answered, and Gron nodded.

"And why would a Thrak turn rogue?" he asked again.

"Because they disagree with King Kronus's reign?" one of the male soldiers asked, and Gron waved his hand in a circular motion indicating for him to elaborate on his answer. "More specifically, his laws. They join the rebels because they do not believe in the human oppression."

"Very good, but also they may turn against all of us. There are some who hunt down humans for sport and Thrakorian's for revenge. Usually they were wronged in some way and seek recompense. Whatever their reasons, you do not take your strength or your training for granted. They are not only stronger and faster than you, but they lack the rules and regulations we willingly live by. They will kill you."

Each student paled at the realization of a very real threat. They'd heard many times during training about rogue Thraks, but had never properly discussed the reasons why they existed, or what they were capable of.

Kyra realized she'd naively thought they were lone-wolf types, living and working off the radar for stolen credits of scraps of food. She hadn't properly considered how a Thrakorian could possibly turn against their King, or why.

"If a Thrak's husband or wife turned rogue, would they follow?" she asked, trying to put herself in their shoes.

"Quite possibly," Gron answered. "Their loyalty to their partners would know no bounds. It stands to reason they would follow them into the unknown." She got it. If Silas came to her and told her he was turning against what they'd been taught, she knew there would be a part of her that would consider going with him. No matter how loyal she was to their extraterrestrial overlord and his race, there was always part of herself that wasn't completely convinced. A part that she'd pushed aside in the line of duty. If he begged her to question their new world, she would, and could understand why others might be swayed in the same way. Gron coughed loudly and brought everyone out of their thoughts. "This brings us very nicely to your next challenge. Follow me," he told them, and left the computer suite in a quick march that had them all clambering for the doorway. He led them into the very back of the huge building, and into a padded training room very much like the one where Silas had trained her in self-defense the year before.

Kyra knew exactly what was coming. "The longest anyone has lasted before yielding is twenty seconds. Who thinks they can beat it?" Gron asked them, and the group immediately formed a line behind the tallest and strongest of the human bunch. She had no illusions that she would last more than a few seconds, but she was ready to give it her best shot, and took her place in the queue.

Each trainee took a turn in trying to fend off Gron's attack, and each was subsequently floored and bested within seconds. Kyra watched as they all tried the same standard methods of self-defense, and failed. She noticed the pattern, and when it was her turn, she knew exactly what she had to do.

Gron stood just feet away, his shoulders and arms bulging with muscle, and even on her tiptoes, she only just about reached his chest. He was by far the biggest she'd seen, and Kyra knew she had no chance of fighting him. Instead of attempting to block his fists like the others had done, when the attack came, she ducked it and ran to his back.

She took off for the door and was halfway there, when she was tackled from behind and pulled down to the floor with a hard thud. Gron's immense frame overlapped hers, pressing into her back, but she still refused to yield.

With jabbing elbows and core strength developed over years of training, she didn't hesitate to go full-throttle. She fought herself into a small gap beneath his arms, and took the opportunity to twist onto her back. Gron growled as she connected with his ribs, but it wasn't enough to stop him. Only when he had her pinned down, bound by his incredible mass, and wrapped in her own twisted arms did she give in. She cursed him in anger, but then lay flat on her back, gasping for air when he released his grip and stood over her.

"Run, surely that's the only way?" Kyra asked with a scowl.

"Quite right, but at least try and take your opponent down first. That was the mistake you made," Gron answered, offering her a hand up. "But you lasted twenty-two seconds by my calculations, so well done." His grin was infectious, and she returned it involuntarily. Kyra then watched as the rest of her class tried the same tactic she had, and many made it into the teens with their scores, but she was the overall victor.

After their defense class, they were dismissed. It felt good to end the year on a high, and when it came to finishing up and packing her room, she was more than happy with her progress.

There were many ways in which she still needed to

clear her head of the doubts and opposing ideas she still had about their leaders, but being away with McD would help with that, she had absolutely no doubt about it.

***

After hours of travelling, Silas finally pulled Kyra through a security door and into a huge apartment building in the center of Manhattan. He used the chip in his wrist to gain access into the elevator, and pressed the button for the twentieth floor. When they reached it, he led her out into a hallway with just two doors, and opened the left one using a key from his pocket.

"Welcome to the McDermott's New York bribe," he murmured, but wrapped an arm around her as they crossed the blissfully silent threshold. "We will not be disturbed this time, I've been guaranteed it."

"Good," Kyra replied, and she ran through the huge room to peer out the window at the night's sky and the vast city all around them. Just like Los Angeles, there was a combination of old and new buildings, and each was alive with energy and life. She wondered what sorts of people were living in the city, and if they even had lower-class areas there anymore. She hoped they wouldn't have to worry about having to deal with any undesirables, and then mentally kicked herself for daring to think such a thing. Luxury was becoming easier to accept and expect nowadays, and sometimes Kyra hated the person she seemed to be becoming.

"You're so beautiful in the moonlight," Silas told her from the doorway, where he'd seemingly stayed in wait for her to take it all in. "The only thing wrong with this picture is that you're still dressed." The view suddenly lost all of its appeal, and Kyra padded to the only room he'd lit via the control panel on the wall. She dropped her clothes as she went, and gasped when she opened the door wide and found the biggest bed she'd ever seen inside.

"Where do you want me?" she asked.

"Everywhere," was all he answered, and it was more than enough.

CHAPTER TWELVE

On the morning of their final day in Manhattan, Kyra rolled out of bed with a groan and forced herself into the shower. The hot jets were bliss, as had been their entire stay, and she smiled to herself as she ran her hands over her body with the soap. Silas had made up for their lack of private time and then some during their break, and she knew they'd each be arriving back on base with stupid grins on their faces and unavoidable springs in their steps. They hadn't seen another soul the entire two weeks, nor had they seen the ancient sights the city had to offer, but she didn't care. All each had cared about was getting some rest and relaxation with the person that mattered most, and they'd gotten it.

The pair soon gathered their things and left the solace of the apartment behind, and she was sad to go. Kyra was quiet at first, but then leaned into Silas's hold, needing to feel his grip again.

"Tell me we'll come back next year?" she begged as they watched the apartment building disappear out the cab window. "One more year and I'll be a Sergeant. We can live together, eat our meals in our own home, sleep together…"

"Not if you go elite," he replied coldly, and pulled away. Kyra watched him warily, and wondered if perhaps he might be jealous. She'd always hoped she might get chosen to move onto elite training, and hadn't counted on something pulling her in the opposite direction. Part of her hated him for it, but knew it wasn't his fault. Silas wanted them to be together, and Kyra knew if it were her being left behind, she'd beg him to stay. She couldn't bring herself to confront him about it, but remained out of sorts until they climbed aboard the hovercraft that'd take them back to L.A.

"Whatever I do, or wherever I go, I'll always come home to you, Silas. We've made it through so far, no matter the times apart, or the pressure from your family. Don't push me away because you're scared to work hard to keep us together, or else you'll lose me anyway."

He was instantly enraged, and threw down their packs in a huff before storming off toward the bathroom. She watched him go, and hated seeing him so angry. Nothing would keep her away from him, but she wasn't going to fall behind just so they could be together for longer, and he had to understand that. Kyra hoped their first fight wouldn't come after such a wonderful summer break, and especially not because of his feelings towards her career. She'd fought hard to get where she was, and thought he'd known her ambition to succeed would always come first over her personal life.

She let him stew on it, and busied herself with her notes until he came back over and handed her a bottle of water he'd bought from the vendor at the end of the craft. Kyra thanked him and took a long sip while watching his body language carefully. He was poised and quiet, but too calm. Silas was clearly trying hard to keep his emotions under control, and she decided against pushing him. The rest of their journey was done in relative silence, and when they reached the bus heading to Fort Angel, he finally spoke up.

"I don't want you to go," he admitted, and pulled her to one side before they climbed aboard. "I love you so much, and part of me thinks I'll go mad knowing you're far away. Even thinking about you spending your days with all those geeks doesn't stop me from exploding with jealousy. I keep imagining you and some clever scientist getting to know each other, and you falling for him. It makes me want to puke even thinking about the day you might call and say we're over."

Kyra was in utter shock. He'd never spoken this way about his feelings, and now she knew why. Despite the tough-guy exterior, Silas desperately needed her affection to keep him steady. He'd been the same over and over again throughout their relationship, but she hadn't seen it before. When things were on his terms, there'd been no need for him to press the issue. She'd been the one following his lead all the way, but now the dynamic was changing, and he was evidently feeling vulnerable.

"If you believe I'd do that, then you need to re-evaluate our relationship," she told him. "Never have I so much as looked at another man since you. My passion and drive is otherwise focused solely on my career, so I suggest you pull your head out of your ass and see what's right in front of you." It was her turn to get angry now, but she forced it aside and took his face in her hands. "Me, in case you didn't realize. I'm here right now, and for the foreseeable future. If that changes, then we'll deal with it, but don't ruin what we are because of your fears of what we might end up being."

Silas seemed genuinely shocked. His eyes bore into hers, and Kyra lost herself in his gaze. "If you push me away, you'll never know what we might've been. Don't ruin us by tormenting yourself with the *what ifs*, just let it be," she added.

"All I see is you, Kyra. All I want is you. Nothing else matters, just us. I'm sorry," he replied, and laid a kiss on her cheek over the X shaped scar and she had to force herself not to flinch. She'd never liked him touching it, but it wasn't because it hurt or anything, it was because that mark still belonged to someone else—even after all this time.

After a couple of minutes spent stealing one last kiss,

they were aboard the bus and on their way back to base. Another year of training was due to begin, and no matter where they ended up, Kyra somehow knew whatever happened was meant to be. Now twenty years old, she had no doubt she loved Silas, but also that they were still very young and had a long way ahead of them yet. She would never rush or throw her dreams away for his benefit, and didn't care if it made her selfish or wrong. It didn't feel greedy to want what was best for her own life ahead of any others, nor did it feel wrong earning those merits through her hard work and resilience. If it was, she didn't need to be right.

***

"I'm late," Brona mumbled into her coffee a few mornings into the next round of training, and she stared at her with tears in her eyes. "Over a week. What do I do?" she implored, and Kyra's heart ached for her dear friend. She wasn't sure there was much Brona could do, and guessed telling the truth might be the only option she had. These kinds of secrets had a way of exploding at the worst possible moment, and as much as it was wonderful news, Kyra wanted to shake her for not having been more careful.

"You need to speak with Lt. Psy, but he might halt your career if you drop out of secondary training now." She was trying to make Brona's options clear, while still being honest and gentle with her clearly worried friend. "Would you keep it if you were, you know?" she asked, and Brona nodded in response.

"Jett would take care of us, I know it. But, I'll be gutted if I had to drop out now. What do I do?" she seemed so lost, and Kyra knew she needed her strength to keep her head clear.

"Get a test, you need to know for sure. If you are pregnant we'll go and see Psy together and find out what your options are. Okay?"

"Okay," Brona replied, and she seemed better already. There were so many advances in birth control nowadays this shouldn't have happened, and she wanted to kick them for being another statistic. Kyra bit her tongue though, and gave her friend a supportive squeeze while they packed up their breakfast bowls.

They went their separate ways to training, and Kyra was glad she could help even just a tiny bit. She spent the better part of that morning wondering if Brona had done the test or not, and when lunchtime came around she sped straight to the canteen to find her. Brona was nowhere to be seen, so she tried her room, but still nothing. Kyra was on her way to the Medical Division's training center when one of the students stopped her.

"Brona's been rushed into surgery," the young girl informed her, and Kyra stared at her open-mouthed. "She collapsed in class and was taken for investigation, next thing we heard she was having surgery, but no one knows why."

"Does Jett know?" she asked, and the girl nodded.

"He's with her. West wing of the female ward," the girl added, seemingly knowing that would've been Kyra's next question. She thanked her and ran as fast as she could to the ward. On her way, Silas intercepted her. He was about to ask why she hadn't gone to lunch, when realization swept over his puzzled face.

"What's happened?" he asked, grabbing her tight.

"Brona…. She's not well," Kyra told him, and was almost unable to come to terms with it herself. Her mind was racing with what if's and how's, and she knew she just needed to get to her friend. Silas let her go, and followed her lead straight into the medical building and up to the ward. A nurse directed them to Brona's room, but she hovered outside, unsure if it was her place to go in unannounced. Kyra knocked, and waited for an agonizing few minutes until Jett popped his head out and joined them in the hall.

"Hey," he said groggily, and Kyra hugged him instinctively. She hadn't cared for many people in her life, but Brona was one of those she held most dear, and the sheer thought of her in pain was heart-wrenching. Everything in her wanted to scream at Jett to hurry up and say something, but instead she kept a tight hold on him, silently willing for the words she knew were agonizing for him to say. "She thought she might be pregnant, but it turns out she was far from it." His voice faltered, and Kyra quickly directed Jett to a nearby seat. "Some kind of infection. They've given her a full hysterectomy."

"Oh no," she replied, instinctively putting her hand over her lower abdomen, where a twinge niggled from within, as though her body was crying out in sympathy for her friend. "How is she?"

"Not great. She's gone from planning a family, to having to deal with the realization she'll never have one. I don't know how to ease her pain," he replied honestly, and she hugged him again.

"You can't possibly understand where her head is at. Just be there for her and deal with the torment alongside her. Stay here and take a breath, I'll go in," she offered, and Jett seemed grateful for the chance to have a break. Silas told her he'd let her superiors know she'd be out for the rest of the afternoon, and while she was glad, a pang of fear rang in her gut. She'd make up for the missed hours and then some, she knew it, but for now she had to prioritize her friend's needs over her training. No matter how determined she was to succeed for herself, there were evidently moments that were more important than those plans, and now was one of them.

She pushed open the door and crept inside the small room. Brona lay asleep on the bed, wrapped in white linens so symbolic of hospitals. She looked pale and weak, and stirred only when Kyra took her hand and sat down.

Brona burst into tears, and not a single word was said

as Kyra climbed up onto the bed and held her in her arms. They cried together for a long time, and she only let go when Brona stopped clinging on so tightly. She hadn't needed to say a word, and was simply there for her heartbroken friend in a way that needed no words or promises, any reasoning or bargaining. Silent grief overwhelmed them both, and it was a long time before either said a word.

"I'll never be a mother. I'll never give Jett a family or hold my own child in my arms. In what world is that okay?" she asked, and Kyra got the impression her question was rhetorical, so simply held on tight and let her grieve.

She continued to hold Brona for what felt like hours, and only let go when Jett and Silas came to find them. Kyra and Jett swapped places, and she didn't envy him the task of nursing Brona back to health. She would be there as much as possible, of course, but knew it wasn't her place to be there through the thick and thin of it. She just hoped Jett was up to the task.

On their way out of the medical building, hers and Silas's fight was long forgotten. When times were hard the silly little things had a habit of falling away, and only the most important stayed behind. She stumbled, fell, and then cried in his arms when he caught her, and Silas didn't leave her side all night, regardless of the rules they'd both promised to adhere to. Certain circumstances called for certain measures, and she was glad he didn't leave her alone.

Kyra then threw herself into work to distract her from the awful news. During her downtime she spent hours relaxing with Brona in the hospital while she healed. She never once tried to tell her she'd be fine, or that it was for the best. Instead, she spent every visit reminding Brona of how she loved her job, and the reasons why she'd joined the army. Her love of life, and ferocity of spirit were what'd brought her to this base, and by reminding her of that passion, Kyra helped her mend a part of her heart that'd been broken. Brona eventually went back to her training, a little more lost and quiet than before, but on her way back to being her old self for sure. There might never be the full smile she once had, or the twinkle in her eye when she laughed loudly, but she was coping, and routine was good for her.

"Who can tell me some of the physiological differences between humans and Thraks?" Sentinel Gron asked the class a few weeks back into their second year.

Many obvious answers were given regarding the height and strength differences they'd already covered, but other than that her classmates seemed surprisingly uninformed.

"Thrakorian's age much slower than humans," she said, after raising her hand and Gron had given her a nod.

"That's right, our bodies are healthier and stronger in ways that far surpass human evolution. We age slower, heal faster, and have a larger brain capacity." He then went on to tell them a little more about their race, and Kyra wondered why they needed to learn about their differences beneath the skin. Thrakorian's were a genetic distant-cousin of sorts to humans, but they'd seemingly got all the good parts, and she kind of felt like Gron was simply giving another lesson on how much better Thraks were than them. She wondered why they'd bothered keeping them alive. Why they were training them and urging their society to thrive and better itself. There were too many things that didn't seem to add up, and her code-breaking brain didn't like being left in the dark. Kyra had to remind herself that she was nobody, and that any details Gron was purposely leaving out must be for reasons far above her station. She also knew her sadness was creeping into her work, and guessed her impudence regarding his self-important lessons was wearing her patience thin.

In contrast to their first year when she'd welcomed the break from hours spent behind a computer screen, this year was the opposite. Whenever they'd completed their sessions spent with the Thrakorian teacher, Kyra felt relieved to head back into the computer suite to get back to their technological training. They'd moved on from older style machines to state-of-the-art systems with a wide variety of features and advances, and this was where she felt she belonged. They spent the afternoon running through a simulated program that required the use of special gloves, rather than a mouse or keyboard. Using their hands to direct and zoom in, the trainees watched via cameras mounted on the heads of computerized ground troops as they sought out a rebel stronghold. They were informed that the footage wasn't real, but each decision they made might either progress and infiltrate the rebels successfully, or lead their soldiers into an ambush. As Intelligence soldiers they had to be sure of their decisions, and of the consequences should their instinct be wrong.

Even though she knew it wasn't real, Kyra took the simulation as seriously as if she was assisting a real team. She imagined Silas being beneath the mounted camera, and knew she would do everything she could to ensure the success of his mission and his safe return to base. After having been taught the correct tactical terminology for the program, they began their first exercise in the imaginary field.

"The objective is to investigate unnoticed, get as close to the camp as possible undetected, and then attack with precision and as few casualties as possible," Gron told them. "Don't try and tell them how to fight or anything like that, imagine these are experienced soldiers. Your role is intelligence. You're looking through their eyes in search of clues and intel. You're after answers, not blood."

Kyra watched the desk intently, and had to stifle her gasp when the flat screen seemed to lift up and come to life before her eyes. She was immersed in a virtual world, running along and watching the scene as though she were really there, while her hands worked fast to move her focus around at the markings on the walls and the onlookers around the scene, where she searched for anything that might seem out of place. When she found a symbol carved into a wooden shutter, she spoke.

"Cease," she said, and her command immediately halted the troops. She then reached up with her right hand and pinched her thumb and forefinger over the symbol, and then opened her hand again to zoom in. There seemed to be a similarity to another she'd seen a few feet back, but this one had the number twelve emblazoned atop it. "Time check, please." The simulated soldier lifted its wrist, and showed her it was almost noon. "Forward." She knew she needn't say more, and always tried to remember Gron's words about knowing her place in the mission. During a live patrol, the soldier's would have both tactical and intelligence operatives in their ears, and too much chatter was off-putting. Simple commands that took no time to process and allow them on their way were what she had to provide, otherwise she'd let them all down if they failed due to her timewasting. She spotted another marking, and another. Soon the trail turned west, and so did their platoon. "Turn into the alley," she commanded exactly two minutes later, and they did as she told them. "Cease, and stay hidden. Time check?" It was one-minute before noon, and exactly sixty-seconds later, a group of what looked like civilian humans tore their way down the road her troops had just been in. They were rebels though, Kyra could tell by the patches sewn into their jackets, and she also knew they would've quickly taken out her platoon if she hadn't ordered for them to hide.

When the men and women had gathered together and gone, she took her computerized unit further into the area, where they discovered the rebels, took them out with stealth and accuracy, and then obliterated their entire congregation. It didn't matter that it wasn't real, her work was sound and her methods worked well. Kyra's confidence was growing, as was her skill, and she felt bad for having let her upset over everything with Brona come between her and her training.

The simulation then ended, and Kyra lowered her hands, but wished she could do it all over again.

"Well done, Millan. Nice work realizing the numbers were timings," Gron told her, and she thanked him. She then watched as the others finished their simulations, and was pleased she hadn't taken too long or failed like some had. This was what she wanted, there was no doubt in her mind, and Kyra let herself daydream about someday working in one of the huge operational skyscrapers around the world overseeing missions like this for real. Her heart raced with excitement at the sheer thought, and she was filled with renewed ambition.

CHAPTER THIRTEEN

By over halfway through her second year, Kyra was studying day and night in anticipation for her final secondary exam in a few months' time. They'd covered almost their entire syllabus, and Capt. Quinn was now using the time to go over their work again in summary, while introducing them to some of the more obscure insider secrets behind their ruler's reign.

"This little beauty," she said, pulling a small creature that looked like a squid from a vase of water on the front desk. "Is a creatura. Who knows what that is?"

Blank faces greeted her, and she seemed pleased to discover that no one was any the wiser. She was being careful to hold it by its back, and they quickly learned why. "I need a volunteer…" Capt. Quinn pointed to one of the students in the front row. He stood and joined her, but clearly wasn't pleased at having been chosen for the demonstration. She placed the creatura on his arm, and its tentacle-like limbs made immediate contact. He hissed but kept still, and they all watched enthralled as their teacher took his cheeks in her hands. She turned his face down to meet hers, and watched for a few seconds before opening her mouth. "Tell me a secret," she then asked.

"When I was twelve I stole rations from my sister, and I didn't care when she went hungry. I did it so often she got too skinny, and I had to stop." He seemed surprised at his answer, and clearly had no control over the words leaving his mouth.

Quinn then released him, pried away the creatura's tentacles, and chose another recruit, and another. They each had the same reaction he'd had, and gave up a secret they seemed embarrassed or ashamed to admit.

"I wet the bed until I was fifteen," one of the young men answered, and he was met with sniggers from the others.

"I'm in love with Sofia," another man answered, and he turned a shade of crimson Kyra had never seen before. It was funny watching the students offload a secret or two, but she breathed a sigh of relief when the creature was put away, and wondered what she might've answered if pulled up in front of the others.

"The longer they stay connected to you, the more secrets you will reveal. These creatura's were created by Thrakorian scientists, and are one of the best methods of interrogation we have access to. They are invaluable in the use of extracting information from rebels," Quinn told them.

The class was then dismissed, and Kyra jumped in surprise when she felt a strong hand on her arm. She turned and looked up into Gron's scowling face. She hadn't even heard him come into class, and wondered what he might need from her.

"I saw you," he said, stepping closer. "I saw you take a breath when the creatura was put away. What secrets are you scared of revealing, Corporal?"

Kyra shook her head, and peered up at him pleadingly. The last thing she needed was Gron thinking she might be hiding something important, or him doubt her reasons for having joined the Intelligence Division.

"Nothing, sir. I promise," she replied, and knew her voice was shaking. "I would simply be embarrassed by the response I fear would come out, and didn't want the class knowing my secrets."

Gron took her elbow and led her over to the front desk. The others had all left, and she knew without having to ask what he was going to do. The creatura attached itself to her hand when he pulled it back out from its vase, and she instantly felt euphoric. Her mind was alive with memories, hopes and dreams, and she suddenly became aware of Gron's intense violet eyes peering into hers.

"Tell me your secrets, Kyra," he said, and his voice seemed so very far away. Everything inside of her wanted to obey, and she opened her mouth without any resistance from her usually so tight-lips.

"I'm in love with someone other than my boyfriend," she replied without any hesitation, and he laughed.

"With who?" he asked, and she had the feeling he thought it might be him. Kyra felt her cheeks burn as the answer forced its way out of her.

"King Kronus…" he raised an eyebrow at her. "I've loved him ever since Invasion Day." Gron pulled the creature off her, and the second the contact was broken, her dream-like haze also lifted. "Please don't tell anyone," she whispered in earnest now that her embarrassment had kicked in.

"Lots of silly human girls have a crush on the King, of course they do," he replied without any care for her humiliation. "You're too clever to become another of his groupie humans who're desperate for an audience in the hopes he might choose you for his lover, aren't you?" She nodded. "Good, because it'll never happen. He's betrothed to a Thrakorian noblewoman, and has never so much as looked at a human. Keep your crush to yourself, it's a pointless dream anyway." He stormed away, and Kyra moved quickly back to her desk, where she gathered her things and followed him out the door. Despite feeling ashamed, she was glad she'd appeased his curiosity on the subject, and hoped they'd never again have another lesson on the creatura and its power to incite truth from its host.

As she walked the long corridor back to her block, Kyra couldn't help but think of Gron's reaction to her revelation. She knew holding onto her feelings for Kronus was a foolish dream, but it was one that wouldn't go no matter how many times she tried to tell herself it was pointless. He was a god to them, and therefore it stood to reason that many of his loyal subjects would love him, despite his apparently being betrothed to another. The power, status and unattainability had to be the appeal, that must be it. No human could possibly be worthy of a place beside him, and she knew it would never happen anyway. The King never left his private island estate, and those who were handpicked to serve him would never betray his secrets or abuse their position. Even Kyra knew he only entertained Thraks socially, and by the time she'd settled in the seat beside Silas for dinner, all thoughts of King Kronus and his piercing gaze were forced out of her mind.

***

In the run up to their final exercise, Kyra knew she was able to give less and less of her free time to Silas. He seemed determined to try not to complain, but every now and again would make an offhand comment that would send her exhausted blood boiling. She felt like he was intent on distracting her from her work at times, as though he might even be doing it on purpose, and soon they were quarreling and bickering on a far too regular basis.

"I've never stopped you from studying, or demanded your time and attention," she growled at him after another row one night, in an attempt to stop her voice from becoming too raised. "Why do you insist on undermining me?"

"I've never once told you not to follow your dreams, or said you couldn't do it," he replied with a frown. "All I asked was if you could spend one night off because I'm going away again tomorrow. I'm important too, right? Not just your career?"

His words hit her like a blow to the gut, and she knew he was right. She hadn't made him feel wanted in the slightest, and knew she'd prioritized work over everything in her life—especially him.

"I know," she groaned, shaking her head sorrowfully. "But I just can't give you the time you want, Silas. I need you to be patient and wait for me, like I've always waited for you." They had planned to spend the night in his room, but now she wanted to be alone. Kyra grabbed her things and walked to the exit, but Silas followed her. He reached across and slammed the door shut when she tried to open it, and pinned her to the back of it. With her cheek touching the cold wood and her stomach forced against it, the air rushed from her lungs, but she resisted her urge to cry out in surprise. His lips were right by her ear, and his show of power and brute strength both scared and excited her, along with his dark tone.

"I'll wait, but you're not going without me. Promise you won't try and leave me behind," he begged, and pressed into her harder. "You're mine, Kyra. All mine. There won't be anywhere on Earth I won't follow you."

"I'm not something you possess, and I won't have you ordering me around, Silas. Remember who you fell in love with, and that I won't stand for you telling me what I can and cannot do." She shoved him back off her, opened the door, and took off before another word could be spoken, because she knew she might say something they'd both regret.

After their row, and the strange way Silas had tried to lay claim over her, Kyra decided to put a little distance between them, and was glad he went away for a few days on exercise. She spent the time keeping herself occupied as much as possible, which wasn't difficult given where they were at the end of their intense training program. She didn't say it out loud to anyone, not even Brona, but she was starting to wonder if things were really going in the right direction for the pair of them. Instead of dwelling though, she worked even harder than she had before to fulfill her dream of finishing secondary training on top. She aced all of the final assessments, and the day before their exercise, Lt. Psy asked her to visit his office.

"You wanted to see me, Lieutenant?" she asked, and then took a seat when he offered her the one opposite him at his desk.

"Yes, Corporal. I wanted to give you this," he said as he handed her a small box across the table. Kyra knew exactly what ought to be inside, a rank slide, and she accepted it from him with a smile. She opened the box to reveal the badge that indicated the rank of Sergeant, and looked back up at her Commander in surprise. "You're headed for great things, and for formalities sake I need to give you this before I recommend you for elite training." Kyra swallowed the lump in her throat. "When you cross that line tomorrow, I promise you now that I'll give you the rank of Lieutenant, and my recommendation letter, if you come in the top-five."

"But I still need one more?" she asked, and knew she must look like a deer in the headlights. His old face cracked with its wrinkles when he grinned, but it was still one of the most beautiful smiles she'd ever seen.

"No," he answered, and grabbed a file from his drawer. "I have your letters here from Lorde Sharq and Sentinel Gron." Kyra coughed as she inhaled sharply.

"He… he gave me a recommendation?" Lt. Psy nodded.

"He believes you can do it," he replied, and she was pleased he was using his gentler tone. She had a feeling she might cry any minute, and wasn't ready to get told off if she did, but somehow his softer tone soothed away her tears. "Top-five. You give me a high placing tomorrow and the rest is yours for the taking. I'll recommend you for elite, and promote you to Lieutenant. We'll have you loaded on the course after summer leave."

Kyra couldn't believe her ears. She was dumfounded, and found herself nodding over and over in the only response she seemed capable of. "You may go," Psy added, and she was glad. After a fumbled thank you, she found herself out in the same hall where Silas had first made a move on her two years before, and she peered into the same shadow thoughtfully. Things had changed so much since then, and she wondered where they might end up after summer break. How was she going to tell him she'd almost made elite? Instead of being excited to tell her boyfriend the good news, she was terrified of having another row with him over their future, and it made her realize even more that they were potentially on their way to being over.

She headed straight to Brona's room instead, and they jumped around together excitedly, while trying to suppress their girly screams. Her friend had reacted in exactly the right way—explosive excitement with congratulatory hugs and kisses, and she loved her even more for it. They chatted for a while, each of them wondering what the future might hold, and Kyra promised they wouldn't lose each other. It didn't matter if she was stationed overseas for the rest of her training, they were friends forever, and she meant it. They promised to stay in as much contact as possible, and when she finally left, it was with the biggest smile on her face.

Silas was waiting outside her block, and he took one look at the new badge on her chest and pulled her into the shadows with him.

"I'm sorry for how I acted," he told her, kissing her neck softly. "Please forgive me? I'm really pleased for you and your promotion. Can we go and celebrate?" Kyra's earlier resolve melted. She wondered if Silas had come around by himself after all, and hoped this reaction might signify the change in him. He pinned her to the wall and she let him scoop her into his arms. Their mouths found each other's, and they let the fraught tension dissipate via their intense kisses. "I'm so proud of you," he whispered while pressing into her.

"We're strong enough to stay together no matter what, Silas. I know it," she replied, and pressed her hands against his chest lightly to let him know she had to go. She had a very long day the next day, and needed her rest. "We'll celebrate tomorrow."

"Did he say he's recommending you?" he asked, and Kyra nodded.

"If I place in the top-five. You, Psy, Gron—everyone. You've really pushed me and helped me to succeed year after year. Thank you," she told him, and placed a gentle kiss on his cheek before sliding out of his grasp. Silas didn't say a word, but he watched her go without argument, and Kyra was glad. She headed straight up to her room, and fell into bed for what she knew would be a restless night, but still a much-needed bit of quiet relaxation time before the intense exercise the following day.

CHAPTER FOURTEEN

Kyra and her fellow secondary phase training graduates were led into a vast mountainous simulation area the following morning, where they formed a semi-circle around Lt. Psy.

"This year's final exercise is nothing more than a simple race to the finish line. There are no points to accrue, simply the possibility of recommendation after assessment from your instructors and myself. Those deemed worthy of graduation at this level will be awarded with their next rank, and any offered a place in the elite training will be given the relevant promotion and paperwork," he informed them all. Many shuffled nervously under his scrutiny, but Kyra was ready, and more determined than ever to succeed. "The finish line is at the far end of this terrain. You should complete the course as quickly as possible, but remember it is forbidden for any soldier to stop another recruits' progress, and you will be disqualified for doing so. There will be other elements for you and your fellow graduates to overcome in order to reach the end as quickly as possible, so focus on them rather than competing with your comrades. See you at the finish line." He gave them a wink, and then jumped on the back of a vehicle that reminded Kyra of Silas's motorbike, only larger. The driver then sped away, and within seconds the trainees were left alone. A loud buzzer then chimed, and they were off.

Many of the soldiers headed north, while Kyra stopped

for a second and took a look around. There weren't any clues yet, so she took off in a straight line for the finish behind the others.

On her way, she quickly started to notice markings on the trees. They were far more primitive than the ones she'd spotted on the final exercise before, and they were clearly meant to look like natural marks. She inspected one, and then the other, and followed her gut instinct to go around the path the others had made before her. Some of the soldiers close by seemed to be watching how she chose to proceed, and while part of her wanted to shout at them for not following their own instincts, she decided against it. Instead she ran on ahead and soon lost the stragglers in the thick brush of trees and heavy moss.

Kyra carried on and on, all the while searching for clues or more markings. There weren't any, and when she stopped to catch a breath and check her perimeter again, she was surprised to hear someone running towards her. Expecting another recruit to come bursting out of the forest, she prepped herself, but then was slammed into from her side and thrown to the ground by strong hands. She jumped back up and faced the man who'd tackled her, and gasped when she saw Silas dressed as a rebel. He'd clearly been drafted to play enemy in their exercise, and wore a smile that made her instantly wary of his motives.

"I knew you'd go around," he told her, wringing his hands and cracking his knuckles. "You're too clever, Kyra. I told myself you'd see the markings and take a different route, and it seems I was right."

"You've got an unfair advantage, Silas. A normal rebel wouldn't know me like you do," she replied, and he simply shrugged. Kyra turned to run away, even if she had to go back a few feet to do so, but he pounced. Silas pinned her to a nearby tree and pulled her arms behind her back, locking her wrists together in his strong grip. From one of his pockets, he then produced a piece of wire that he wrapped around them. "This ought to hold you for a while," he said, and rage bubbled up inside of her.

"You're doing this on purpose so I fail, aren't you?" she demanded, and pushed back into him so he stumbled away. Kyra turned to face him again, and knew she was right simply by the look on his face. It wasn't even a guilty expression, but one of smug dominance, and she hated that he clearly thought he'd won. "We're done, you hear me? DONE!" she screamed in his face.

Silas slapped her hard across the cheek, and while she cried out in shock, she wouldn't let him break her. A crazed laugh escaped her lips, and it shocked her to hear it. "Is this the real Silas McDermott finally coming out? The one Tarquin warned me about? I should've known you were no good," the spite in her tone was so vile, and she knew before it even happened that the second hit was going to be ten times worse. He couldn't seem to control himself, and punched her straight in the mouth. Kyra fell back and landed against a nearby tree with a painful thud. She spat the mouthful of blood onto the floor beside her, while Silas paced the small space like an animal in a cage.

With every ounce of strength she had, she twisted her shoulders and slid her hands beneath her backside to pull her arms around to the front of her. She needed the advantage, and had taken off again before he'd even noticed, and ran like her life depended on it. There was no looking back, no staying to fight. Kyra knew she had to get away from him as quickly as possible, and used everything she'd learnt to ensure she got away. Tears were streaming down her face, so much so that when the finish line appeared fifty feet away, she had no idea how many other trainees were already on the other side of it. She sprinted as hard as her exhausted body would take her, and knew the shock was wearing her down just as much as the exertion. Had Silas really just done that? Could he be capable of worse? She was terrified he might just be. Her head was pounding, as was her lip, and Kyra roared in pain as she crossed the line. She then fell to her knees as she was informed she'd come in sixth place.

A medic cut her free from the binds and tended to her wounds, while Kyra stared off into the distance. She paid no attention to her cuts and bruises, and didn't feel the pain, but her heart felt broken and she knew tears were streaming from her eyes. He'd won. Silas had managed to take away her future, and all because he didn't want to lose her. He'd done it anyway, and she knew there would never be any going back to the way they were before. They were over, and while she felt sad, there was also a wave of relief that hit her along with her sorrow. She had no strength left to fight or flee, and felt like an empty shell when she lined up with the others to be told their official result. She saluted Lt. Psy along with the rest of the trainees, and watched in horror as he shook his head at her as though disappointed that she'd let him down. Kyra wanted to scream at him and tell him how Silas had betrayed her, but she held her tongue. He was playing a rebel, after all, and a rebel would've detained or killed her if it were real life. She had failed, and would have to deal with that failure if she was ever going to move on. Right now though, she felt like crawling back to the gutter and staying there.

"Come and see me first thing tomorrow, Sergeant," Psy instructed her when he'd dismissed the troops, and she nodded. He wouldn't offer his recommendation, she knew he'd never go back on his word, but hoped he might at least offer her some kind of comfort.

Kyra went straight home. She didn't stay to celebrate with any of the others, or discuss their time in the exercise like many were doing. She just wanted her bed, and climbed in without even showering.

Insistent knocking woke her a few hours later, and she climbed out of bed with a wince and a groan thanks to the aches and pains that'd now set in. On the other side of her door stood Brona, and she was clearly upset at not having been given a full report by her best friend. She took one look at Kyra's bruised face and pained eyes, and her anger quickly dissipated.

"Oh, no. What happened?" she asked, and stepped over the threshold into her room. Kyra didn't object at the intrusion, and flung herself back down onto the bed with a sob.

"I came sixth," she told her through gritted teeth, and began to cry harder. Brona didn't ask any more questions. She knew exactly what that placing meant, and simply laid down on the bed to hug her friend; while she let out the pain there was no hope of hiding. She wrapped Kyra in her arms and held her tight, and didn't let go. Kyra was so grateful that Brona wasn't firing questions at her or demanding to know what'd happened. She was simply there, and it was exactly what she needed while she let the pain consume her.

***

The next morning, and after just a small amount of fretful sleep, Kyra got washed and dressed in sad silence. Under the watchful eye of her best friend, she tried her best to pull herself together, but was clearly failing miserably.

"Do you want me to get Silas?" Brona asked, and she seemed surprised when Kyra shook her head no.

"We're over, B. There's nothing there for me anymore," she answered, and turned to the mirror again so that she could finish tying up her hair. "And no, I don't wanna talk about it."

"Okay, but you know I'm here whenever you do," she promised, and Kyra nodded. She took a deep breath and sighed.

"I'll be fine, but I need to make it through this morning and get away from here. Thank goodness for summer leave. Whatever role Psy wants me to take when we get back, I'll just have to accept it," she replied, and stood to give herself the once over. She'd gotten ready in a daze, working on autopilot, and was surprised to find she was actually quite presentable—if you didn't count the split and swollen lip.

Kyra knocked and entered Lt. Psy's office a short while later, and shut the door behind her before saluting him and taking a seat. He was clearly dismayed at her score, but was a combination of regret and warmth as he watched her with both a scowl and a soft gaze.

"We didn't quite get you there, did we?" he asked, looking down at a file she assumed held her records. She knew her two recommendation letters must be in there, and hated that she'd only just missed out on a third because of Silas and his selfish actions. "I'm keeping these, though." His gaze snapped back up to meet hers. "Come back after leave and take your place in the training program as a Junior Commander. You'll be assigned a role in the Intelligence Division training program, and eventually we can talk again about getting you a place in the elite training."

"Thank you, Lieutenant. I appreciate you taking the time to talk with me, and can assure you I did everything I could to get the best placing possible yesterday. I've let us both down by failing, and I'll never let it happen again." She stood and saluted, and left before her trembling lip gave way and the tears she'd hoped had dried began to fall again.

"Sergeant Millan," a deep voice called when she was out in the corridor, and she turned to greet its owner with an obligatory salute. "Commiserations, I had hoped you'd make the elite program's next intake, but perhaps next time you'll be ready," Sentinel Gron told her, and she forced herself to smile.

"Thank you, sir. I intend to come back fighting, but for now I'm just ready to get away and clear my head," she answered honestly. He reached out and touched her bruised lip gently, and she watched as his brow furrowed. "It seems I'm not the code-breaker I thought I was. But I learned a valuable lesson, though."

"You didn't head north with the rest of them?" he asked with a furrowed brow.

"No. I went around after spotting some crude markings on a tree, but I was wrong and still encountered a rebel." He nodded and stepped back, dropping his hand to his side.

"Enjoy your leave, Sergeant," Gron told her, and she saluted before he turned and walked away without another word.

Kyra packed up her things and headed to the gates of Fort Angel, where the various buses sat waiting for the soldiers to board. She wasn't sure where she was even going this time around, and sadness panged in her gut at the realization.

Silas was waiting beside a bus that read 'Manhattan,' and she almost resisted going to see him, but when their gazes locked, she knew it would be impossible.

"Will you come with me? We can talk, sort things out..." he asked when she neared the bus, but Kyra ignored him. She walked around behind it in search of some privacy, and Silas followed like she knew he would. When they had far fewer eyes on them, she stopped, turned and scowled up at him. "I'm sorry," he said, clutching his chest with his hand. "I was so terrified of letting you go, but now you're staying and we can make a go of it again. Let me show you how much I care about you. I love you, Kyra. Please let me show you how much. Come to New York and we'll get married. Let me spend the rest of my life making it up to you..."

She stood in shock for a few seconds, opening and closing her mouth while Silas stood waiting patiently for her answer. His words were still settling in, and his strange attempt at a guilt-ridden proposal just made her angry. It wasn't romantic in the slightest, and she knew he just wanted to control and own her; it was the only reason why he wanted her to be his wife. That way, she'd never be free, and he was a fool if he ever took her as weak enough to accept.

Kyra curled her fist and hit him as hard as she could straight in the cheekbone. She didn't want the hassle of dealing with a bloody nose, so had struck the side of his face instead.

"Don't talk to me ever again. Don't even look at me again. We are more than over, Silas. We're dead, and you killed us." She stormed away before he could reply or speak, and had the biggest grin on her face.

Kyra took a deep breath, boarded the bus to Los Angeles, and watched as he stumbled into the Manhattan bus with his face buried in his hands. She spoke to no one, and held her head high, despite trembling in fear of the unknown that lay ahead. No matter what though, she was proud for standing up to him. Being alone was better than being with a man so desperate to keep her under his control that he was willing to sabotage her career in order to do so, and the journey back to L.A. was long and lonely, but also a very freeing one.

CHAPTER FIFTEEN

Kyra checked her credits in the machine on the wall outside the terminal building, and was astounded yet again at just how many she'd managed to build up over the past three years of service with the Human Royal Armed Forces. There was no time or need to enjoy her wealth, for it still felt very surreal, and all she wanted was somewhere quiet to hide away for the next two weeks to clear her head. She then headed straight for the nearest travel information desk, and spoke with a middle-aged woman behind the counter.

"I'd like to find a room to rent, please," she asked, and judging by the woman's reaction, she wasn't the first homeless soldier she'd dealt with in her time behind that desk. Kyra guessed she normally might deal with businesses or upper-class humans, rather than beaten and exhausted young women, but her kind smile said she understood that soldiers often weren't keen on going back to their old homes during summer leave.

"There aren't many places available, I'm afraid," the lady replied, and began searching her computer for options. "We normally book these further in advance, did your plans change suddenly?"

"Something like that," Kyra replied with a frown. "Breakup," she added when the woman's stare didn't let up.

"Ah, I see. Well, we do have a few basic rooms for rent in the lower-class areas?" Kyra shook her head, there was absolutely no way. She would rather spend double the credits and stay somewhere better, even if it meant travelling to another city in order to get a place. "Okay, well how about a room at The Crowned King in the city center? It's just over one-hundred credits per night, but that includes all the food and board."

"Yes, that sounds lovely. Thank you," Kyra answered, and she passed her wrist over the electronic reader beside the desk.

"Your bill will be settled at the end of your stay, but I see you've plenty so you needn't worry. Enjoy your break," she told her, and Kyra accepted the reservation details with a smile. She thanked the woman and followed her directions through the city to the hotel.

When she arrived, it felt almost unreal. She'd never seen anything like it, and gasped at the fantastical luxury and elegant style she'd somehow managed to get a room in. She couldn't wait to get out of her combats, but at the same time the thought of wearing her only civilian outfits wasn't entirely welcome either. Those clothes reminded her of Silas, so she promised herself she'd find a clothing store as soon as she'd checked in.

"Welcome to The Crowned King, Sergeant Millan," said the doorman after she'd swiped her arm over a device in his hand that read her microchip. He knew her name from the small screen that confirmed her reservation, and welcomed her in like an old friend. She wanted to play it cool, but wasn't used to such service, and fumbled over her response. The man just smiled sweetly and directed her to the desk, where she checked in properly and took her key. A young woman then escorted her up to her room, and even opened the door with a flourish of whimsy. Kyra giggled and followed her inside, and then had to hide her surprise at the stunning luxury of the room. A huge bed was in the center of it, draped in crisp white cotton and numerous pillows and cushions. Heavy drapes gave the room some privacy, and a bathroom the size of her bedroom back on the base, was to her left.

"Breakfast, lunch and dinner are served downstairs in the restaurant. Timings and the menu can be found in your brochure," the woman indicated to the desk where a few leaflets had been delicately arranged for the visitor's use. "We have numerous services available during your stay. Downstairs is a bar and relaxation area if you'd like to unwind in the company of the other patrons. We also have a tailor on-hand if you would like to purchase any clothes, and a hairdresser for any personal needs. Please call the desk to make any bookings."

Kyra thanked her, accepted the key back from the woman, and then locked the door behind her—just to be safe. No matter what, she was still uneasy and wanted to be sure Silas couldn't track her down and come inside. Thanks to the setbacks in both her personal and professional life, Kyra was desperate for some solitude in order to get her head straight, and her career back on track. She ran a deep bath, complete with far too many bubbles, ditched her glasses, and climbed in. It'd been so long since she'd had a soak that it took her a while for her to settle amidst the hot water, but soon she was drifting in and out of sleep, while images of King Kronus filled her head. He was a welcome sight, and put out his hand to help get her free from the thorns, but then he changed and turned into Silas. He grabbed her roughly, and pushed her down onto the ground before binding her wrists in a rope.

"You're mine now, Kyra. Always and forever," he whispered into her ear as he climbed over her. Everything turned black, and she was somehow in a cage with Silas standing watch. His eyes looked black in the darkness, and she cowered in fear before him. "There's no escape this time, and no one will find you."

Kyra woke up screaming. She coughed as a wisp of bubbles caught in her throat, and began sobbing into her hands. It wasn't long at all before those sobs turned into full-blown wracks of terrified tears, and she clambered out of the bath in a rush. She wrapped herself in the hotel robe and climbed into bed, where she continued to cry over every last ounce of pain and hurt she'd been trying so desperately to overcome. Silas had betrayed her, pure and simple. He had acted selfishly and purposely sabotaged her exercise to try and keep her under his control, and there would never be a world in which they could overcome such selfish treachery.

Kyra was determined to pull herself together by the time she went back to Fort Angel in just under two weeks' time, though. She had to show him he'd lost. Silas might've succeeded in halting her progression into the elite program, but she wasn't going to give him the satisfaction of seeing her anything other than focused and fighting. She also promised herself she'd prove to Lt. Psy she deserved that recommendation letter regardless, and when she dragged her sorry ass out of bed hours later, she set about planning how she might do it.

After wandering around her room in a thoughtful daze for a while, Kyra got dressed and headed down to the lobby. There she booked in with the hairdresser and tailor for the following day, and had some dinner in the huge dining room. There were many other guests there too, but she wasn't in the mood for chitchat, so kept her head down and her focus on the delicious meal. Afterwards, she had every intention of going to the computer suite to look into which roles she might like to pursue in the rank of Sergeant for the Intelligence Division, when Kyra spotted the bar. There'd never been much of an opportunity to drink in the past, but now she welcomed the chance to drown some of her sorrows, and vowed she'd go to the computer suite the following day.

"A beer, please," she ordered, and the barman smiled kindly as he poured the drink. She swiped her hand over the chip-reader on the counter, and he nodded when her details came up on the screen in his hand.

"First one's on me," he said as he put the frothy drink

down before her with a smile. "I'm guessing it's time for summer leave at your base?"

"Sure is, and thanks," Kyra replied, taking a sip. It tasted good, but also reminded her of hot days spent drinking cool lagers with Silas in the Hawaiian sunshine, and she had to stifle a shudder. "I'm Kyra by the way." She reached out her hand, and he shook it.

"Blue," he replied, and she was clearly looking confused. He laughed. "It's my nickname," Blue added with a smile. "Mind if I ask why you're here all alone, Kyra?" His expression turned serious.

"Well, I kinda do…" he held up his hands as if to say he understood if she'd rather not answer, but she decided to anyway. "I broke up with my boyfriend this morning, so needed to make new arrangements. This hotel seemed like a nice place to hide away for a week or so until I go back to work, and luckily there was a room available."

"Nothing to do with that split-lip you're sporting, is he?" Blue's gentle expression suddenly turned fierce, and his protective tone surprised her. They'd only just met, yet he seemed genuinely concerned for her, and it felt odd to find such a kind-hearted soul so ready to care about her troubles.

"It might do, but believe me I got him back just as bad—if not worse," she replied with a forced smile. Blue laughed off his dark mood, and went back to wiping down the quiet bar.

"Good to hear it," he told her. "I'd expect nothing less from an army-chick anyway." He then gave her a wink and moved down the bar to serve some new customers, while Kyra took her beer and found a seat where she could watch out the window at the passers by. She didn't know what was going to happen when she went back to Fort Angel, but nothing was set in stone. The future was uncertain, and she just hoped once she settled back into a regimented routine at the base, she'd get used to whatever role Lt. Psy decided was right for her.

The drinks went down far too easily, and before she knew it Blue was getting ready to close the bar for the night.

"Care to join me for something stronger?" he offered Kyra a shot of whiskey, and she accepted it. The beer had given her a nice buzz, and she hoped the liquor would provide the perfect nightcap. She downed it, and he did the same with his, before pouring them another. "Wanna come to a late-night place down the street for a few more?" he asked, and she immediately knew he was after a little more than a couple extra drinks.

"I'm not looking for a rebound fling, Blue," she answered, and stumbled towards the doorway to the bar. "Thanks, though." As much as she was trying not to act all girly, the small bit of attention was flattering, and Kyra had to smile. While he didn't fight her refusal, it seemed Blue couldn't help from calling over to where she stood waiting for the elevator.

"Maybe a drink tomorrow then?"

"Maybe."

***

The next day, Kyra was measured for her new clothes, and then sat down in the chair in wait for the hairdresser she'd made an appointment with. Her long, dark hair was falling in waves around her shoulders and almost as far down as her waist, but she felt brave enough to ask for something very different.

"Hello, Sergeant Millan. I'm Deidra and I'll be your stylist today," a middle-aged woman told her after greeting her warmly. She then began running her hands through Kyra's hair thoughtfully. "What were you hoping to have done?"

"I'm contemplating chopping it all off, what do you think?" she replied, thinking she was definitely ready for a new look.

Deidra's eyes widened, and a look of excitement swept over her face.

"A bob would suit you perfectly. I'll shape it around your face and cut it high at the back. When it grows, you'll have a good few months until it hits your shoulders and you'll need it cutting again. How does that sound?"

"Perfect, let's do it," Kyra answered, and her stylist quickly got to work. She was pampered and made a fuss over the entire time, and when the hairdo was complete, she gasped at her reflection in the mirror. "It's amazing! Thank you so much," she told Deidra with a wide smile, and even hugged her once she'd finished saying her goodbyes. She swung by the tailor on her way back upstairs, and was pleased to see he was finished with her outfits. The portly old man insisted she try everything on, and she felt amazing in the new dresses he'd hand woven especially for her. Even the pants and shirts were the perfect fit, and she walked away a new woman. The renewed and revitalized Kyra Millan was slowly coming out, and she liked how it felt to reinvent herself.

"Wow, check this out. Talk about new and improved," Blue teased when she entered the bar that night, and she felt her cheeks burn under his gaze. He didn't take his eyes off her though, and it felt good.

"Yeah, yeah," she brushed his comment off as casually as possible and took a seat at the bar. He delivered her a beer without needing to be asked, and she thanked him.

They chatted about everything and nothing, and before long some of the other patrons joined in. Chatter and laughter soon filled the small bar, and Kyra genuinely started to enjoy herself. She drank more than she had the night before though, and found herself swaying when it was time to use the bathroom. She emerged to find two shots of whiskey waiting for her, which she promptly downed, and then it was her turn to buy a round.

"Tequila!" she roared, slamming her hand down on the bar with a grin, and Blue gave her a polite curtsey.

"Whatever the lady wants," he replied, and poured her the required amount of shots, which he delivered with salt and slices of lemon at the ready. When it was nearing closing time, he asked her again if she'd like to go out, and again she politely declined. She had no plans that involved men at all, and despite him being perfectly cute enough, Blue didn't stand a chance with her, and she told him so.

The next day she slept late, lazed around and did hardly much else. She was simply counting down the hours until the bar would open again, and was there within minutes of opening time. Kyra wasn't a fool. She realized she might not be dealing with her recent past as well as she'd thought, and kept reminding herself the answer was certainly not at the bottom of a bottle, but still she went back again and again. By the sixth night, Blue was already joking about her not being able to stay away, which was actually kind of true. He made it out as if she couldn't resist spending time with him, rather than the drink, but they both knew she was looking for the escapism she found when the world fell away, and only her drunken happiness was left.

"What's he doing here?" Blue asked nobody in particular towards the end of his shift that night, and Kyra followed his gaze over to the doorway, where a huge man had just entered the small bar. His face was hidden by shadow, but it was clear he was Thrakorian by his sheer size, and when he walked toward the bar, Kyra gasped in shock. She turned to hide her face from Blue's newest customer, and he noticed her reaction right away. He stiffened and stood taller, but it didn't matter in comparison to the huge man towering over him. It was a well-known fact Thraks didn't drink alcohol, so they all knew his presence here must mean only one thing.

"I'm looking for Kyra Millan," Sentinel Gron asked,

and Blue shook his head.

"I haven't seen her this evening, sir," he lied for her, and Kyra cringed. She watched from her spot a few feet away, and guessed Gron hadn't noticed her thanks to the new haircut. A million and one questions were going through her mind, but she couldn't get them straight through her drunken haze.

"That's funny, because according to her records she purchased a drink here not fifteen minutes ago," Gron replied in his ominous deep tone, and he gripped the bar with is powerful hands. "I'll happily shut this place down and put you out of a job if I have to, human," he growled. "Would you care to explain to the local police how you were unwilling to provide information when a Thrakorian demanded it of you?" The entire bar had gone silent, and each of the usually so chatty punters were watching the exchange in shock. Kyra quickly started to feel terrible for letting Blue deal with her hard-ass of a boss. She had no idea why he was here looking for her, but guessed she'd better find out.

"Sentinel Gron, sir," she called over to him, and the intimidating man turned towards her with a scowl. "What's this about?" she asked, and swayed as she peered up his mammoth frame to his face. Gron caught her by the lower back, and helped her stay standing.

"You're drunk," he answered, and she burst out laughing.

"And you're very observant."

"Let's go to your room so you can sober up. We'll have to have our conversation in the morning," he steered her away, and Blue appeared as if out of nowhere to block their exit.

"Is this the man responsible for your busted lip, Kyra?" he asked, standing tall in defiance to the scary extraterrestrial before him. "Because if he is, I don't think it's a good idea for you to leave with him."

Gron leaned down to speak quietly, and Kyra watched

in horror as he overshadowed Blue with both his huge body and frightening demeanor.

"Your concern for her is very touching, but you'll find I'm her Commanding Officer, not her boyfriend. As if I'd touch a human," he snickered at the insinuation, and Blue immediately backed off. Kyra gave him a nod, and he let them leave, but she felt his eyes on her all the way over to the elevators.

She and Gron rode up to her floor in silence, but all she wanted to do was giggle. Kyra knew she was swaying after all the alcohol in her system, and bumped into her mammoth guest on more than one occasion, despite the smooth ride. Inside the room, she threw down her things and grabbed another beer from her stash in the bathroom, but he took it before she could even touch her lips with the bottle, and poured it down the sink.

"Hey!" she argued, and stormed into the bedroom, where she stripped down to her underwear and climbed into bed with a huff. "I think you'll find this is *my* summer break, so two weeks to do as I please. I don't have to take orders from you." Kyra winced and her hands flew to her mouth. She'd completely forgotten whom she was talking too, and tears immediately sprung at her eyes. "I'm sorry. I'm so sorry."

"As if I care," Gron answered with an impatient sigh, and he took a seat in an armchair across the room. It was the only other piece of furniture there, and despite it being a tight fit, would have to do. "Go to sleep," he barked, and shut off the light. Kyra lay back and tried to get comfortable. She curled around herself fetus style, but still couldn't switch off.

"Why are you here?" she eventually whispered into the darkness. Panic had pierced her drunken haze, and she was worried she might be in trouble.

"I'll tell you in the morning. Go to sleep now, Kyra." She curled even tighter into a ball, and willed sleep to take her, but it was no use. After lying there for at least another hour, listening to Gron's shallow breaths across the room, impatience began to creep in. She wondered if he was asleep or not, and got her answer when she climbed out of bed and padded over to the bathroom. "Leave the beers where they are," Gron called over to her, and she mumbled a dopey affirmation, before stumbling inside and using the toilet. Kyra then pulled a baggy t-shirt out of her drawer to cover herself properly, and headed back to bed.

"Why don't you guys drink?" she asked the shadow where she knew he was still sitting. Gron moaned something about her being a pain in the ass, and she heard him click his neck as though stretching.

"Alcohol doesn't affect us the same way it does humans," he answered, and when she stayed silent, he seemed to know she was waiting to hear more. "Rather than having fun, we get emotional. Mostly tearful, like a silly girl, but it can also make us angry." Kyra couldn't stop from laughing loudly, and she was sure she heard him laugh too. "More so than usual," he conceded. She snuggled back under her sheets with a smile, and was glad she finally felt at ease enough to drift off at last.

Sleep descended, but with it brought strange dreams of being chased through the woods and bound, gagged, beaten and kept prisoner in a muddy cage. She tried her hardest to fight against the faceless captor, but it was no use. He cut her arms and legs with a curved blade that scooped through the flesh and left her blood dripping onto the floor. Rats and mice licked at both the crimson droplets and her wounds, and she could do nothing but cry in vain for help that didn't come.

When the morning sun's rays pulled her from the dream, Kyra groaned, but was actually grateful for the rude awakening. She sat up, grabbed her glasses from the bedside table, and put them on while blinking away the sleep. Gron wandered out of the bathroom, his hair wet from a recent shower, and she watched him through pounding eyes.

"You really are here, then? I didn't dream it," she asked, and he nodded.

"Seems to me your dreams are far worse than a simple visit from your superior officer. Care to tell me what had you crying out and flailing around in your sleep?" She shook her head. "Hmm. I thought not."

Kyra climbed out of bed and headed to the bathroom before either of them said another word. She knew he didn't really care about her nightmares. He'd made it perfectly clear in class how he felt about humans. But at the same time, every now and again that kind side of him seemed to come out, and she didn't know how to deal with it. She took a shower, brushed her hair and teeth, and got dressed. Only when she felt ready to face whatever he'd come to tell her, whether good or bad, did she emerge.

"So, what's all this about then?" she perched on the end of the bed, and noticed that he'd straightened it in her absence. *You can take the soldier out the army, but you can't take the army out of the soldier,* she thought with a smile.

"I've reviewed the exercise footage," Gron replied, and she felt her brow furrow. She'd had no idea their training was recorded, and apprehension sent her heart flying into her mouth. "I know Sergeant McDermott tried to detain you during the exercise. One might argue it was his role as a pretend rebel to do so, however I believe he was wrong."

"Why?" her hoarse voice was barely audible, and Gron stared into her eyes.

"He shouldn't have been there. He was supposed to go straight to the central camp with all the others. Silas had an unfair advantage, and knew you were clever enough to see the symbols. He sat in wait and attacked when you bypassed the rebel area, is that a correct assessment?" Kyra could do nothing but nod, and he seemed pleased. "He wanted you to fail, didn't he? He didn't want to lose you, but…"

"But he did anyway because I couldn't forgive him for

sabotaging my career," she finished his sentence for him. "What made you suspicious?"

"Your reaction the following morning. If you took another path, you should technically have crossed that line in first-place because the others all encountered rebels and had to fight their way out. I needed to see for myself what had affected your time, and was disgusted when I saw how he'd treated you."

"I thought you didn't care about humans?" she asked, and had attempted to add a teasing element to her tone, but it just came out as bewilderment.

"Let's keep it our secret," Gron told her, and tears quickly started falling from her tired eyes. She buried her face in her hands, and let them fall. "I came to tell you Lieutenant Psy has reconsidered his recommendation on the grounds of an unsanctioned personal agenda by one of the Training Commanders."

"What?" She looked up from her hands.

"You've made elite training, Kyra. When leave is over, pack your bags and head out on the first transport to Alaska," he said, and handed her the three signed recommendation letters, along with a badge signifying her new rank of Lieutenant. She took them and continued to sob for a few minutes, while Gron waited patiently for her to calm down. He didn't offer her a shoulder to cry on or a hug like Brona would've, but he stood guard over her, and his presence helped Kyra deal with the realization that something life-changing had just happened.

"You couldn't have told me this last night?" she teased when she'd found her voice again, and Gron laughed.

"You were a mess, and I mean it. Stay off the booze from now on, okay?"

"It's difficult not to try and escape your thoughts when you're told everything you've worked so hard for was just ripped away. And all because the person you thought you could trust betrayed you…"

"Well not anymore, and trust me, he'll be dealt with."

Kyra actually cringed at the thought of her being the reason for Silas getting punished, and despite him having hurt her far deeper than just physically, she shook her head.

"Please don't stop him progressing further. Silas believes in himself for the first time since he joined up, and I'd never forgive myself if he lost that again. Give him extra duties, or send him to a base where they only serve gruel and have to live in the dirt." She laughed at the sheer thought, and Gron smiled.

"I'll see what I can do, and all I'll get Psy to say is that you've been reassigned." Kyra liked the sound of that, and felt her burdens lift from her once heavily laden shoulders. Gron stretched and grinned, clearly having had enough of the depressive conversation. "So, how about you show me around the city before I head back to base? Starting with breakfast," he added, and beamed when he saw the shock on her face. "Thraks need to eat too, you know?"

She knew all right, but never suspected one would want to spend time with her doing so. She guessed it was out of nothing but pity. He was clearly making sure she was okay before leaving, and wondered if he needed convincing that she'd be in the right place at the right time come the end of the week.

They left the bedroom and wandered down to breakfast, where they were met with confused stares. Humans still really had no clue when it came to Thrakorian's. Those middle-class humans staying in the hotel clearly had enough credits to have learnt a thing or two, yet still acted like Gron was a walking sci-fi show for them to watch with interest. He either didn't notice or didn't care, and part of her wondered if he quite liked being both feared and coveted at the same time. Most humans would give anything to have a Thrakorian friend or lover, but ninety-nine percent of the human population was denied anything of the sort. Only those already on the inside had them kinds of relationships, and they would never share their powerful lovers with the world, or their insider knowledge of them. She'd been lucky, or privileged enough to learn because of her training, but everyday humans weren't so well informed. The mystery was clearly an aphrodisiac, and Kyra told him her thoughts as they ate huge portions of food and drank numerous coffees together.

"So, in short—Thraks equal gods, or so you'll have us believe…"

"You're spot-on, and damn right. You humans had every chance to take care of yourselves without our help, and you failed. Since we came along, you've not only thrived, but come back from the brink of chaos and eventual extinction." He told her matter-of-factly. "I knew you were ready for elite. Your mind really does see right through all the dirt and madness others get hung up on. You see the anomalies, truths and injustices in every waking moment. You'll go far," he added, and she blushed.

"I can't thank you enough for not only finding me to tell me the wonderful news, but also for having believed I'd been wronged. You're actually a pretty nice guy, Gron."

He quickly shushed her, and she laughed. He had a reputation to protect after all.

Kyra expected him to leave straight after breakfast was over, but Gron surprised her again by dragging her out into the bright sunshine with him. He hailed a cab, and ordered the driver to take them downtown. She was surprised by his choice of destination, and instinctively went to pass her wrist over the chip-reader, but he stopped her.

"Thrakorian's don't pay for cab journeys, or anything else for that matter," he said, and she sat back in the seat, shaking her head incredulously.

"Then why do we?" she asked, watching him intently.

"Because when you had free reign you nearly ruined both your race and this planet. Control is key to keeping your kind in check, and part of that is ensuring you work for your meals and the roofs over your heads. We know the value of a hard day's work, and do it each and every day without the need for monetary gain or putting a value on our efforts. Human's need reminding of their misdemeanors, and the credit-system is the perfect way."

"The cattle control their own food, shelter and lifestyle—how convenient," she replied, and stared out the window as the city flew by.

Before long, the cleaner and less cramped roads and buildings started to disappear, and the lower-class areas of the city she knew far too well came into view. The cabbie eventually slowed, and stopped outside a building Kyra had promised herself she'd never visit again. The Violet Street foster homes were just as they'd been when she left three years before, and she begrudgingly climbed out of the car when Gron led the way. He instructed the driver to wait for them, and she was glad to hear it. Hopefully it meant they weren't staying long.

"What do you see on these streets, Kyra?" Gron asked, and ignored the surprised faces of the men and women trying to figure out why they had a Thrakorian visitor. "Do you see a childhood spent in poverty? A youthful innocence taken from you by the pressures of society? Or perhaps a life you vowed to yourself you'd never come back to?"

"Can I choose all three?" She squirmed under his scrutiny.

"Of course. And don't ever forget it," he replied. "Next time someone gets in your way, you never stop fighting back. I want you to promise me you'll never live in a place like this again. Pack your bags and board that hovercraft for Alaska when summer leave's over. Never look back to here, or Fort Angel again. You're worth more, so go and get it."

Kyra's heart suddenly leapt at the sheer thought of what path her life was about to take. Everything was going to change, just like they had three years ago when she'd taken Silas's hand and joined the army. But this time, nothing would stop her from staying strong.

"You got it, boss," she promised him, and beamed up at the mammoth man in the dingy light of the dirty slums.

That night, and each one after, Kyra went back to the hotel bar to enjoy her last few days away, but she decided against ordering beers or shots. She stuck to water or soda, and found she could still enjoy the company of the men and women enjoying their beverages, without the buzz she'd become so reliant on. Blue tried to question her about her Thrakorian visitor, but she politely told him to keep out of it, and was glad when he let it go.

Her last few days were spent without tears or the black cloud that'd been looming over her, and instead she actually felt excited about going back to work. She spent her time preparing herself for the hardcore training she knew would come during the elite phase, and by the time she boarded the ship heading to the Alaskan training base, Kyra was absolutely raring to go.

CHAPTER SIXTEEN

Hundreds of other elite trainees travelled alongside Kyra on their long train ride north to Alaska. Once a thriving country, it was now a restricted area used solely for training the elite forces. In her research, she hadn't found much information readily available to the public, but knew it was now a hive full of highly motivated and well-trained soldiers ready to further their careers, rather than towns and cities full of civilians like it had once been.

At first, only a few of the soldiers on her intake spoke to one another, and the silence was deafening. Either nerves or excitement seemed to be getting to them, but by a few hours into the journey, they were all chatting and getting to know each other. The fresh start felt good, and it was liberating to meet other soldiers headed to the elite base with aspirations of a future as upper-class officers, and potentially even Gentry.

Kyra wandered the train in search of a face she recognized, but instead found a small group of fellow Intelligence Division soldiers, and joined them at a large table they'd taken over.

"What are you pursuing?" she asked a few, and each took it in turns to offer their specialty. There were mostly strategic intelligence, computer programming, and technological science students, or like Kyra, code-breaking. They all chatted long into the night, and it felt good talking with like-minded people who not only knew the subject matter, but also actually engaged in debates with her over some of the lessons the likes of Gron and Capt. Quinn had taught them. Each training base seemed to do things differently, and it was a breath of fresh air engaging with others who were just as passionate about their jobs as she was. Kyra eventually settled back in her surprisingly comfortable seat and got a few hours' rest, while the whirr of the engines lulled her into a thankfully dreamless sleep.

When dawn came, so too did the end of their journey. She stretched and grabbed her things, rubbing her eyes groggily, but was alert and quick to pull out her jacket to see off the chill that'd descended. The freezing blasts that hit the trainees faces as they disembarked was sure to wake up any stragglers, and many groaned against the stark change in temperature. Platoon Commanders were there to greet them, just like they'd done at Fort Angel, and Kyra followed the line heading to the right, where a banner indicated the Intelligence Division. There were no buildings on the horizon, only the handful of entranceways like the one beside the banner. After a better look, she saw that it led inside a domed bunker ahead of her that was covered with snow. From above it'd surely look sparse, and Kyra couldn't wait to see what was inside.

She stood with the others and trembled against the cold. They'd been given warm coats, but the arctic chill still permeated the down, and she couldn't wait to get inside. A human woman wearing the rank of Captain stood before them, and she glared at the newcomers as though completely indifferent to their discomfort.

"You'll soon get used to the temperatures here in the extreme north, and this is actually the mildest time of year," she informed them with a smile once all were present and correct. "Welcome to Elite Base North, where you will be trained not only in your Division, but also as elite soldiers in general. Here your hard work and due diligence will pay off in leaps and bounds, but only if you stay focused, otherwise it'll be back to the middle-ranks for you." She stared them all in the eye, and Kyra was careful not to avert her gaze when theirs locked. "My name is Capt. Kash, and I'm the Commander of the Intelligence Division's training section. You'll be seeing a lot of me, and believe it when I say, you're lucky to have me as your leader. Follow me." Kyra wondered what she meant by that, and envisioned other leaders who might take pleasure in pushing their trainees to their breaking point, or perhaps only let their class favorites progress. She hadn't heard of favoritism in the military before, but guessed it must happen across the training bases.

Their group did as they were told, and each sighed in relief when they entered through the doorway and hit the warm air within. It was just as she'd imagined, and the narrow hallways quickly opened up into a maze of passages and archways. They finally found themselves in a canteen, where a handful of soldiers were sat drinking coffee, and Capt. Kash stopped.

She turned to face their group again. "This base is built entirely underground, and each Division is linked by a series of tunnels. It'll take no time at all before you're familiar with it, but in the meantime you've all been provided with a map of the building in your new rooms. Speaking of," she told them, and started walking off down another passage that led away from the delicious smell of food. The trainees were taken to a corridor marked 'D' and Kash grabbed a small device from its holster on the wall. Kyra recognized it as a handheld information console, and watched as their superior called up the logs. "Your rooms are all on this corridor, go and dump your things, check out the maps and other information provided, and then come and meet me back in the canteen in an hour." Kash handed the device to the closest trainee, who then started reading out the names and their associated room number.

Kyra headed off in search of hers, and ran her wrist over the lock to open it. She still marveled at the technology behind the microchips implanted in their arms. The complex transponder allowed them to live and survive so fluidly within their new home and work areas, and by simply emitting just the small amount of information required by the readers at any given time. Never once had she needed to go and investigate any problems with her microchip or her clearances, and she often wondered whether it was a computer system or a team of human soldiers that maintained the seemingly faultless system. Of course, the chips also meant they were always traceable, like Gron had made clear when he tracked her to the bar, and it made her a little uneasy at the same time.

Her new home was clean, spacious and surprisingly light for an underground fortress, and she quickly set about unpacking her things. Kyra spent a few minutes making sure her room was properly tidied, and then sat down to peruse the information Capt. Kash had advised would be left for her. A small tablet device was waiting on the desk, and she powered it up. The screen showed Kyra where each division studied and slept, and where the other areas of the huge base were located. This building alone was miles wide, and distant areas were connected via a train line she was sure they'd be shown at some point over their first few days. Each section had a state-of-the-art simulated training area like at Fort Angel, and Kyra hoped they might be sent in a simulated desert terrain soon. Despite the freshly pumped warm air, she already missed the heat of L.A. and the intense barrenness of Death Valley. She suddenly found herself wondering what was going on right now at the base her friends thought she ought to be returning to, and smiled at the reaction she was sure Silas had given upon hearing she'd been accepted into the Elite program after all.

A quiet knock at her door pulled Kyra from her thoughts, and she opened it to find a short, slightly rounded girl on the other side.

"Hello," she said, reaching her hand out, and Kyra shook it. "I'm Gabriela, or Gaby for short. I'm pleased to meet you."

"Kyra, and likewise," she replied, feeling a little unsure of what to say next.

"I live directly across from you, so I thought I'd stop by and say hi. Do you want to walk back to the canteen together? I'm giving myself plenty of time just in case I get lost along the way," Gaby told her, and Kyra agreed that it was a good idea. She nodded, grabbed her things, and then followed her new friend down the hall. They turned in the direction Kash had taken them, and soon got chatting as they followed the path to where they hoped some breakfast would be waiting.

"I just graduated secondary training from Fort Baker outside of New York, heading down the computer science route, how about you?"

"I've just finished secondary too, but I'm hoping to specialize in code-breaking. I trained at Fort Angel in Death Valley."

"Where did you live before you joined?" Gaby looked sheepish at asking, but Kyra wasn't ashamed to answer her honestly.

"I was a foster kid from downtown L.A."

"Me too, but from New York," Gaby replied, and they both grinned. "Far away from where we once were, hey?"

"Yeah, and never going back," Kyra agreed. She liked Gaby, and hoped they might end up being good friends. There wasn't a place in her life for a new man, but a new best friend? She downright needed one of those. Brona was carrying on with her medical training at Fort Angel, and Kyra wasn't sure they'd even see each other again. She missed her already, but knew they'd both have to accept the changes life had thrown at them, and try to remain in contact wherever possible.

The training was as grueling as Kyra expected, and then some. Weeks went past in a blurred routine of meals and lessons, training and simulations. Each of the trainees was put through so much, and she wondered when she'd ever see the other side, let alone the natural light of day again. Living underground did have its perks though. The chill was kept to a minimum, and there wasn't any risk of insect bites or rainy weather ruining their days, but the sunshine was a tormenting memory she daren't access, because it made her feel utterly homesick in a way she'd never imagine possible.

By the end of her first year in elite training, she felt like a well-oiled machine rather than a person anymore. She was desensitized to so many natural human emotions because of their intense seclusion while at Elite Base North, and Kyra often felt like she was akin to a computer running on programming and codes, rather than a member of their new society.

When she travelled south on the long train ride back to Los Angeles for summer break again, there was nowhere she wanted to stay, not even the Crowned King. She wasn't the same person she'd been the summer before, not by a long shot, so decided to board a train or bus heading anywhere that looked good. She had plenty of credits, as well as her free travel warrant, so decided to let her gut lead the way.

After waiting in the terminal building for a little over an hour watching the timetables, Kyra made a decision, and climbed aboard a ship going west to Japan. She hadn't heard much about the ancient country, but was open to learning all about the different cultures and history behind the people there. Everything she owned was in her backpack, and she didn't feel the need to add more to it, however it was an exciting idea travelling to places she'd never dreamed of before. Gone were the days of different languages across the globe, so she knew there wouldn't be any problem finding places to stay or tour guides for her holiday. The Thrakorian's had ordered that all regional or cultural dialects should be ceased, and all humans now spoke a single language no matter their heritage or race, as there simply was one race now—human. Kyra had to admit it made things easier, but at the same time she loved hearing the strong lilts and odd sounding words coming from the mouths of those old enough to remember their mother tongue, and she wondered if they dreamed in forbidden languages or wrote secret letters in their strange script.

Japan was a stunning mixture of ancient beauty and modern technology, and there she found an underground group of hackers who adapted any console they could find to improve and play with the mainframes. It was perfectly harmless, and highly exciting for an enthusiast like her to get involved in, so she didn't worry about joining their fun. Kyra spent the entire two weeks testing and reprogramming computer systems with the men and women who were pioneers in the apparently new field, and she wondered if perhaps the Intelligence Division might look at recruiting them before too long.

The small band of supporters sought change and a move into the more digital world for the human race, and all while working with their leaders' technology to revolutionize the old and give birth to a new era of machinery. She loved being in Japan, and absorbed every element of the culture she could. On top of her underground activities, Kyra made sure to experience everything else the country had to offer. She ate every variant of food she could find, and walked through both the bustling cities and the tranquil fields that were so close together it felt like a marvelous contradiction.

She'd set out on a journey to clear her mind, and it worked. When she stepped off the hovercraft in Los Angeles's terminal building again the world felt small, and she yearned for the peace she'd hoped would stay with her longer. Her Asian paradise already seemed so far away, not just half a day's travel, and she took a moment to grieve it.

While sat nursing a coffee and whiling away the few hours wait she had until their train would disembark for

Alaska, Kyra began watching the busy terminal, especially the people all milling around it. She spotted mothers with their children, soldiers with their comrades, and then something else caught her eye. It was her job to notice things out of the ordinary, and all of a sudden not all seemed right. Every moment of training came back to her in a flood, and it made her stomach lurch.

There were two men were standing not far away, leaning close to each other and whispering intently in one another's ear. The closeness wouldn't normally bother an everyday passer by or casual observer, but Kyra's gut immediately flared. The men weren't lovers, and they certainly didn't seem to be friends either. Their exchange was all business, and methodic, like every movement had been meticulously planned. She immediately wondered if they might be up to no good. When the two men moved down toward the train tracks, Kyra followed her instincts, and took after them. She watched from afar, sipping her coffee from its paper cup casually, so as not to alarm them, and spotted a black smudge on the wall to one edge of a turnoff, which they coincidentally took. Something about the marking stirred her even more, and she continued to follow the men. She watched as they came to a stop, checked their periphery, entered a control room, and then left again a few minutes later dressed as policemen.

Kyra could tell they weren't enforcement officers, and somehow knew without a doubt that something bad was about to happen. She looked for a nearby device to alert her superiors to a potential threat, and found an old style telephone that was attached to the wall. She lifted the receiver, and hoped for the best. The lines were long since dead, but should've been replaced using cell receptors, and as soon as she heard the dial tone, Kyra knew the real police would be on the other end of the call no matter what buttons she pressed.

"This is Lieutenant Kyra Millan, Intelligence Division," she said quietly into the receiver. "I believe there to be a potential threat to the L.A terminal building, and I'm requesting permission to take the suspects into my custody for questioning. What do you recommend?"

"We see you, Lieutenant. Which are the suspects you are concerned about?" a female voice asked from down the line, and she turned briefly to look at the two men, who were now hovering by the tracks. They were standing close to each other again, whispering intently while watching the crowd, and still looked out of place among the travelers.

"Two men, dressed as police. In my line of vision now," she told the call handler before turning back, and knew they had seen her on their cameras.

"Thirty seconds until Thrakorian infiltration. Please stand by," the voice told her, and then the call ended abruptly. Before she could even think or move, a squad of around thirty huge men and women stormed the station. They moved stealthily through the sea of people, and the tactical advantage was marvelous. It was clear to Kyra where they were going, however the two men seemed oblivious to their presence until it was too late thanks to their covertness and speed. They tried to fight, but were quickly reprimanded by the powerful Thraks and taken away, while she and the other humans watched on with open mouths.

Next thing she knew, they were being evacuated. A loud voice sounded throughout the crowd via hidden speakers, issuing directions to the nearest exits and informing them that all trains and other crafts were grounded until further notice. Kyra followed the crowd and started walking back to the entrance, when a huge hand fell on her shoulder and halted her.

"Lieutenant Millan?" the burly Thrak soldier asked, and she nodded. "I need you to come with us for debriefing," he told her, and she knew there was no other choice but to comply. Kyra followed him back over to where the rest of his squad were combing the area and taking photographic evidence of the scene. She stayed quiet while they did their thing, and was surprised when she was ushered into their truck and taken to the nearby precinct. She'd never been involved with the police in her life, and felt odd riding in the back of a van with five heavily laden Thrakorian's. The foster kid inside of her wanted to run away in fear, but the soldier element won over, and she kept her cool.

CHAPTER SEVENTEEN

"Lieutenant, it's a pleasure to meet you," a young woman greeted them inside the entrance to the police precinct, and Kyra shook her outstretched hand. "I'm Bow, the call handler you spoke with."

"It's a pleasure to meet you, Bow," she replied, and followed her further into the depths of the huge building. "I hope my instincts were correct with those two men in the terminal?"

"It's not my place to say, but I can tell you that you caught the attention of our Commanding Officer, Paladin Forst. He was quick to act on your call, and would like to meet with you," she told her, and Kyra had to stifle her shock. She'd never dreamed of meeting one of the highest ranking officer's in the Thrakorian army, and wondered if he might be waiting in the back to interrogate her about why she'd acted the way she had towards the two men. It would be hard to explain, but every moment of it had been pure instinct, and she barely even remembered a moment-by-moment account of the capture. All conscious thought had left her when she'd found a fragment of chaos within the apparent normalcy of the terminal, and everything after that had been natural, learned responses to the scenario.

"Of course," Kyra replied after a thoughtful second, and Bow smiled warmly in response. She led her down another hall, and then ushered her into a small room with just a desk and two chairs inside. Bow then frowned when she saw the look of alarm cross Kyra's face.

"This is just temporary, after your statement you'll be shown to Paladin Forst's office," she informed her, and turned to leave. Even after the assurance, unease rumbled in her gut, but Kyra did as she'd been asked and took a seat.

"Wait!" she called when Bow was about to close the door, and she stopped mid-way. "I'm supposed to be boarding a train to Alaska. Can you please make sure they're aware of the situation?" Bow gave her a small nod.

"The entire world knows there was an attempted rebel attack on Los Angeles, Kyra. Until we have the all clear, all movement in and out of the city has been halted. You needn't worry about your superiors in Alaska, they've already been made aware of the situation."

Kyra appreciated the reassurance, but couldn't stop thinking about what'd just come out of Bow's mouth. Evidently she had been right earlier on, and those two men were rebels who really had been up to no good. She yearned to discover what they'd been planning, and hoped her host officers would give her the full account before she left.

It wasn't long before she'd told her story to a pair of human policemen, and then to a Thrakorian Inquisitor. She kept her cool, and had told each of them the truth of how she'd come to notice the two men in the Terminal, and why she thought them suspicious. Only once they seemed convinced did the clearly seasoned officers lighten up, and it was a relief to be left in peace after hours of debriefing. An older, grey-haired Thrakorian man then came to get her, and asked Kyra to join him for some coffee. She saluted him before he even introduced himself, and knew that he must be Paladin Forst.

"How is it that a young woman just four years into her training, spotted two rebels in a crowd of hundreds of humans?" he asked, and she watched in surprise as he poured her drink and stirred in her preferred amount of sugar and milk, without needing to be asked her preference. She guessed her file really must've given him everything he needed to know about her, and the only thing left for him to wonder about was what went on in her mind.

"I'm very good at what I do, sir," she replied with a smile. "My superiors throughout my training have attested to my natural skills as a code-breaker, and I've learned to trust my instincts."

"That's what I like to hear, especially when it comes to our Intelligence Division trainees." He watched her for a moment, and then passed Kyra a file. Inside it were photographs from the scene, along with stills taken from the camera footage of both her and the two men. "Show me how," was all Forst added, and he took a seat in a large armchair next to her. Her formal debriefing might be over, but she had the feeling the interrogation might not be as finished as she'd assumed.

"Here," she pointed to the scuff on the wall that she'd taken for a directional sign. "This is how they knew where to turn and get their fake uniforms. Someone else masterminded this attack, and planted the clues for them beforehand. It'll be worth you checking the tapes back to see who left this mark."

"Couldn't it simply be a line of dirt from the tracks?" Forst asked, and he watched her intently.

"Absolutely not," she answered. "These terminals are pristinely clean. This mark has been put there in the hour or so leading up to the men's presence in the building. Whoever left the uniforms and directions must've left more clues, or perhaps another item for the fake policemen to find." Forst grinned across at her, but it was a dark smile that gave her the creeps, rather than one to bask in.

"You're right. A bomb was found attached to the undercarriage of a train heading east. It would've been filled with soldiers heading to their base, but instead my team managed to deactivate it and remove the device following your discovery."

Kyra felt like she couldn't breathe.

"Are you serious?" she blurted out in surprise, and then apologized a second later.

"I'm absolutely serious, Lieutenant. Whatever your training or gut instinct told you, it was spot on. You saved thousands of lives today, and ought to be proud." Forst took a long sip of his drink, and his wrinkled eyes never left her face.

She stared back at him; unable to even think of anything other than the words he'd spoken. Kyra took the wizened man in. She guessed Forst must be somewhere around six hundred years old, and that he must've seen a lot in his time. His approval meant more to her than she'd ever imagined she needed.

"Thank you, sir. I have to admit I'm in shock, so please excuse my awkwardness. I'm truly honored to serve, and knowing I saved those people is a profound honor I'll never forget."

"None of us ever forget that first pivotal moment in our lives, so you're right to want to cherish it," he told her, and stood. "I want you to stay on with us while we investigate these rebels and the attack they'd planned. Your training base has been informed of our need for your insight, and the report from me will count towards your elite exam, so don't worry about being left at a disadvantage—in fact it's far from it. I want fresh eyes and a keen instinct on this case, and you seem capable of providing both."

"Sir, I…" she didn't know what else to say. He was patient though, and gave her a moment to calm down before giving her a nudge.

"This is the chance of a lifetime, Kyra. Don't let it pass you by," Forst offered with a warm smile this time. He seemed so wise she couldn't question his advice or deny his request. There was something else there too though, and despite his huge size and clearly powerful build, she saw something gentle shine out of him now that he'd dropped his guard a little.

"I don't intend to let anything pass me by, sir. I'll stay." She then followed his lead and walked in silence behind him through the narrow corridors leading towards the back of the precinct. They walked through a doorway, and the largest group of Thrakorian soldiers she'd ever seen in real life appeared before her and her high-ranking escort. Such mass gatherings were rarely seen, other than on television or in the newspapers, and Kyra could see why. It was an intimidating group, and she instantly shrunk back, as if she wasn't already tiny enough in comparison to them.

In a move that surprised the life out of her, each of them started clapping. Her face burned with instant heat, but she felt amazing, and looked every man and woman there in the eye, rather than at the floor like she'd done at first. Her moment didn't last long, but it'd been wonderful having received recognition for her hard work and intelligence that'd led to the successful capture of the two rebels.

"The prisoners are with Inquisitors now, Paladin. So far nothing more than what we already know, but they've only just made a start," a Sentinel soldier informed Forst, and he nodded.

"Very well, we'll observe the interrogation from the control room," he answered, and ushered for Kyra to join him. She did as she knew was expected, and followed his lead without question or comment. The last thing she wanted to do was be seen as a hot-head who thought she knew everything, but she also wasn't keen on them feeling like they were babysitting an inexperienced novice in the field either. Kyra decided that if she were asked a question or her input was required, she would speak up, otherwise she'd simply stand back and keep an eye on everything. This experience would no-doubt provide a bigger lesson than any theoretical simulations she could do back at base, and she believed Forst when he'd told her staying wouldn't hinder her training. If anything, she'd be much better off when it came to her final exams.

They came to a stop, and Kyra watched the huge screens from beside Paladin Forst. They could see the two men were being question separately, and each was already squirming under their Thrakorian Inquisitor's scrutiny. She didn't envy them one little bit.

"Whom do you work for? What are they planning?"

"Freedom, that's what I serve. Humans deserve autonomy from the oppression of a governing race who is not indigenous to this planet or are wanted here," the man answered. He had so much venom in his eyes at addressing one of the very creatures he was speaking of that it shocked her, but neither the Inquisitor nor Forst seemed surprised by it.

"Humans are free in many ways. We provided education and purpose, leadership and structure to ensure you survive and thrive. We do not govern this planet using fear or violence, and yet you insist on hurting your own race to try and harm ours. That's not freeing your people, it's genocide," the Inquisitor answered, and the man swore. He rose to the bait just like the Thrak had seemingly planned, and soon started shouting his mouth off.

"Genocide? You dare talk to me about killing innocent human beings? Your people steal lower-class humans from their beds with no reason or rhyme, because you think they won't be missed—well they are! You poison water supplies to kill off underachieving areas of the world and kidnap entire families to serve in your homes as slaves. Inconvenient pregnancies are practically non-existent now thanks to your doctors and their so-called 'unavoidable hysterectomies due to complications.' It's obvious you're slowing human reproduction, but will you tell me why?" He paused for a breath at long last, and the Thrak sitting opposite him didn't move or say a word. "I thought not."

Kyra had to stop herself falling to her knees in shock.

Not once had she ever contemplated that Brona's operation two years before might not have actually been for the reasons they were given, and now the man's words resonated somewhere deep inside of her. Uncertainty quickly followed the agonizing barrage of emotion she suddenly felt, and she did everything she could not to turn to the huge Paladin beside her and demand to know if it were true. Kyra balled her hands and squeezed as tightly as her muscles would allow in an attempt to keep still. She even focused every ounce of mental strength she had to ensure her breathing didn't speed up in her fury. In the end, forcing the thoughts away was her only hope, and she wished with all her heart that one day her doubts would be cleared on the subject, not confirmed. There were times in her life she'd questioned the Thrakorian's methods or what she'd learned, and she hated how often it was continuing to occur.

By the time the Inquisitors were finished with the two rebels, there was very little of them left. Kyra wasn't forced to stay and watch, but she did to show solidarity regardless of the still niggling guilt in her gut. The men were beaten, questioned, tortured and treated with chemicals and toxins from synthetic creatures in order for the Thraks to get their answers. The scene was gruesome, and she knew it would stay with her forever.

With her help, they then worked long into the night decoding what the men had said while piecing the information together. She was still convinced they were lower-level insurgents, and was sure this wouldn't be the end of the rebel attacks. Kyra made sure to say so via her final report, and none of the Thraks working with her disagreed. The data was then put together and relayed to a team in England, where she knew the Intelligence Division's Gentry would go over it with a fine toothcomb and get back to the precinct on the next course of action.

After two days of solid work, she was exhausted, and

stood to attention outside Forst's open office door to wait for what she hoped was his permission to return to Elite Base North.

"As well as providing the initial alert, Millan has been an asset to the case," she heard him on the phone with someone while she waited, and her ears pricked up at hearing her name. "Yes, I believe so too. Very well." He put down the receiver and grabbed his file. Kyra wanted to cough, or shift in her stance, anything to remind him of her presence. She was also desperate to know what'd just been said, but Paladin Forst ignored her. He signed a few forms and then reached into a desk drawer.

When he stood, Kyra saluted. "Lieutenant Millan, in recognition for your work in apprehending two rebels intent on taking the lives of thousands of innocent human soldiers, I hereby grant you the rank of Colonel in his majesty King Kronus's Human Royal Armed Forces. As per the Besieger's orders, I have been asked to invite you to join him in The Tower, where you will be rewarded for your bravery." He handed her a document validating her rank, along with a new badge with the corresponding emblem on it. Kyra ran her fingers over the symbol, and couldn't quite believe this was happening. She took a deep breath and swayed on her usually so steadfast feet.

"The Tower? As in…"

"The Tower of London, yes," Forst answered before she could finish her train of thought. "Or what's left of it. The Gentry from every area reside and work from England, and The Tower is the base of operations for the Intelligence Division," he told her, and she remembered Gron's explanation of the fortress isle from their training. "The Besieger wishes to speak with you face to face, and sooner rather than later. You're to leave right away, and the Inquisitors are flying back with you, so you won't be alone." Kyra could think of nothing worse than spending several hours in a small hovercraft with two such scary and intimidating Thrakorian's, but knew she had no other choice. After watching them work though, she truly hoped she was never on the receiving end of their skills. She couldn't put together the smiling and kind-looking men she'd talked to after the interrogation, and the men who'd tortured those two rebels, or the end result. What was left of them had barely been alive, and she doubted they'd stayed that way for long.

Kyra did as she was asked though, and grabbed the backpack that held her tiny amount of belongings. She followed Forst out of his office and down the hall to where the two Inquisitors were waiting patiently for her, and her discomfort was renewed despite their warm smiles.

"It's an honor to have my presence requested, sir. Thank you for the promotion, and for your confidence in me," she replied, saluting the Paladin.

"Until we meet again, Colonel," Forst replied with a smile, and he walked away, leaving Kyra with her scary escorts to the English isles.

CHAPTER EIGHTEEN

After the first hour aboard the small hovercraft, Kyra finally started to relax. Neither of her Thrakorian companions made much effort to talk with her, both seeming happy to sit quietly and read, and she soon gave in to her exhaustion. She woke hours later, and was surprised she'd been asleep for so long. Kyra checked the time, and knew they were almost across the pond to England. She looked to her right, but the window didn't reveal anything but ocean and she wondered if they were running late. The tiny craft's attendants were soon busy delivering a simple breakfast of power bars and coffee to the two Inquisitors though, and she guessed they still had a little time. She fixed her hair and clothing, accepted some food, and took a seat at the small table, where she buried her head in a newspaper.

"Do we make you uncomfortable?" the younger of the two asked her, and Kyra frowned as she peered over the tabloid at him. She knew better than to try and lie to either of them, even about something so small, so figured honesty was the best policy regardless of their informal setting.

"You might say that, sir," she replied with an awkward smile. "But something tells me you get that a lot?"

He laughed and nodded. Kyra wanted to see him now as the kind looking Thrak with a warm smile and a gentle laugh, but she also couldn't get the images out of her mind of him torturing that rebel man. Her allegiance was with the Thrakorian's, there was not a single doubt in her mind about that, but she also maintained a healthy fear of them regardless of her relaxed attitude with those such as Sentinel Gron towards the end.

"We're like any other soldier—dedicated and fearless when required, and resolute to our rules and training, but outside of that we're normal Thrak guys." She didn't think that could really be possible, but presumed they were trained to turn it off again after the interrogations were over.

"Do you have families? Children?" she asked, genuinely interested.

"You've got me there," the same soldier replied with a laugh. "I don't trust anyone, especially women. You could lie to me about the simplest thing and it'd mean the end of us. Many of us Inquisitors are the same, so most stay the 'lone wolf' types. How about you? Or does the geek life get in the way of all that too?" he asked with a wink, and Kyra shrugged.

"It does, but my ambition is what keeps me away from the guys I train with. I let myself get distracted once before, and it didn't end well."

"I know, I read about it in your file," he said, and Kyra suddenly remembered exactly who she was dealing with. "Sorry, but I had to do my due diligence before debriefing you. That and we are an honest profession, so I have a tendency to blurt things out and piss people off."

"You certainly managed that," she answered, but forced herself to laugh it off and give him a smile. "It doesn't matter now, he failed and I made elite. I like to think just knowing that was all the kick in the balls he needed."

"Damn straight, Colonel." He replied with a nod, and then looked out of the nearby window. She followed his gaze and saw land on the horizon. They let the conversation drop then, and before she knew it they were heading in to land.

She'd never traveled so far or so fast before, and actually had to get her bearings when their small hovercraft came to a stop. They were met at the dock by a combination of Gentry human officers and Thrak soldiers, and each were welcoming and kind to her while she tried her hardest not to look like a lost little lamb. She followed their lead, and was glad none seemed interested in making small talk.

Kyra was then shown to a huge bedroom, which was to be hers for the duration of her stay, and was then left to freshen up before her meeting with the infamous Besieger. A member of the Kings Guard Service, the Besieger was the official capturer of both rebels and rogues. She'd experienced a mere snippet of his specialty, and had no idea what to say or how to act with one of the Thrakorian's top ranking officers. Kyra racked her brains to try and at least prepare some witty conversational pieces in case he was one for small talk, but wasn't sure how to deal with a man she was sure must be one of the older and more battle-hardened of the extraterrestrial bunch.

She showered and changed into fresh combats, being sure to position her new rank badge perfectly over her chest. Kyra stood staring at her reflection in the mirror incredulously, until a knock on her door pulled her from her reverie. She took a deep breath, opened it and followed her usher through the maze of corridors to an elevator. Once inside, she could finally figure out where they were within The Tower. She could see the ruins of the old castle all around her as she took in the sights of the once iconic city, but now an intimidating Thrakorian stronghold was nestled within its walls. There were numerous underground bunkers, like where she'd just been in her guest room, but now she was heading into the clouds on a fast-moving course to the thirtieth floor.

The view was astounding, and Kyra took it all in as much as she could in the short time she had before they'd stopped and were walking down a lavishly decorated corridor, and into an even more decadent office. A Thrakorian man stood waiting for her, and in a surprise move he hugged Kyra tightly after she saluted. The Besieger was shorter than most of the Thraks she'd met previously, but he also had a much kinder smile and it reached his eyes, which was something she'd rarely seen in others of his kind.

"Colonel Millan, how wonderful to meet you," he said, and indicated that she was to take a seat next to him at an intimate dining table in the opposite corner of the room. Sitting down to chat so informally felt strange, and Kyra knew she must look uncomfortable, because he smirked. "I'd like to get to know you a little before work commences on the information we procured from those rebels. Would you care to join me for some lunch?" the Besieger asked with a smile, and Kyra finally took the offered seat.

"It'd be my honor, sir," she answered, and watched in awe as servants started filing in with a meal that'd clearly been ready prepared. There were meats, fruits, and vegetables the likes she'd never even seen before, and wine so clearly expensive they were each only given a mouthfuls worth to match the course. Kyra had never eaten anything like it, and savored every mouthful. "This looks amazing, I don't think I've eaten this well in my entire life," she added, and he smiled, as if he had hoped she'd react that way. The Besieger himself, it seemed, was taking great pleasure in treating the simple girl from the slums to a decadent meal, as though she might be more than just a guest in The Tower. The realization that she'd almost made it to the top, albeit as a guest, both delighted and scared her, and she ate her tiny portions of mouthwatering food in silence.

"I'm sure you'll get used to living this way in no time. After all, the human Gentry are privileged, pompous elitists with a strong sense of entitlement, and a desire for all the finer things this planet has to offer. You'll have to learn to fit in—or lie through your teeth," he answered with a gentle smile, and pushed a plate of sweet buns towards her. "Try one of these." She did as he told her to, and groaned appreciatively, while he gave her that sly look again. "You fascinate me, Kyra. I want to know what on Earth created a mind as valuable as yours in this dreadful world I've come to call home. Will you let me figure you out? Will you give me the opportunity to see you in action, and tell me how you do it?"

She felt hot under his intense gaze, and wondered for a moment if she needed to consider whether or not he was hitting on her. Kyra hadn't done too well in the romance department, and sure hoped she wasn't about to have to fend off the advances of an older and clearly very clever Thrakorian. He seemed intent on discovering how her mind worked though, rather than anything else.

"Of course, sir. But I won't be here long, surely?" she asked, and all he did was hum in reply. His response made Kyra suspect that her visit might not be for the few days she'd expected, and hoped she might get some information in the form of an official order, rather than the cryptic requests she'd had so far.

"Please, call me Thrayke," the Besieger told her when the next course had been delivered, and she shook her head no. It wasn't protocol to converse so informally, let alone dare to call him by anything other than his title. "At least in privacy? It's my given name after all, and only the few men above or of equal rank to me in the Thrakorian army ever call me by it. I will admit I've missed the sound of my name on a feminine tongue."

Kyra stopped eating and looked at him. She took a moment to really see the man before her and attempted to figure him out. He didn't seem interested in her sexually, but his expression of longing seemed genuine enough. Thrayke was smaller than others she'd met, but absolutely more commanding than Gron or Forst. They'd been intimidating and scary, and she'd had to fight to see the softness lurking beneath their armor, but Thrayke had shown her that gentleness right from the start. He'd earned her respect because he'd shown an interest in her mind and skill, and had respected her regardless of her race. He was slowly winning her over without a show of dominance or power, and she appreciated the difference in tact.

"Are you lonely, Thrayke?" she asked before she could stop herself, and wanted to die of embarrassment the second the words left her mouth.

"Tremendously," he answered, and his honesty startled her. "Don't you get lonely, Kyra?"

"Sometimes, but then I remember the days I spent with those who didn't deserve my time, or those that no longer have a tomorrow to wake up to. I hold my head high and remember how lucky I am. All I ever wanted was to have a purpose and a cause to serve." She grabbed another bun before the servants could take the basket away, and watched him absorb her words in apparent awe.

"How are you so young? It's as if you've lived a thousand lives, not just one," he finally asked. "What an enigma you are."

They whiled away the next hour talking about all sorts, from politics to the state of the human race, from both before and after Invasion Day. When their meal was over it was time to go down to the control room and start analyzing hers and the Inquisitors' work. Thrayke peered down at her as he pulled back her chair in a gentlemanly way, and she watched him intently.

"Thank you for a wonderful meal, Thrayke," she told him, and basked in the smile he gave her at hearing his name on her lips.

"You are most welcome, Kyra. It was an absolute pleasure," he answered, and then together they traveled down the elevator to the bustling computer suites below. Silence had descended along with them, but she didn't feel uncomfortable, and was surprised by how relaxed she was around him.

The room that'd been designated for their use was cramped and hot thanks to the numerous bodies inside, and a huge table stood in the center. It was shaped like an octagon, and Kyra followed Thrayke's lead to stand at one edge. He reached down and activated the touch-sensitive computer system within, and quickly started pulling up the data. The team watched the tapes back in full, including the footage from the terminal, and then started picking apart every aspect of the raid, and the resulting intel from the two rebels.

Days later, and after very little time to eat or rest thanks to the heavy workload, Kyra was released and given permission to take a break. She went straight to the bedroom that'd been given to her when she'd arrived, and crashed out on the bed.

For the first time in a long while, she dreamt of King Kronus. He was reaching out to her through the thorns with a gentle smile and the same tender gaze, and when she was through them, Kyra found a feast-covered table awaiting her. When she tried to eat anything though, it turned to dust as she bit down, and soon she was coughing on the dryness.

"If you want this, you have to earn it," he told her, taking a bite of an exotic-looking fruit. Kyra watched as the juice dripped down his chin and he chewed on the soft, moist flesh. She reached forward and gathered the juice on her fingertip, but as she raised it to her mouth he grabbed her wrist harshly to stop her. "You've heard the stories," Kronus said. "If you want this you have to choose. Do you keep your wit, intellect and freedom, or do you become my mindless slave? You can have anything you want as long as you surrender entirely, and I mean it." He licked the juice from her finger with a sly smile. "If you're my property you're to have no opinion, no thought of your own. You're to do exactly as you're told, and when you're told to do it. Only then will you be worthy enough of a seat at my table."

"No, that can't be the only way?" she begged, trying to wrench her hand free from his mighty grasp. "I've figured you out. You're not the scary monsters you'd have us believe, and you don't want us to worship at your feet. There are holes in your propaganda, lies that are slowly unraveling. You're race appreciates intellect and talent, it doesn't admonish those with it."

"Appreciate it?" He laughed loudly, making clear fun of her foolishness. "It scares us, that's why we keep those like you so close, so we can monitor you. Humans like you have been given your rewards not out of appreciation, but out of preservation. My people are so determined to rule your race entirely that we seek out those who have natural strengths and harness them for our own. What you think is your reward is simply another noose around your neck, and if you fail or abuse your gifts—that noose will be your undoing." He laughed maniacally, and she began to cry.

Kyra shot awake, and tried to stop herself from trembling. Her dreams were always fraught with her fears come to life inside her mind, but this time it seemed her subconscious had brought out more than just her doubts and fears, it'd completely opened her mind to truths she'd forced herself to ignore. She hadn't seen the Thrakorian's as puppeteers and oppressors before, but now her doubts were fully alive, and it scared the hell out of her to even consider they might be justified.

CHAPTER NINETEEN

The same human servant who'd escorted her to Thrayke's office on the first day, woke Kyra early the next morning, and was clearly trying to hide her smirk when she answered the door looking disheveled and still half-asleep.

"The Besieger would like you to join him for breakfast, Colonel," she informed her, and Kyra nodded in acceptance. "I'll wait here while you get ready."

After a shower, she felt much better, and soon her stomach was rumbling at the offering of another freshly prepared meal. She'd already started preferring the delicious home cooked dishes to the soldiers' regular meals of rations. The meal substitutes in the shape of the power bars or smoothies she'd grown used to over the years in the army were now off-putting in comparison. She followed the woman up in the elevator again, and straight into Thrayke's office. As she crossed over the threshold, Kyra saw a table filled with wondrous treats and fresh fruit, and her dream quickly came back to her. She felt uneasy, and suddenly the idea of partaking in the meal before her seemed like a bad idea. Slavery was not on her agenda, not now, not ever. Although, Thrayke had never treated her as though he wanted that kind of relationship, so she felt torn.

He welcomed her warmly, and began talking animatedly about all of the things they'd discovered, and new laws that had been implemented overnight following their success. His enthusiasm was infectious, and her mood had lifted before she'd even sat down. Kyra helped herself to sweet biscuits and fruit, and then had to try the fried eggs with bacon and cheese.

"You're first mission was by chance, but also a tremendous success. I bet you're starting to wonder where you might possibly go from here?" he asked, and she suddenly found it hard to swallow the food in her dry mouth. Was this the moment he gave her the ultimatum like she'd dreamt of, or would he be stealthier in pursuing his target than the fictitious Kronus?

"My guess is back to Alaska to complete my training?" she answered, and strangely found herself not wanting to go back. Kyra hated how mixed her feelings were towards her new life. It all seemed to be moving so fast. There were questions she had but daren't ask and they were haunting her so much it was sure to make her crazy.

Kyra knew she was in too deep. Her mind wouldn't stop questioning, or stop doubting, and she was sure it would get her into trouble sooner or later. There were parts of her that doubted the integrity of Kronus's reign, as well as admired and served it. She worshipped and adored him like a good and loyal subject, while still questioning his motives and agenda in secret. Her friend had seemingly been left barren because of the Thrakorian regime, and yet she still couldn't bring herself to believe the worst in the beings that'd ruled them through kindness rather than oppression.

"Surely you know by now you don't still belong in training?" Thrayke asked, and Kyra stared down at her hands.

"Perhaps, but I'm scared to ask what else might be available to me otherwise. I lost my chance to succeed before, and I don't want to lose it again."

"You won't," he tried to assure her.

"But what might I have to sacrifice first?" she had to ask the question, and still couldn't bring herself to meet his gaze.

"To become an elite officer you must first prove yourself worthy, but to become Gentry? That's a status afforded only to those so loyal to the crown that they are no longer one being, but part of a whole. If you accept it, you must willingly forgo friends, family, time for yourself and your basic needs," he said, leaning closer. "But in doing so, you'll open up a world of knowledge, rewards, and limitless possibilities. The list goes on. If that's something you can do, then accept. I can guarantee the day of reckoning will come, and you'd do best to ensure you're on the winning side of the divide when it does." The sinister promise came as a shock, but Kyra hoped he simply meant it as forewarning of potential changes ahead. Those humans in higher standings would surely fare better than those further down the pecking order in the event of further chaos to their current rule. Just like on Invasion Day when Silas's family had been cared for, while she was left to die in the slums with her slovenly parents. She wondered if perhaps another cull might come, and knew she'd rather be where she was now than where she'd been last time.

"But what price must I pay? Do I have to become a mindless soldier, or a forced subservient in order to attain my place among you and your Gentry? I cannot hide behind pretense or lies, I need you to tell me honestly," Kyra said, and she could feel herself caving. "What do you want from me?"

Thrayke seemed to respect that she was no longer interested in word games or politics. Playing nice had brought them here, but she needed answers or else she might just be tempted to walk away. His expression turned from that of a man looking upon a gift he admired, to one he craved.

"Isn't it obvious? I want you, Kyra." He reached forward and took her hand in his. "I want you to be mine, but not at the cost of your freedom or your integrity. I want you to come to me willingly, and know that the rewards you are given are for your service, rather than my personal interests. I want you to accept this, and know there are no caveats." Thrayke took the final badge she could ever wear from his pocket and handed it to her. "Your companionship is my reward, but I want it voluntarily, and I'm willing to wait. Until then, I'll settle for us being friends. How does that sound?"

Kyra stared down at the unthinkable rank slide in her hand. At only twenty-two she'd just been offered the position of General, and knew she would likely be one of the youngest humans to ever have been awarded it. Thrayke clearly wanted her to stay, but seemed intent on there being no direct asking price for her promotion. She was happy to continue being his friend, but guessed his generosity and friendliness would be short-lived if she kept him waiting too long for more.

"Have you been with human women before?" she asked, and flushed when he had to stifle his laughter. Thrayke quickly exercised control over his features, and grew serious again.

"Yes, but not many, and not for a long time. I don't have the same aversion to your race as some others of my kind do, and I'm willing to show you how much I care if you give me the opportunity. Don't hide your naivety, Kyra. It's part of the reason I find you so endearing," he told her, and she tried her best to shake the unease in her gut. Her dream was still in her mind's eye, haunting her and affecting her ability to make a decision.

"Very well, but I need time to get used to this, and to settle in if I'm to stay. Can you give me that?" she asked, and was relieved when he nodded.

"I can give you anything you want, don't you realize that by now?"

"Of course I do, but what I need won't come from your pocket, or be a gift thanks to your standing in the army. It'll come from the kindness you've shown me, and the promises you've made. I need to trust in them," she answered, and he suddenly sat up a little straighter. "I will never become your slave, or your mistress. I will be your friend and comrade, and we'll see how things go from there. Is that acceptable?"

"Absolutely, and I wouldn't have had it any other way," he replied with a satisfied smile.

"I should've known the moment I climbed aboard that hovercraft to England that I wouldn't leave again," Kyra teased, and she swapped her old rank badge with the new one.

"Even the most astute of minds miss the obvious at times," he replied. "But what's most important is that you embrace your destiny here and strive for greatness. It's all yours for the taking, so do it."

***

Months of long days and short nights kept Kyra both busy and exhausted in the aftermath of her initial investigation into the rebel activity in L.A. but she'd already begun to love living and working in The Tower. After a short settling-in period and lots of adjustments to the formal and methodical working patterns, she was finally asked to work on cases of her own. There were both open and unsolved incidents for her to take a look at, and plenty of chances to decode data or hack into rebel computer systems, so she soon learned to thrive on the chaos rather than fear it. Hard work was good. It helped focus her mind and keep her thoughts from overwhelming her, and all the while she had her friendship with Thrayke that was blossoming in the background of her day-to-day workload.

Thanks to a bout of rebel activity in Eastern Europe, the Besieger and his vast army of Thrakorian soldiers were busy traveling back and forth between locations across the continent. Kyra had started to look forward to his return from operations, and was always eager to sit and eat a meal with him, while he caught her up on the outside world she'd already begun to lose touch with. Thrayke often brought back oddities he found on his travels and somehow knew she'd find fascinating, like strange delicacies, souvenirs, and photographs of the ancient ruins she'd heard about but never seen. She would pore over them while he told her about the mission, and she'd given up trying to hide the fact that she truly enjoyed his company.

He remained true to his word and never pushed her, but even she could tell that they were slowly crossing that void between friends and lovers, and was surprised it didn't scare her more. Kyra hadn't let anyone in since Silas, and had never even considered that she might fall for a Thrakorian. Her crush on King Kronus had stemmed from a childish fixation she'd never been able to shake, but with Thrayke things were very different. He treated her like an equal, and in his company she soon forgot she was a member of the inferior race only distantly related to their highly evolved one. Thrayke regarded her as a woman, but never the weaker sex, and he'd not once belittled or tried to control or manipulate her like Silas had.

"I want to take you out tomorrow," he told her one evening over ice cream, a welcome indulgence she'd never thought she'd have the chance to taste. "I've cleared your schedule, and authorized the excursion." Thrayke seemed a little uneasy, but she decided against questioning his cryptic invitation.

"Well in that case…" Kyra left the *"I have no choice,"* unsaid, but watched him with a smile so he knew she wasn't displeased with his offer. "Where are we going?" she added, but he shook his head.

"You'll see," was all he answered, and leaned forward to pour her more wine.

The next morning, she was woken early by one of Thrayke's minions, and directed to a small hovercraft in the same dock she'd arrived in. She climbed aboard, and saluted both the Thrakorian soldiers and their master, who each nodded in response. In public, she and Thrayke maintained a professional relationship, and even behind the doors of his office they still hadn't strayed out of the realms of friendship. The small craft took to the air, and within minutes they were travelling through the heavily fortified city of London and it's numerous Thrakorian skyscrapers, and then out the other side into the fields and dense forests that'd been left to grow wild over the past eighteen years.

Kyra stared in awe, and caught Thrayke watching her from the front of the craft with a sly smile. He knew she'd love to travel the world, and even a small escape from the urban density of the city was a welcome change of scenery. Her cheeks burned as she contemplated just how well she'd let him get to know her during her time in The Tower, and she smiled to herself.

Before long the craft slowed, and they landed by a small cluster of buildings hidden amongst the trees. Just she and Thrayke disembarked, and Kyra peered up at him in surprise, but was sure to remain quiet rather than question him.

"Follow me," he ordered, and took off towards the largest of the buildings without another word. Kyra did as he commanded, but when two human nurses and what looked like a team of Thrakorian scientists greeted her at the door, she started to panic. She had hoped Thrayke was taking her on a date, but now her elation at having left the confines of the city was quickly subsiding.

"What is this place?" she asked him quietly, but he shook his head to silence her. Kyra wanted to run, but instead her loyal bones and muscles followed his orders, regardless of her desperation for answers. While her mind tried in vain to figure out what was going on, her deceitful body walked down the corridor after the nurses in silence.

"Please undress and put on the gown provided," one

nurse said when they reached a small room, and she ushered Kyra inside. Thrayke came in with her, and when they were finally alone he wrapped her in his arms in an attempt to soothe her fears. She fought his grip though, and felt tears pricking at her eyes.

"You need to tell me what's going on right now," she snarled as quietly as she could, and pulled away from his hold. "What is this place, and why did you bring me here?" The powerful Thrak suddenly paled and sighed as though regretful, but she couldn't let herself feel sorry for him. He should've told her the truth the night before, and every second that ticked by in his silence was agony. Were they going to hurt her? Do strange procedures, or run tests? Kyra threw herself at him and pounded on Thrayke's chest with her fist in her first ever show of defiance toward him. "Tell me why we're here, dammit!" her words seemed to shock him from his reverie, and he peered down into her eyes solemnly.

"We're here because they're going to cure you," he whispered. Kyra guessed her scowl must've given away her confusion, because he quickly explained himself further. "We've figured out how to isolate the malfunctioning codes in human DNA that make your kind weaker, and we've corrected them. I took samples from you, and the scientists have created a serum specifically for your genetic code. They're going to cure you of any illnesses you might ever have developed, and stop the aging issue."

"Aging issue?" her voice was hoarse. While she was surprised and even amazed by the wondrous scientific advances they'd made, she was still angry that he'd deceived her.

"After today you're aging will slow, like ours," he said, and cupped her cheek with his palm. "You'll live for another five or six hundred years." Thrayke leaned in and kissed her, and in her shock Kyra didn't resist him. It'd been so long since she'd had physical affection, and she needed a show of his now if she were to even consider accepting this strange gift.

"Why me?" she asked when Thrayke finally let her go. "Are all Gentry humans getting this serum?"

"No, it's still in the early stages. You've been handpicked to receive the treatment, but you're classed as a test-subject."

"Test-subject?" her anger was rising again, and her mind was suddenly alive with all the ways in which this might go horribly wrong. "What if something happens? What if I react badly or the serum doesn't work?"

"You won't. The serum is one hundred percent effective, Kyra." She took a step back and peered out of the huge window at the lush grounds all around them. Birds were flying in and out of the bushes and trees, and they mesmerized her while she tried to process her frenzied thoughts.

"Will it hurt?" she eventually asked, and already knew she was conceding.

"No, but it'll take a while, and you'll most likely have a tough time while you're body is adapting to the genetic changes. Your brain will struggle to process its organic rebirth, but once you're on the other side, it'll function at an even higher capacity than before." Thrayke came close behind her and leaned down to offer her a soft kiss on the neck, and Kyra welcomed his touch again. She leaned back into him and sighed. "I'm not promising you perfection, but I can promise you're one of very few human's who've been offered this procedure. I can't give you love, marriage or a family, but I can offer you your health and a long life. I guarantee we'll have a lot of fun together, and I'll never hurt you." Kyra wondered how she'd gotten in so deep without realizing it, but also knew there was no going back. She wanted what Thrayke was offering, and when his lips pressed against her neck again to deliver another tender kiss, she knew she'd already accepted.

"I guess I'd better get dressed then?" she replied, and slowly began removing her clothes. He stepped outside while she changed and ditched her glasses, and after she'd taken a few deep breaths, Kyra let the team of scientists and nurses back in.

Thrayke stood on the periphery while they got ready, clearly not wanting them to know why he had chosen Kyra to receive the serum, and she wondered how they'd chosen their test subjects thus far. While she pondered, a nurse instructed her to lie back on the bed and hold out her hand. When she hesitated, the young woman touched her shoulder with a light and clearly practiced bedside manner.

"This is just an IV. It'll be connected to a drip so that you're properly hydrated during the administration period."

"Will it be bad?" Kyra had to ask, and the woman pursed her lips. She was clearly annoyed that her patient didn't already know all of the facts, but they clearly weren't about to hold-off on her treatment now that everyone was present and ready to continue—even if she wasn't fully prepared.

"You'll sleep a lot, and when lucid you'll be hazy. Most patients have hallucinations and blank spots in their memory, but some others let their fears come to life and overwhelm them. Try to stay calm, otherwise we will be forced to restrain you, but I promise that by the time you come down from the final dose, you'll feel absolutely wonderful."

Without another word she pushed the needle into Kyra's vein and connected her to the IV. Another needle was then pressed into her neck via a pressurized gun, and she knew the first dose had already been administered.

Within seconds, her vision started to blur and her body ached from head to toe. The twinge started dull, but then radiated outward from inside her bones, and she began to fidget. The nurse wrapped the hand with the IV needle inside in gauze, and then secured her arm in place using a thick belt. It reminded Kyra of an old horror movie she'd watched when she was younger, in which a young woman went crazy and was strapped to a table, while doctors gave her a lobotomy.

The men and women watching over her didn't move or speak while the nurse completed her initial treatment, but she watched them in fear, scared they might be about to do the same to her as the doctors had to the poor girl on the old screen. Kyra forced herself to calm down, and let the sane part of her still barely conscious mind rule her body. She followed the advice the nurse had just given, and refused to let her fears overwhelm her.

"Very well, there's been no adverse reaction," one of the Thrakorian scientists told the nurse with a nod, and she hated how cold he seemed towards both her and his human employee. "Administer the doses as per the schedule until all have been absorbed. We will check back periodically."

"Yes, Lorde Greegis," she replied, and Kyra watched through heavy eyes as he and his team left. She was glad. Having them stood staring at her was intimidating, and now she would be free to give into the drugs so they could do their work to her body. Thrayke took her hand as she was about to fall into a dopey sleep, and she forced herself back awake.

"Don't fight it. The serum is basically breaking you apart and then putting you back together again, but it'll be easier on you if you don't resist. I'll stay as long as I can, but I'll never be far away. I promise," he said, and kissed the back of her hand.

"It's okay, it was just the roses hugging too tight," Kyra mumbled, and he laughed. She smiled, and knew she'd just spoken what he would've considered to be nonsense, but she didn't care to tell him why she'd said it. She was staring down at her bare arm at the scar she bore there, and her mind was alive with hallucinations that she was up on that rooftop again. This time, unlike in her dreams, it felt so real. She could smell the flowers and felt the chill of the night's air on her skin. "I know you aren't real, but I'm glad you're here," she said to the fantastical King, and he grinned down at her.

"You're just a child, Kyra. I don't know why you'd ever think I could love you." When he spoke it was with such a kind expression, but nasty words, and she shook her head.

"A child can love as deeply as an adult, perhaps even more so because they don't fight their feelings. Be kind or leave me alone," she replied, and then groaned as a wave of nausea hit. The dull ache in her bones was radiating outwards again, but now the pain was escalating. Kyra felt like she was tearing apart from the inside out, and could feel herself going from hot to cold and back again in quick succession. She felt the sting of another needle in her thigh, and within seconds, blackness enveloped her. She welcomed it, and let herself fall deep into the forced slumber in the hopes that it'd be over by the time she awoke.

CHAPTER TWENTY

"There are bugs all over me, help me get them off!" Kyra screamed, and the nurse flew to her side. She grabbed Kyra's free hand and held it away from her arm, somehow having known she was about to scratch her skin clean off.

"There's nothing there, see…" Kyra looked down, and sure as she'd said, there was nothing. "You need to rest now, we're almost done," the nurse assured her with a warm smile, but Kyra wanted to scream at her that rest was impossible with all the horrific side effects the serum was causing.

"How many doses left?" she forced herself to ask instead. She was coming around, but hated the lucidity, because she knew it simply meant the next shot was imminent.

"Not many," Thrayke's voice answered her from the doorway, and the nurse backed away from Kyra's bedside. He took his usual seat by her and tried to hide his grim expression.

"What's the matter? Isn't it working?" she asked, suddenly afraid that all the hard work was going to be for nothing, but he shook his head.

"I need to go to The Tower, but I'll be back in two days—I promise. You'll have finished your treatment by then, so I want you to rest up and wait for me, okay?" The last thing Kyra wanted was for him to leave, but she knew it must be important, as he'd stayed close by the rest of her time under the care of the strange facility otherwise. She wondered just how long it'd been, and guessed three or four days, but couldn't be completely sure.

"You know where I'll be," she tried to answer nonchalantly, and guessed he saw right through her fear, but didn't call her out on it. "I'll see you in two days."

"Two days," he told her insistently, as though making sure it'd sunk in, and he kissed her forehead gently before walking away. Kyra let out a sigh, and then jumped when the nurse came over with her next dose. She'd almost forgotten she was there, and felt her cheeks burn at having been seen with Thrayke during such an affectionate moment.

"It's okay, we all know you two are seeing each other," the nurse told her. "My advice—enjoy it while it lasts." She pressed the gun to Kyra's thigh, administered her dose, and then walked away without another word.

Her vision grew hazy and her lids heavy, but she wanted to know what the nurse had meant. Kyra mumbled something, but knew nothing had come out but garbled slurs, and gave up. She let her head fall back against the hard pillow, and stared at the ceiling. Bats were flying around her lampshade, and she giggled. They turned into dragonflies and then fairies while she watched, and only when the light was hurting her weary eyes did she let them fall. Dreams of birds soon filled her darkness, and Kyra was among them, soaring through the trees and across stunning fields in search of a place to rest her tired wings. She ducked her head and ate a worm, but instead of the delicious meaty flavor she anticipated, rancid bile filled her mouth, and she woke up retching.

"Shouldn't she be through the nausea by now?" a deep voice asked a figure to Kyra's right, and the soft sound of her nurse answered in a forced sweet tone.

"Everyone is different. There are two doses left, and I'm certain it's worked. Look." Kyra felt the sheet being lifted from her thighs, and recoiled at having her bare legs shown to her visitor.

"As if I'd be interested in what's under this gown," the man's voice chastised, and Kyra quickly realized it was the same scientist that'd overseen her arrival, Lorde Greegis. His hands pressed against her skin while her eyes finally cleared from their blurry haze, and she could see he was checking where the nurse had been using the serum gun to administer her doses. "The marks have already healed, that's a good sign. Very well, I'll leave you to complete the treatment."

Kyra was glad when the door closed behind him. She pulled the sheet back over herself and held her arm out to the nurse, who quickly gave her the penultimate dose.

"See, you're stronger already," she said, patting her on the shoulder, but Kyra didn't even attempt a reply. She turned her head and stared out the window, wondering when the sky had turned purple. The pink clouds billowed across her view, and she stared at them for so long her eyes felt dry when she tried to blink. When she managed to open them again, fear gripped her gut. Two zombies stood staring in at her from the other side of the glass, each dressed as a policeman. She knew right away it was the rebels she'd caught at the terminal, and that they were long since dead.

"I'm sorry," she whispered, and began to cry.

"Don't be sorry for our deaths, be sorry for your failure," one replied. "You're failing the human race every day that you serve them…" he coughed and sputtered, spitting out rotten teeth on the ground before him, while the other scratched at an oozing welt on his cheek. She tasted bile again, but wasn't sick, and guessed there probably wasn't anything left to bring up.

"You think you're protected and respected, but they only care about what you can do for them. You're innocent, but the Thraks don't care. If you fail or disappoint them, they'll kill you," the other added.

"No, I don't believe you," she mumbled, and shook her

head as hard as she could to try and rid herself of this hallucination.

"They've given you a tremendous gift, Kyra. Ask yourself why? Slaves aren't always forced. They can be bought too. They need humans, you just need to figure out why," the first answered. The two zombies stumbled away, and Kyra was allowed just a moments peace before two more took their place.

"Look at you, Kyra. Look at what you're letting them do to you, and how much you care for those disgusting creatures. After what they did to us, how can you bear to serve these aliens?" her mother asked, and Kyra couldn't answer. She felt like she was about to explode with heat and the pain suddenly radiating from inside her chest. It made her choke and gulp deep lungful's of air, and she prayed for respite that didn't want to come.

"You can't even answer us, I always knew you'd be nothing but a disappointment," her father sneered, while Kyra gasped for air and they simply continued to stare. She wondered if they were there to watch her die, and then their sinister smiles confirmed it. They wanted to see their foolish girl perish thanks to her own stupidity, and she screamed with rage.

The bed then felt like it was shaking so hard she might fall off, but when her hands and ankles were strapped to it using the belts either side, she quickly realized it was her shaking, not the bed. Her nurse was working franticly, and all Kyra could do was watch. It was then she knew she must be dying, because she was no longer watching from atop the bed, but above it completely. She was floating higher and higher, and felt nothing but freedom. No fear or desperation filled her heart, she was simply gone, and when she watched the nurse stab a huge needle through her chest, the pain didn't even register.

She wanted to tell her to stop. There was no need to worry, she was fine and would be gone soon, but her nurse kept going. The electric shock was the first thing to register, and Kyra's cerebral form was suddenly sucked downwards. The second burst of electricity sent her crashing back into her body, and with it came pain, sickness and regret.

Kyra coughed and sputtered, and each breath was agony to lungs that'd seemingly closed during her temporary holiday. Gritty eyes peeled open, but only long enough to register the relief on her nurse's face before she fell into a deep sleep. This time there were no dreams waiting for her, or even a comprehension of time passing—just bittersweet emptiness.

**

Birds were singing somewhere, and the sound eventually pulled Kyra from her slumber. Her window was open, and the sound of chirping was so loud she was sure one must've come inside, but when she opened her eyes and took a look around, there weren't any to be found.

"You're awake," the nurse said, and Kyra turned her head to find the soft voice she now knew so well.

"So it seems," she had to whisper because of her dry throat. "Is he back yet?" she asked, and the nurse seemed to know she was asking after Thrayke.

"He did return, but was called away again I'm afraid. He'll be back in a few days, so you've got plenty of time to rest," she answered, and Kyra forced her weary muscles to move so she could sit up.

"He came back?" she asked, confused that he'd left again. She took a long drink of the water offered to her, and her body seemed to absorb and use it to heal and restore her vitality right away. Within seconds she felt better, and wondered if these were the kinds of changes she'd have to get used to now that she was on the other side of her treatment.

"Yes. You almost died, Kyra. Since then you've been asleep, and it's been almost six days."

"I guess that explains it," she answered, trying not to let it worry her that she'd been effectively comatose for almost a week.

"Explains what?" the nurse asked, and her eyes widened. "You remember?" Kyra nodded, and downed more water. She didn't want to go into detail about what she'd seen or felt towards the end of the treatment, in fact the entire week or so she'd been receiving it was one she'd happily forget entirely if she could.

With every passing minute she felt stronger, and was determined to get back up and running as soon as possible. Kyra slid to the edge of the bed and got ready to test her legs. She'd been bedbound the entire time, and while she no longer felt weak, she was sure she'd at least wobble on her first try. Surprisingly, her body was not only strong and ready to be used again, but she felt better by the second.

A shower and some fresh fruit was the next saving grace, and before she knew it her natural strength and muscle tone was back, and then some. Kyra's memory was also improving, as was her basic cognitive function. That afternoon another scientist came to her room and ran some tests on her, and she scored far higher than she had previously in even the basic skills and practices.

As far as she was aware, the treatment was a success, and she couldn't wait for Thrayke to return so she could show him the results.

The next morning, Kyra awoke to blissful silence and welcome solitude. After having her nurse nearby through the thick and thin of the treatment, she was grateful to be by herself again at last. She decided a walk was in order, and got dressed in fresh combats and a vest she found in one of the drawers. Renewed strength radiated from within already, and Kyra silently thanked her body for accepting Thrayke's gift. She knew he'd been responsible for bumping her to the top of the list for the treatment, and wondered how long she might have added to her once so short lifespan.

She tried the patio style door, hoping to go out and enjoy the sunshine, but it was locked, so instead she took off out the main door and down a long corridor. Kyra passed room after room, and all of them were empty. She wondered when or if they would be filled with other humans having the same treatment she'd had, but also considered how they wouldn't want to give this scientific advancement to just anybody. After a while, she tried another door, and felt an icy chill run down her spine the second she stepped inside. A curtain was drawn around the end bed, but she noticed a figure lying there, and had to see. When she rounded the white screen, she wished she hadn't. A dead man was lying on the bed, and his cadaver was in the middle of what looked like a post-mortem examination. Many of his organs were lying in dishes on a table to the opposite side, and his body laid open and bloody right before her eyes. Kyra's hand flew to her mouth, but she couldn't take her eyes off him. Even in her shock, she was fascinated by what she'd found, and grabbed the chart that was lying by his blue feet.

"Colonel Summers, treatment successful," she murmured as she read his information aloud. "If your treatment was successful, why are you dead, Colonel?"

"Curious little lady, aren't you?" a deep voice asked from the doorway, and Kyra turned to see the same scientist she'd had a number of run-ins with standing in the doorway. "I see you've met Colonel Summers."

"What's the meaning of this?" she asked, and threw down the chart as the huge Thrak approached. She peered up into his eyes with as much strength as she could muster. "Lorde Greegis, I'd like to know what happened to this man," she demanded, and he scowled down at her.

"I killed him," was his answer, and there wasn't even a flicker of guilt on his face when he said it, in fact she was sure she caught a smile curling at his lips. He grabbed Kyra roughly and twisted one arm behind her back as he turned her to face the dead body again. There was no way she could fight him, even with her renewed strength, so she gave in to his hold. Fear flared in her belly, and it sent her mind going over the various ways in which she might try and out-maneuver her powerful foe if he turned nasty, and she cursed her smaller size and human weaknesses.

Greegis pressed his mouth to her ear, and she shuddered as his breath fluttered along her face and neck. "Even when the trials are successful, we still like to dissect our subjects to make sure we know the full extent of this serum. We can't let you all walk away with power, health and added longevity, while you give us nothing back in return. This is a research facility, General. We procure test subjects and monitor the effects of the serum for analysis—before, during and after the treatment is complete. His organs will be tested and stored, as would yours if the Besieger hadn't forbidden it." He spoke the awful promise so slowly and eloquently it seemed even more sinister, and she shuddered.

Kyra writhed and tried to pull herself out of Greegis's hold. She hated how tightly he held her, and his words felt like ice cutting deep, dripping glaciers down her spine. The sheer thought that the trial subjects had thus far been used as nothing more than lab-rats made her want to vomit, and she was desperate to get away from both the body of her fellow candidate and Lorde Greegis as soon as possible.

"I'll tell him if you hurt me," she tried to threaten, but his laugh stopped her from saying anything more. Greegis threw Kyra down onto the ground and held her there without even breaking a sweat. He still held her wrist tightly, and started twisting. He didn't stop when the ligament tore, and he didn't stop when she screamed and begged him to. Only when a loud crack echoed through the vast room did he let go, and he stood over her with a threatening smile while Kyra curled into a ball and cradled her already rapidly swelling wrist.

"Tell Thrayke, see if I care. This is my facility, and I

promised I wouldn't kill you—nothing else. I suggest you get out of my sight before I break the other one, and stay in your room until he comes for you. If I catch you snooping around again, I'll make sure you happen upon another *accident*." Kyra didn't even look back. She forced her legs to carry her out and back down the hall. When she made it to her room, and the bathroom, she puked up everything her tense stomach had tried desperately to keep inside. The pain in her wrist was excruciating, and the broken hand lay limp by the basin while she struggled to pull herself together. Shock and terror held her captive in her trembling body, and she could barely breathe, let alone move from her position on the floor. After what felt like hours spent curled around the toilet, she managed to stand, and cleaned herself up before climbing into bed.

The pain was miraculously easing already, and she inspected her wrist, expecting to find a completely useless limb that'd take weeks to heal. Instead, the bones were already beginning to fuse back together. The swelling had gone down, and the bruises were clearing. She fell into an exhausted sleep while her new and improved body continued to work its magic, and when she awoke, Thrayke's smiling face eased every one of her fears and doubts. She didn't care if he'd known the truth all along about what was going on in this facility, he'd kept her away from the same fate as the other subjects, and she would be eternally grateful.

"Hey sleepyhead," he said, and took her hand in his. Kyra was glad it was her good hand, and sat up so she could properly greet him. When she moved the broken wrist, she was surprised to find there wasn't any pain, and looked down at it in surprise. It was completely healed, and she bet Lorde Greegis would've known that when he'd done it. She'd never doubted his intellect, but this display of cunning wickedness made anger flare from within. There was nothing to show Thrayke, no injury or even a simple bruise or weakness. Greegis had known she'd have no proof to show her powerful friend of her mistreatment while recuperating in the facility.

"Hey yourself," she replied, forcing her angst away. It was no use clinging to her hatred of the evil scientist, so she pushed aside her fears in preference of focusing on the good and not the bad. "I hope you're here to take me home?" He seemed surprised by her forwardness, but Kyra wanted out of this facility as soon as possible, so would do whatever it took to ensure Thrayke didn't leave without her again.

"I need to check your charts first, but if Greegis gives you the all-clear, we'll be back in The Tower by nightfall." He kissed the palm of her hand, and then leaned into her. "I'm glad you made it through. I could tell the treatment was hard on you, but you did it. You're one of the first humans to have had the serum, and it's a secret project. When we return you're to say you were deployed to another area temporarily."

"Anything you say, boss," she replied playfully, and was happy to go along with whatever story he wanted if it kept them both safe from others like Greegis. Kyra wanted him to see how well she was feeling, even if she had to fake it a little, and it seemed to be working. Thrayke grinned broadly and helped her up off the bed. He looked her up and down, as though making sure she was still whole, but also seemingly checking to see if he could spot the improvements. She wouldn't tell him how she'd discovered the extra healing abilities already, so simply strutted her way over to the bathroom to brush her teeth and hair so he could see for himself that she was capable of going about her business without any help.

Kyra stared at her reflection in the mirror, and was surprised how well she looked, considering only hours before she'd uncovered some terrible truths about her serum and its inventor. Her skin was bright, as were her eyes and teeth. Her dark hair was shiny and smooth, with just the right amount of volume. She'd kept her short bob, and loved how easy it was to take care of. A quick stroke of the brush and it was good to go, and she followed it with her usual routine of moisturizer and a little mascara. It was then that Kyra realized she hadn't worn her glasses in days. The case lay on the counter by her toiletries, and she left it there. If the serum had corrected her eyesight, then it was just another reason why it'd been worth it, so she would happily get used to having benefits such as perfect skin, hair, and vision.

When she was ready, she walked back out to meet Thrayke and took his hands in hers, before climbing up onto her tiptoes to kiss him. He seemed impressed, and kissed her back passionately. "Did you notice I'm not wearing my glasses?" she asked him, and he nodded.

"Yep. I like Kyra-two-point-oh very much, even her ass is cuter," he teased, and she giggled. "Let's get some air," Thrayke then offered, and he led her over to the huge glass door. She went to tell him it was locked, but they opened without any issue, and she wordlessly cursed Greegis again for his successful game playing. Kyra wondered if he'd led her out through the corridor on purpose, and thought that maybe he'd wanted her to find Colonel Summers's body. Perhaps it was his sick way of ensuring she truly knew her life had been spared by her friend in high places, and still only with Greegis's permission.

They walked out into the sunny garden, and she tilted her face upwards to let the rays warm her skin. Kyra closed her eyes and let Thrayke lead her, completely trusting him to keep her safe, and they slowly wandered a few feet into the meadow. His words from before her treatment returned, and Kyra found herself thinking about the promises he'd made.

"You did all of this for me, Thrayke, but you don't love me, or want a future together?" He came to a stop and sat down on the lush grass. Kyra joined him, and then followed suit when he leaned back and stared up into the clouds thoughtfully.

"I've never been in love, Kyra. I've had relationships, but they've never lasted more than a few months, so I've gotten used to being alone. You're the first woman I've worked with that I've developed feelings for, and I love that we've let ourselves move slowly, but I can't envision us going further than where we are now." He let out a deep sigh. "Modern-day Thraks simply don't fall for humans. In fact, many of us make fun of those who came here centuries ago and fell in love with their concubines. I'm not ashamed to be with you, but I don't know if I can offer you more…"

"It's okay," she answered, and climbed into his arms. Kyra loved that he wrapped himself around her tightly, and let herself relax in his hold. It was a welcome relief to let the rest of the world fall away for a few minutes, and she listened to the thundering heart hammering in his chest. "I don't know if I want more either, so let's just have fun and see where this world takes us. Thanks to you I have a long life ahead of me as well, so there's no need to rush. How old are you anyway?" she had to ask, and peered into his face, taking him in. Thrayke had just a few wrinkled lines on his face, and a tiny sprinkling of silver to his dark blonde hair. He was freshly shaven as always, and smelled of lavender and bergamot, or perhaps it was the garden, she couldn't be sure.

"I'm three hundred and twenty," he answered, and ran his hand over her cheek into her hair. His piercing blue eyes bore into hers, and she was instantly mesmerized.

"You look older," she teased, and loved the grin he gave her in response.

"It's called 'war-hardened,' but you'd know nothing about that, you're just a baby," he joked in response, and Kyra pouted.

"Did you have wars on Thrakor? I didn't think it was volatile there?"

"It's not, but the other planets we've colonized weren't always so easy to conquer as Earth." He shrugged unapologetically when she slapped him on the arm, and she had to admit it must've been relatively easy on Invasion Day. "I've served King Kronus for fifty years, but before that I was assigned to his father's Guard Service, and was on the first wave of harbingers each time we took a planet for the Princes or Princesses to rule."

"I guess it was a welcome relief when you were offered the role of Besieger? How many siblings does King Kronus have anyway?" she asked, and was glad he was being so open about his monarchs and their history.

"Sixteen. He's the youngest, so yes. To be allowed to settle here permanently was a reward for my service. Seeking out and crushing the rebels brings me a joy I can't even begin to express. We are a reasonable and peaceful race, but we're also predatory. Hunting is a serious sport on Thrakor, and when we're wronged—there's no mercy." His expression turned wistful, and Kyra guessed he must have been relishing in some memory she couldn't quite understand the joy of, but hoped his hunting instincts might be something she could come to appreciate.

She was proud of her work with the Intelligence Division, but hadn't had to fight or kill in the line of duty, and didn't want to. Kyra still felt guilty at having those two rebel's deaths on her soul, and wondered if she'd ever be able to forgive herself for that loss of human life. No matter the pride in her work or the knowledge that she'd been right to stop them, it was all still a bittersweet victory. Whereas for Thrayke, guilt seemed like it wasn't even a factor, and she actually envied him for it.

She could hear the air filling and leaving his lungs, and the rhythmic sound lulled her into a happy and relaxed state. The craziness of the past few weeks was left behind, and despite them still being at the facility, that too felt blissfully far away.

"Where were you on Invasion Day?" she asked, and snuggled deeper into his hold.

"I invaded Europe. The Tower of London was an

unfortunate hit, but unavoidable as the human parliament were hiding out inside it in an attempt to escape. During my reconnaissance visits, I'd always visited England, and while I hated destroying vast areas of it, I enjoyed taking control and building things anew. The Tower was my creation, hence why I insisted I live there and keep a team of my most valued advisors within its walls."

"Whoa, that's incredible," she replied, and stared off at the tree in the distance. "I was in Los Angeles. My parents were killed in the blast and I was taken into foster care. The rest, as they say, is history, but I always knew I wanted to serve." No matter how close they'd gotten, she still couldn't find it in her to tell him the truth about the roses and Kronus's treatment of her that night. She wondered if she'd ever tell another soul about it, or keep it with her until the day she died, whenever that might be.

"I saw your file. Even through school you excelled in computer science, and I'm pleased you had a strong ambition to enlist. The Intelligence Division is where you belong, not the L.A. slums." Thrayke kissed the top of her head, while Kyra wrapped her arms tighter around him.

"Forgive the intrusion, sir," a voice them chimed from a few yards away, and she looked up to see one of Thrayke's soldiers standing to attention in wait for his superior's reply. He was clearly uncomfortable, and she wondered if he'd been the unlucky soul who'd drawn the short straw, and had to be the one to disturb them.

"What is it, Sentinel?" he asked, but didn't let go of Kyra right away. He took his time releasing her, and it was a surprise, because normally he wouldn't show her any care or affection in front of the others if he could help it. They both stood and she quickly saluted the Thrakorian soldier. No matter her rank in the human army, any Thrakorian was classed as above her and deserved her respect.

"Good morning, General Millan," he said with a smile, and then turned back to Thrayke. "We're needed back at The Tower. Some time-sensitive intel has been sent in from Bangkok, and the soldiers are on their way to rendezvous with us in London now."

"Very well," he replied, and turned to Kyra. "I have to go, I'll send the ship back for you in a few days."

"No, I'm coming," she insisted. There was no way she was going to stay behind, absolutely not. "I can recuperate at home from now on, and I'm certain I no longer need to stay here. Please." She knew she was downright begging, but also that she'd get on her knees and beg harder if that was what it took to get her on that craft. The sheer thought of staying behind in Lorde Greegis's care made her want to cry, and Thrayke seemed to sense it. He stepped closer and spoke quietly in her ear.

"Why don't you want to stay? Has something happened?" He was bristling with anger, and she forced herself to smile and shrug off her worry.

"I just want to come home, that's all," she assured him, and Thrayke nodded, but didn't seem completely convinced. He took her hand and led her back to the facility, where she packed her things while he cleared her discharge with the scientists. Lorde Greegis wasn't pleased, and insisted they give her a once over before they left, much to Kyra's dismay. He was rough with the needles as he drew her blood, and lacked any bedside manner when he poked and prodded at her, but in the end she didn't care.

Climbing aboard the hovercraft was one of the best moments of her life, and she didn't look back. By the time they were airborne and on their way back to London, the tense fear snaking in her gut had subsided, and a genuine smile was on her lips. Home was good. It meant safety and security, work and routine—and she couldn't wait.

CHAPTER TWENTY-ONE

Despite her elation at having left the facility behind, being back at The Tower also meant Thrayke was too busy to spend time with her. He was off with his Thai-based comrades being filled in on whatever it was they'd discovered there. He had to keep the details quiet though, and was his usual secretive self with cases she wasn't working on, but Kyra could understand his reasons for not letting her get involved. It would be seen as a huge indiscretion on his part to allow a human officer, even Gentry, knowledge of a case she had no business working on, so she never pried, and Thrayke seemed to appreciate it.

After a few days of quiet solace in her room, she took a walk and ended up on the roof of the huge skyscraper. It was cold and windy atop The Tower, but the view was fantastic, and Kyra loved the thrill of being so high up. She stood there for a while, until the cold started getting to her, and then climbed the stairs all the way down to her floor, rather than take the elevator. She then headed to the gym, canteen and back to her room again, and by that point had decided it was time she returned to work. Boredom was not what she'd signed up for, and she set her alarm for early the next morning.

Kyra went for a run and had a power bar for breakfast, and then went back to work. Starting with simpler tasks, she set about catching up on mail and any leads regarding her current cases. With fresh eyes she was able to spot new clues, and knew her heightened brainpower was thanks to her treatment more than the respite. Kyra was soon absorbed in her work, and quickly spotted flaws in the systematic code-breaking skills she'd previously used. She suddenly knew better than to stick with the simple methods and protocol, and let her mind wander. It wasn't long before she found connections she had astonishing explanations for, but they were there, and the logic worked in decoding the clues based on her findings.

By the next evening she'd discovered what she thought might be a new coding system being used by the rebels, and sent a request to the Besieger's office asking for a meeting with him to discuss her breakthrough. During working hours she always maintained her professionalism, and knew Thrayke appreciated her going via the right channels in requesting a meeting with him. Their private lives were nobody else's business, and she was as keen as he was to make sure it stayed that way.

The following afternoon she had a reply from Thrayke's secretary, and was invited to visit his office an hour later. Kyra accepted, and then got back to work. She re-checked her data and by the time she was heading upwards in the elevator to see him, was convinced her findings were correct.

"I didn't know you'd gone back to work?" he asked when she'd shut the door behind her, and she could tell he was angry at not having been informed of her movements.

"I didn't know you were back from Thailand," she countered, and watched as he dropped his dominant façade and regarded her with a smirk. "Laying low in my room just wasn't for me, I needed to get away from those four walls."

"I don't blame you," he said. Thrayke beckoned her over to him, and she stepped into his outstretched arms. "It's good to see you busy. The spark is back in your eyes, and I can see you're excited about something. What is it?"

"I think I've cracked one of their symbols, not just the

use of it, but what it actually means." Kyra stepped back and peered up at Thrayke with a smile. "I think this could be something groundbreaking."

"Show me everything you've got," he answered, and they both quickly slid back into work mode. Kyra laid out her files on the desk and showed him a symbol much like the others they'd found around the rebel-infested areas. These markings had been spotted all across the world, and each time the soldiers had tried to figure out where they'd led, the trail had gone cold.

"They aren't directions or markers like we've normally seen," she told him. "They're an invitation."

"How?" Thrayke asked, and she could tell he was excited by the possibility of her being right.

"The variations aren't directional, they're a code. None of our computers could crack it, and I thought for a minute I might've been wrong, but then I considered they might be using more primitive approaches to confuse the technological code-breaking equipment. I spent all night going through every possibility imaginable, and came up with this," she said, and handed him a scribbled sheet with her workings out on. To anyone who didn't know the codes or systems used by their Division, it would've seemed like a mess of numbers and letters, but as he read it Thrayke's eyes widened. He looked back across at her, and positively beamed.

"They're coordinates and dates."

"Yes," she agreed, and showed him her clearer sheet of answers. "All across the world on different dates. I think these are invitations for people to join them, and now we know where and when."

"I need to take this to the Chief of Defense, Kyra. This is big," he replied.

"Told you," she said, and squealed in surprise when he yanked her across the table and into his lap. "Why, Besieger Thrayke, this is rather inappropriate behavior, don't you agree?"

"I don't care," he replied, and his mouth locked over hers. She was up in his arms before she even knew what was going on, and in his bedroom seconds later. This was it, the moment they went from casual attraction to something more, but Kyra was more than ready to take that leap at last. "I've waited a long time for this," he murmured against her lips as he placed her gently on the bed.

"Then don't wait a minute longer," she answered, and he didn't.

***

Early the next morning, Kyra stirred and opened her eyes to look out the window at the incredible view from Thrayke's top-floor apartment. She was surprised to find him standing there, staring out at the city around them, and she drank in the sight of him. His muscles were defined and rock-solid, and every contour of his body was perfect. Thrayke was a powerful and strong man, but a gentle one too, and she smiled when she thought back to their night together the evening before. She could see him better in the dawn light, and had a clearer view of the array of nasty scars over his back. They were deep, and went all the way from his neck to his thighs in clusters of lined scrapes. Kyra watched him for a while, and saw the beauty in him regardless of those scars, just like he seemed to have done with hers.

"Morning," Thrayke said, and turned to look back at her with a knowing smile.

"It sure is," she replied, and took a long stretch. Her body felt amazing, like she'd unwound in ways she hadn't even realized she'd needed, and she was surprised by how awake she felt after just a couple of hours sleep. She climbed out of bed and pulled on her shirt, and then padded over to join him by the huge window. Kyra felt light as a feather, and floated around him so she stood between Thrayke and the thick glass. She then pressed her back into his stomach while he rested his chin on the top of her head. "You're up early?"

"I don't sleep much, plus I love to watch the sunrise," he answered, running his hands up and down her arms. "And I had important work to do. I've sent a message to the Chief of Defense asking for a meeting, and hopefully he'll see us today."

"Us?" she asked, feeling sure she shouldn't be present during a meeting with the highest-ranking Thrakorian officer below the King, but Thrayke nodded.

"Of course. This is your discovery, Kyra. You deserve full recognition if your theory is correct," he told her, and she trembled against a cold chill that swept down her spine from out of nowhere. The last of her visions during her treatment suddenly returned, and she remembered the warning the dead rebels had given her. She knew they weren't real, but still the message was from somewhere deep within her psyche, and it'd warned her to be careful of being too good at her new job. She wondered at what point her inquisitive mind might be deemed a threat rather than a useful tool at their disposal, and hoped having Thrayke on her side would help prevent those questions being asked of her if they ever arose. He had stopped her from being dissected in the Thrakorian lab after her treatment, and she had to believe he would do it again if her integrity were ever called into question.

"Will you take care of me?" she asked timidly, and gasped when he turned her to face him in one quick and effortless move.

"Of course I will, but why would you ever think you might need protecting?" he demanded, and pulled her close. His lips caressed her neck, and then lingered of one of her scars from the rose thorns. "Where did you get these scars?" he whispered against the silver mark.

"On Invasion Day," she answered bluntly, and then peered up into his eyes in search of answers. She had to trust him, she knew that, but she also needed to know he wasn't keeping her safe just for his own personal thrill. She had to trust he truly believed in her as a soldier and code-breaker, and so would warn her if she ever crossed the line and became a target. "I often feel like there are things I'm not seeing, Thrayke. Important things. I can't know everything, I get that, but I need to know that you'll keep me safe from harm, no matter what happens. Like you did with Greegis."

"You know about that?" He seemed genuinely shocked by her admission.

"Yes, and sometimes I'm scared of being under another magnifying glass in case…"

"In case of what? You're seen as a threat rather than an asset?" he asked, and then leaned in closer. "You can talk to me openly."

"It's something like that, yes," Kyra admitted, and Thrayke sighed, but didn't deny the possibility that it could happen. For the first time she let herself say aloud some of the things she'd wondered throughout the years, and hoped she could trust him not to freak out or cart her off in chains for talking like a rebel. "I often wonder if the human race wasn't just colonized on Invasion Day. The weakest were wiped out, and those incapable of change followed slowly after, because of their resistance. Those humans weren't wanted or needed in our new society, so an evolution of sorts stepped in. Only the strongest survived." Thrayke nodded in understanding, but stayed quiet while she finished her thought, and she was glad. Part of her wondered how she even had the nerve to speak her doubts aloud for the first time, and it was painfully ironic that she was saying them to a Thrakorian. "What's left is now a living, breathing civilization, working for survival and under one goal—to serve our King."

"And?" he asked, leaning even closer as though he might be bracing himself for what she was going to say next.

"I can't help but wonder if perhaps freedom is really just an illusion? We've been conditioned for the past eighteen years to serve willingly, but what if it's a lie? I know you can't tell me yes or no, but I guess I just hope that the day I do discover the truth, I'll be on the right side of the great divide—whatever that might be."

"I'd make sure of it. I'll never let anything bad happen to you, I promise. Don't doubt your safety ever again. I swear I'll protect you, on my honor," he replied, and climbed down onto one knee. She'd heard about their solemn oaths, but had never seen a Thrak give one before, especially not to a human, and she choked on her acceptance of his immense pledge.

They were back in bed before she could say another word, and Kyra felt on top of the world. Thrayke showed her just how much she meant to him, despite his previous promises of offering her nothing more than a bit of fun. She loved whiling away the hours with him while the sun crept up over the city and everyone below them got to work, but they were in no rush to leave the comfort and warmth of each other's arms.

**

"Did you have a run-in with some barbed wire?" Thrayke asked later, and he ran his hands over some of the scars on her back. Kyra shook her head no, and looked up into his eyes from where she lay on his huge chest.

"Thorns. I got tangled in a bush trying to escape the fighting, and they cut me," she answered, and still couldn't tell the rest of the story, regardless of how strongly she felt about him. "What about you? Where did you get your scars?"

"Various battles," he told her with a thoughtful sigh. "The worst were after I fought a huge beast on the planet Prothas, now ruled by Kronus's sister, Queen Digrea. It plucked me right off the ground, and dragged me across sharp rocks in its talons." She gasped loudly, unable to hide her shock, but Thrayke just smiled and carried on with his tale. "The animal was intent on eating me for dinner, and it very nearly did. My back was left in pieces, but I had enough strength to finish the beast off before it could devour me. I was fortunate to be alive, and took many days to heal. Some of the wounds were as deep as the bone, but now I feel no pain thanks to the marvels of our medicine."

"You were very lucky," she said, and watched him in awe. He'd mentioned wars and battles before, but never in great detail, and she appreciated him telling her a little more about his past. "Do you have a family back on Thrakor?" she then asked before she could stop herself, and he let out a gruff laugh.

"Yes, but only my parents and siblings. I'm not married or betrothed, if that's what you were wondering," Thrayke teased, and although he was exactly right, Kyra shook her head in defiance.

"No, it was an innocent question. I want to know more about you," she replied, and giggled when he pulled her up for another deep kiss.

"Ask me anything and I shall answer truthfully," he told her, and she believed him. Before she could ask anything else though, their conversation was interrupted by an incoming call to his personal line.

"I'll remember that in the future," she said while he jogged over to his desk, and Thrayke gave her a wink before grabbing the handset from its dock.

"Besieger Thrayke," he answered sternly, and Kyra was careful to remain silent while he took the call. "Yes, sir. Of course." He listened intently to the caller, and then looked over at her with a smile. "Absolutely. I'll send for General Millan now, and we'll be with you in under an hour."

He hung up and then dialed his secretary. "I need a hovercraft ready in fifteen minutes," he told her, and then hung up before she could ask any questions.

"Nothing like being direct," Kyra joked, and then jumped out of bed and into the shower before he had the chance to respond. She was in and out in less than five minutes, and was almost ready to go by the time Thrayke had done the same and came out in search of his combats. "So, we're going to see the Chief?" she asked, tying her boots, and he nodded.

"He wants to see what we've got, and he wants you to explain how you got there. This is good, so don't be afraid," he told her, clearly still thinking back to their conversation earlier that morning. "Chief Rasmos is scary, but only when you're on his bad side, so stay an open book and you'll be fine." Kyra shook her head, and tried to ignore the somersaults going on in her stomach. "One word of advice—if you thought the Inquisitor's were bad, he's their master. He knows everything about every Division, so do not underestimate his knowledge for a second, and you'll be fine."

"Easier said than done," she replied, and rolled her eyes playfully.

***

Ten minutes later, Kyra and Thrayke were onboard a small hovercraft headed west to a region of skyscrapers dedicated entirely to the Chief of Defense and his team. As per normal protocol, Thrayke sat in the front of the ship while she was in the back, and Kyra hated being without him, but it also gave her a chance to go over her findings again. She was surer than ever after another look, and spent the rest of the journey watching the handful of Thrakorian guards that accompanied them. Kyra guessed they were for Thrayke's protection, but also found herself wondering if they might also be there as supervisors of the human guest.

When they arrived, the small team was shown to a huge meeting room, where Thrayke and Kyra were offered a seat and asked to wait for the Chief to arrive. There wasn't another human in sight, and part of her guessed her assumptions might not have been so far fetched. They were clearly not entirely comfortable having her there, but she couldn't understand why. Perhaps they maintained a strictly non-human base for the Chief's operations, but then why would he ask her here? Kyra forced her questions away, and remain silent and poised, and ready to meet with the infamous man.

Ten Thrakorian soldiers of high ranks soon filed in, followed quickly by a grey-haired and incredibly hardened soldier. Kyra knew right away he must be Rasmos, the Chief of Defense. He greeted them, took his seat at the head of the table, and immediately started firing questions at Thrayke. Kyra remained silent, waiting to be spoken to or asked a question, but he never did. She sat there feeling like a spare part the entire meeting, and like a small child in comparison to all the mightily huge Thraks seated around her.

"The theory is sound, now we need to decide how best to proceed," Thrayke finished, and the Chief went quiet. Kyra had noticed Rasmos thought nothing of holding long silences while he made a decision, and she sat watching him while he seemed to be going over the information in his head.

"I need to take council," he finally answered, and looked past Kyra to the other Thraks seated around the table. "What do you suggest?"

"Airborne missile attacks on each area at the given date and time. That'll show those foul humans we're onto them, and have them running back into hiding again, rather than trying to recruit from right under our noses," one offered, and the others nodded in agreement.

"We can send in mercenaries to pose as inductees and take them out during the meeting?" another chimed, and before long they were all discussing the best ways in which they might attack the rebels during the next gathering of potential recruits for the cause.

The group brainstormed for hours, and not once was her opinion asked for. Kyra listened to the huge men go on and on, and all the while she waited in vain for one of them to at least offer her the chance to contribute. She soon began to wonder what she was even doing there, and was more than grateful when Chief Rasmos called a halt to the meeting.

"We'll meet back here in two hours," he told them, and stood. Each of the others climbed to their feet and saluted as he left, and Kyra made sure she stood to attention until a few seconds after all but her entourage of guards had gone. Thrayke didn't even look back as he walked away, and although she knew he was keeping their cover, anger surged from within. She felt like a child. She'd been treated like a useless accompaniment to their meeting, and all while the man who'd sworn to take care of her had let it happen.

Suddenly feeling hot and in need of fresh air, she stormed from the room. Kyra climbed the steps to the roof and didn't even bother to check whether her wardens had followed. She felt more like a prisoner than a guest, and tried to fathom why Chief Rasmos had even bothered insist she attend the meeting with Thrayke. None of them valued her opinion, or had even asked for it, so her journey was a waste of time and resources.

Kyra stood looking out at the clear sky for over an hour. She pieced together all of the conversations she'd had with Thrayke regarding her findings, and what she'd heard during the Thrakorian only brainstorming session. Part of her began to wonder if he'd taken the credit for her discovery, but she couldn't understand why he too had insisted she come if that were the case.

A loud whirring sound soon pulled Kyra from her thoughts, and she looked up to find a large hovercraft looming over the building's peak. She and the handful of guards she'd almost forgotten about each moved to the outer edge of the roof, and she watched as the craft slowly descended before landing smoothly.

Chief Rasmos came out through the doorway. He stopped to stare at her and the others on his route to the craft, and she saw carefully controlled rage cross his usually so stoic features.

"General Millan, what are you doing up here?" he bellowed, and then shook his head. Rasmos looked back at the craft and then to Kyra again. "No matter. Salute and bow to him, but keep your gaze low, and under no circumstances do you make eye contact. Know your place, soldier. Understood?" he asked, and when she nodded he quickly resumed his course to the craft's doorway. For just a moment, Kyra wondered who might be about to step out to meet him, and it dawned on her a split-second later that it must be King Kronus who had come to meet with his Chief of Defense.

Her heart thudded in her chest, and Kyra felt herself heat from the inside out. She watched as he and Rasmos left the craft, chatting intently. Kronus ignored each of the soldiers he passed, focusing solely on his right-hand-Thrak, and when he passed her, all Kyra saw of him was his black sneakers and blue denim jeans. He wasn't wearing uniform, but then again she wondered why on Earth he ought to. None were above him in this entire world, and she didn't need Rasmos's warning to know she was incredibly far beneath him in the pecking order.

"Everyone's here, sire. We're due to resume the meeting in thirty minutes, but only with your permission?" she heard Rasmos saying to King Kronus.

"Excellent," was all Kyra could hear of their leader's response, and upon hearing his voice again every one of her memories came flooding back. Both the reminisced and the fantasized version of King Kronus came to the forefront of her mind, and just like he'd haunted her dreams since Invasion Day, it seemed he was now also intent on dominating her reality.

CHAPTER TWENTY-TWO

Kyra was the first to take her seat back in the meeting room, and was soon joined by the rest of the Thrakorian soldiers—who continued to ignore her. Thrayke came in a few minutes later, followed quickly by Chief Rasmos and eventually, King Kronus.

"The King has taken a look at the report, and isn't convinced of its legitimacy. What say you?" Rasmos addressed the room, and the gang who'd all been so quick to offer up their weapons, mercenaries and foot soldiers were suddenly having second thoughts by the sound of it, and Kyra wanted to scream at them for being such cowards. Her findings were right, and she wanted desperately to have her say at last. She was panting, pursing her lips in an attempt to keep quiet, but she knew it wouldn't be long before she had to at least try. Thrayke twitched beside her, and she couldn't stop herself from looking directly into his intense gaze, where she delivered him a soundless ultimatum. Either he said something, or she would, and he immediately stood from his seat.

"What's left to question, King Kronus?" he asked, and bowed his head to him as he spoke. Kyra watched as he opened the files again and showed him her statement, and Kronus simply shrugged.

"They're recruiting, so what?" he answered with a bored sigh. Kyra wanted to look into his face and try to understand why he'd lost all the soft yet firm passion she'd seen in him so very long ago, but forced her eyes to stay on his hands. She spied a scar on the back of his right hand, and began wondering where he'd gotten it. Perhaps it was at the same time, and by the same thorns as when she'd gotten hers? When Kronus lifted his hand to his mouth, she caught a glimpse of his dark lips and chiseled chin, and watched them for a moment, wondering if he ever smiled. She suddenly became aware that his eyes were on hers, she sensed them, and before she could control her own, her gaze met his. It was just for a second, but she knew she'd remember that beautiful and scary stare for the rest of her life.

He was the same as before, only slightly older, and much more intimidating. His dark hair extended to his stubble-covered cheeks now, and his eyes also glittered with hardness to them he hadn't had that first time. Kyra wondered if he was bored like she'd first thought, or simply unhappy. Thrayke had been lonely when they'd first met, and it'd shown. Was he lonely too? Was there anything she could even do about it if he was? Questions buzzed around in her skull at such velocity that Kyra suddenly felt exhausted, and she forced herself to concentrate on Thrayke's response to his superior's offhand response.

"I urge you, take some proper time to establish whether this could mean a real threat or not. I'm convinced of the legitimacy of General Millan's findings, as will you be, I'm sure."

Kronus took a moment to think Thrayke's plea over, and Kyra felt his gaze on her again.

"You have one minute—convince me," he told her, and she jumped in surprise. After having spent hours feeling invisible, suddenly all eyes were on her, and she had to swallow the lump in her throat before any sound could come out of her tight chest.

Kyra stood and grabbed the file, where she pulled out a photograph of the symbols and her workings out. In a brave move, she pointed to the marking while staring the

King directly in the eye. He was just a foot or so away, yet still towered over her like the behemoth extraterrestrial he was. Kronus seemed so much bigger than she remembered, but she didn't back down. She held his gaze and took a deep breath.

"If I'm, I mean *we're* right, they could already have held hundreds of these summits. As word spreads, any number of new recruits could be turning up to join their cause, and now we know when and where. This is correct, not an assumption. You will have a large-scale rebellion on your hands if you don't put a stop to it now," she told him, and Kronus smirked. He leaned closer, never once letting his gaze drop to the photograph in her hand.

"What makes you think I don't welcome a rebellion? It'll give me just the opportunity I've been looking for to skim away some of the excess population, and give my friends here the opportunity to hunt. I've been thinking how countries like India and Thailand haven't been contributing enough, so why shouldn't I use these gatherings as an opportunity to take the entire country off the map?" Kyra didn't believe him for a second, and shook her head slightly.

"If that was the case you would've followed the advice of these soldiers instead of questioning the credibility of my report," she answered, and willingly let him win their staring competition by looking to her side at the dumbstruck men at the table. As she did, a lock of her dark hair fell into her face, and she instinctively tucked it back into place behind her ear, before turning to look back up at Kronus.

"Everyone out—now," his voice boomed in the small room, and a second passed during which no one moved in their surprise. Kyra was as shocked as any of them by his strange outburst, but quickly stepped back and started towards the doorway behind the others. "Not you, General." She turned back and bumped straight into Thrayke. His frown let her know he was as unsure as she was, but he didn't say a word as he left her there. Even the Thraks guarding her were ushered out by the only word that could overrule their orders from Chief Rasmos—their sovereign's.

"King Kronus, I didn't mean to offend," she began, unsure of how to approach the strange scenario. Being alone with him was making her anxious in many ways, and she wanted to forget all about her childish dreams and the memories that were still with her. She needed to be professional and knowledgeable, not flummoxed and meek. "I wanted to express my opinion, but now I wonder if I came across as rude." She didn't dare look at him, but when no sound came from his side of the table, Kyra was forced to look into his eyes again. The softness in them made her go weak at the knees, and she had to grip the huge chair closest to her in fear she might suddenly fall. He looked more handsome than she'd ever imagined, and she cursed herself for falling deeper into her crush.

"A kiss on your cheek," he murmured, staring at her. Her breath hitched in her throat, and Kyra thought she might cry.

"From thorns that hugged me too tight," she replied, and cried out when he shoved the table aside and stormed towards her. Kronus grabbed her by the chin and turned her face to the side so he could look at the scar.

"Is it really you?" he asked, and she nodded. "Why are you here?"

"Because I owe you my life, and I want to stop the rebels that wish to harm you. I've dedicated my life to serving you since the day you saved me from those thorns, and won't ever stop. I believe this threat is real," she answered from within his firm hold, and flinched when his hoarse voice found her ear.

"Get out of here," he said, and her heart sank. "I want you back in The Tower right away, and I never want to see you again. You're such a fool, Kyra. Such a silly, idiotic girl, and you should be ashamed of who you've become.

You don't owe me a single thing, and I certainly don't want you going anywhere near these rebels. Drop this case immediately and go back to your other work," Kronus added, and he took one deep breath before finally letting her go. He then stormed away without another word, and all she could do was watch in shock. Her heart broke a little with each step he took, and by the time Thrayke came back inside, she was more than ready to leave this terrible meeting behind, and get as far away from King Kronus as possible.

The end of book one in the Invasion Day series.

ABOUT THE AUTHOR

LC Morgans is an author with an obsession for telling powerful stories. Not a day goes by that she doesn't immerse herself in other worlds, and her desire to write about them came from an early age. Shutting off her imagination was never an option, so the stories came to life inside her mind, and in time they'll all make it to the page.

She loves hearing from her fans and you can connect with her via the following:

www.LMauthor.com

If you enjoyed this book, please consider sharing your thoughts by leaving a review where you purchased this novel to help promote LC Morgans' work.

Printed in Great Britain
by Amazon

21546738R00149